MOMENT
IN
TIME

OTHER BOOKS BY
SUZANNE REDFEARN

Hadley and Grace
In an Instant
No Ordinary Life
Hush Little Baby

MOMENT IN TIME

a novel

SUZANNE REDFEARN

LAKE UNION
PUBLISHING

Text copyright © 2022 by Suzanne Redfearn
All rights reserved.

Published by Lake Union Publishing, Seattle

www.apub.com

Amazon, the Amazon logo, and Lake Union Publishing are trademarks of Amazon.com, Inc., or its affiliates.

ISBN-13: 9781542037211
ISBN-10: 1542037212

Cover design by Kathleen Lynch, Black Kat Design

Printed in the United States of America

For my family

All the great things are simple,
and many can be expressed in a single word:
freedom, justice, honor, duty, mercy, hope.
—Winston Churchill

1
CHLOE

The first thing Chloe sees when she walks into the alley is a gate someone forgot to close. The sign reads **NO TRESPASSING KEEP OUT**, but of course dogs don't read. And even if they did, most dogs wouldn't consider themselves trespassers, only humble guests, as is their nature when they are hungry and looking for food—quick to befriend anyone who might offer a morsel to fill their empty bellies.

"Hey, Chlo," Jeff says as he lumbers over to shake her hand. "Thanks for coming."

Towering over her at six eight, Jeffrey Thornton is the biggest human Chloe's ever known, and he might just have the biggest heart. He runs a service called Happy Tails, which deals with stray animals in the city when animal services is closed.

Chloe's who he calls when an animal is injured or distressed.

In this case, it looks like it might be both. The black dog wedged between the dumpster and the building sits lopsided on her haunches, her eyes wide and her ears pinned back against her head.

"Idiot cook whacked her with a broom when he caught her going through a trash bag he left on the stoop." He nods toward the back door of the Thai restaurant beside them. "Waitress stopped him from hitting her again, then called AS, and the call went to me. I think he clocked her pretty good. Looks like she's bleeding above the eye."

Chloe squints to see the injury, but it's dark, the moon and stars obscured by clouds and the only light borrowed from a small bulb over the restaurant's door. The dog's left eye does seem to be twitching, but she can't tell if that's from an injury or stress. The dog looks young—not a puppy but less than two years—and Chloe agrees with Jeff that she's a girl, her face fine boned and feminine.

"Looks like she has a collar," Chloe says.

"Yeah, but no tags."

Chloe looks at him curiously.

"She let me get within a foot, then freaked out when I reached for her, so I backed off and decided to call you."

Jeff was right to be cautious. Even the gentlest dog is unpredictable when stressed—fight-or-flight instinct is as real in canines as humans, and neither reaction is what they want from this girl.

Chloe scans around them. The alley smells of trash and sewer but doesn't feel unsafe, the greatest danger the cold that blows off the bay a block away.

Despite June arriving a few days ago and it being warm everywhere else in California, San Francisco has turned frigid, the grande dame of the West showing her defiance with a mutinous arctic freeze in springtime. The phantom tip of Chloe's left pinkie and her three missing toes pulse.

Bring it on, she hisses silently, the heat in her veins matching the cold in her lungs. *You tried once, but I'm still here.* Her hands ball into fists, and her remaining toes curl, belying her bluster; cold is a nemesis that Chloe knows too well does not care what you think.

Eight years ago, she and her family were in an accident in a blizzard that killed her younger brother and sister. It left her with a few less digits than she started with and scars on her soul that have never quite healed.

"Thanks, Jeff. I've got it from here," she says.

"You sure?" He looks from her to the dog and then back with concern. "I can stay."

"No. I've got it." She glances at the back door of the Thai restaurant. Through the wood, she hears pots clanging along with ugly techno music. "Just do me a favor and let the restaurant know they need to stay out of the alley."

"For how long?"

Chloe looks at the trembling dog, then back at Jeff. "For as long as it takes for me to calm her down and get her out of here. It could be a while."

The last time she needed to wait out a terrified dog—a pint-size terrier mix at least ten years old with trademark signs of dementia—it took almost twenty hours. She shivers at the thought and really hopes this time doesn't take as long.

"Give them my number." She pulls a business card from her vet bag and holds it toward him.

Jeff's eyes catch on her half pinkie before darting away. Though he's seen the injury dozens of times, his reaction is always the same—an empathetic wince followed by a heartfelt frown of sympathy followed by self-consciousness for both.

Chloe can tell a lot about a person by the way they react to her abbreviated pinkie. She refers to it as her humanity meter. Guys like Jeff—good guys with great big hearts—notice it no matter how many times they've seen it and feel enormous compassion each and every time. They are what she calls the golden retrievers of humans—good natured, predictable, and loyal.

Then there are the chows, snooty people who are revolted by the deformity and seem to blame her for getting herself into whatever predicament caused such a disfiguration and who seem upset with her for forcing them to put up with looking at it. Aloof, fastidious, and callous, chows are among Chloe's least favorite dogs.

Her favorite people are what she thinks of as working dog mutts, practical folk who barely notice her pinkie at all before moving on instantly. *Life's tough, and sometimes bad things happen.* Half a pinkie doesn't define her, and they don't define her by it. Surprisingly rare, these unique humans possess an extraordinary combination of grit and soul along with plain understanding and very little judgment.

The final category is a strange one, and it took her a long time to understand it. A peculiar group of people—mostly men—who home in on her wounds like beef-basted bones, their expressions unapologetic as they gape with rapt, morbid curiosity like she's an aberration to be feasted on and relished. She calls them Dobermans because they're almost always high strung and aggressive—though she likes the breed far more than these humans. Like moths drawn to flickering light, they seem to salivate with macabre pleasure at the evidence of suffering.

Jeff takes the card. "They're not going to be happy."

"Which is why I want you to give them my number. They'll be less happy with the attractive nuisance lawsuit I'll serve them for not closing their gate or the animal-cruelty charge I'll file against the cook if I don't get this girl out of here safely."

He smiles and shakes his head. "You'd make a great lawyer if you weren't already a great vet."

"I learned from the best," she says. "My mom's a kick-ass attorney."

There was a time when Chloe wanted to be nothing like her mom. Now, nothing makes her prouder. Except, of course, she has no interest in the law. Her calling is healing, not haranguing, specifically when it comes to animals. She's always loved dogs, cats, horses—anything with four legs.

Though, after the accident, it became more than that. Something inside her altered, and she found herself with a deep, innate understanding of the scared and vulnerable, regardless of genus or species. It was as if suddenly she could feel them, especially the most damaged. It started with Finn, her sister. For months after the accident, Chloe felt as if a vestige of Finn remained, as if she were still there and watching, not yet at peace. Eventually, she moved on, but the window to that understanding remained.

"Okay," Jeff says with some hesitancy. "Call if you need me."

Chloe sets her vet bag on the ground and lowers herself to the stoop. "Will do. But we're going to be fine." Though she's talking to Jeff, her eyes are on the dog, and the pup tilts her head as if listening, considering the words and deciding whether to believe them.

2
MO

A good day.

Mo sighs happily, then opens the fridge to find something sweet to celebrate with.

Brussels sprouts fill two shelves—a large bowl of roasted ones along with a bag of uncooked ones below. *Chloe.* She rolls her eyes. The girl's on either a binge or a budget. A month ago, it was quinoa; before that, beets—the first when Chloe swore off all food other than grains to see how her body would respond, and the second because Costco was selling twenty-pound bags of Chioggia beets at a bargain.

Sweet tooth still buzzing, she opens the freezer. A tub of Ben & Jerry's mint chip sits beside the ice trays and Hazel's assortment of Trader Joe's frozen dinners. *Yes!* She pulls out the carton, thrilled by its heft, at least half the ice cream left.

She considers spooning it directly into her mouth but then thinks of her mother frowning and pulls a bowl from the cupboard.

Sitting at the table with her treat, she opens her computer to admire her accomplishment, starting with CNN. Front and center on the home page in bold letters: BABIES!—FactNews Releases Report Showing the

Reasons for the Disturbing Trend of the Nation's Declining Population Growth.

She spoons another bite of minty ice cream into her mouth and clicks the link to reveal the article. The page opens to six graphics—the entire issue of population degeneration captured in an eye-catching visual snapshot anyone can understand.

The troubling worldwide trend has already been reported on in depth. For years, futurists and economists alike have been sounding the alarm in dry reports in medical and financial journals about the cataclysmic impact continued waning population growth will have on everything from economic stability to mental health. But FactNews took all that bland analysis and turned it into something snazzy, made it "NEWS!"—new, entertaining, worthwhile, and scintillating (the tagline for the company). By boiling issues down to their essence and packaging them in millennial-attention-span news bites, FactNews brings serious issues to the forefront and makes them relevant.

The first image shows the birth rate decline by year (illustrated with a very cute baby gleefully sliding down the slope). The second shows the decline of sexual coupling (cleverly labeled *The Sex Recession*, which is already getting lots of traction on social media). The slope is overlapped by a second, steeper slope showing the precipitous fall of long-term partnering (called *The Love Deep-ression*). The graph culminates in a comic strip *BOOM!* in 2040, when it's projected the family paradigm will no longer exist, with only a small subset of traditionalists still choosing to share their lifelong term with another.

Her phone buzzes with a text from her assistant, Esther: Forbes wants to feature you in their 30 Under 30 List!!! You go girl!

Mo texts back a thumbs-up, then spoons another mouthful of mint chip into her mouth, pride ballooning in her chest. Making *Forbes*'s 30 under 30 has been a dream of hers since high school. It's the business world's recognition of the coolest geeks and nerds under thirty doing the extraordinary. She wonders if they might consider her for featured honoree in the media category. It's possible. This release definitely puts FactNews on the map in the incredibly competitive world of news bites.

She sets down her spoon and returns to scrolling through the article. The graphs go on to show the decline in earnings, homeownership, and savings for young people; the increase in women working full-time along with the correlating increase in age of first pregnancies; and the projection of US deaths outpacing births, overlaid by the correlating decline of Social Security contributions from the diminishing working segment.

The final image is a mountain of hearts with a troop of adorable dogs and cats bounding up it, a sweet illustration of the skyrocketing trend in pet ownership by millennials and Gen Zers. Mo grins at the fluffy, heartwarming ending. *Start and end with a smile,* she thinks. It's what reels them in and keeps them coming back. Already the final image is the angle getting the most buzz, the furry-baby phenomenon a bizarre and endearing side effect of the decline in having children.

As she leans back and thinks about her interview tomorrow with Jake Tapper, her focus narrows in on a particularly cute beagle springing up the slope. If she nails it, there's a chance CNN will retain her as a consultant, a media expert who weighs in on the veracity of the latest headlines, which will further solidify FactNews's position as a reliable source for facts. It almost feels like too much to hope for, but the producer alluded to the possibility when she called Mo about the interview.

The door slams open, and Mo peeks through the archway to see Chloe pulling a canvas wagon through the front door.

Leaping to her feet, she hurries forward and blocks Chloe's path. "Uh-uh. No way."

Chloe casts her eyes to the floor. "Sorry, Mo. I just need to use the bathroom and grab some dog food. I promise, we're not staying."

Mo tilts her head to the side to look in the wagon and sees a black dog curled beneath a beach towel, a bandage around its head.

"I didn't want to come here," Chloe says, "but I didn't know what else to do. I couldn't leave her in the van, in case she woke up. I was careful. Super careful. She's knocked out, and I made sure no one saw us."

Chloe is dressed in her thick Patagonia jacket, silver Moon Boots, and the sweats she normally sleeps in, which means she was probably called out of bed last night for the stray and probably hasn't slept, and already Mo feels her conviction wavering.

Kyle's voice booms in her head. *Repeat after me. No. More. Strays.*

At the time, she repeated it—"No more strays"—fully believing, when this moment came, she would have no problem telling Chloe she could not bring another animal into their apartment.

Seriously, Ace, our apartment is not a halfway house for wayward animals. We signed a lease. No pets.

He was right, of course, and they are now exactly one infraction away from being evicted. But Kyle's not the one standing here looking at Chloe with her bruised eyes and her cheeks chafed red from the cold, towing a sad, shivering creature behind her with its head bandaged.

"What's wrong with her?" Mo asks.

"Dehydration, exhaustion, possibly shock."

Chloe glances back at the dog with deep concern, and the last of Mo's resolve disappears. The poor thing looks wrecked, and there's no way she can simply turn her away.

"I promise, Mo," Chloe says, "I'm not trying to mess things up for you. I'm just going to grab what I need, and we'll be gone before anyone even knows we were here."

Mo steps aside, then follows Chloe into the kitchen. Chloe pulls a water bottle from the cabinet, and the dog startles at the noise, then whimpers. Mo squats beside her and strokes her sleek black fur. "Shhh. You're safe."

The dog shudders beneath her touch, then settles.

"Will she be okay?" Mo asks.

"Hard to say. I hope so."

Chloe puts the water bottle in the wagon, then goes to the pantry, pulls out a bag of dog food, and scoops the kibble into a baggie.

Concerned by the amount she's packing, Mo says, "You're taking her to the shelter, right?"

Chloe doesn't look at her as she mumbles, "Not tonight."

Mo looks at the clock on the oven. It's only six, and the shelter stays open until eight. "Why?"

Chloe intentionally keeps her focus on her task. "I'll take her in the morning. She needs a night to rest."

Mo's worry grows. The last stray Chloe brought home stayed with them nearly a week before Chloe felt he was strong enough to take to the shelter, and this dog looks far worse off.

"Where will you stay?" she asks, her voice tight, knowing Chloe is broke and doesn't have money for a hotel.

"The van," Chloe says with a shrug like it's no big deal.

"The van" is Chloe's veterinary van, a heap of rust with a heater that provides about as much warmth as a matchstick with a fan blowing on it.

"You can't stay in the van!" Mo practically yelps. "It's freezing outside." This week's been the coldest June week in the city's past fifty years, the temperatures at night dropping into the forties.

Chloe ignores her. Sealing the bag, she sets it in the wagon beside the water bottle.

"At least wait a bit before you go," Mo says, her pulse pounding with the thought of Chloe and the dog spending the night in the van on the street while she is warm and safe in the apartment. "The dog's asleep, and you're already here. It makes no difference if you leave now or in a few hours. You should at least eat something and get some rest."

Chloe shakes her head, her copper bangs swaying. "Not a chance. You're not getting evicted on account of me."

"We're not going to get evicted," Mo says, unable to believe the words are coming from her mouth. If Kyle could hear her, he would not be happy. But he can't hear her because he is six thousand miles away, and Chloe and the dog are here, and it's freezing outside.

"How long is she going to sleep for?" she asks.

Chloe skews her mouth to the side. "Maybe another two or three hours before I need to put her out again. She's really strung out, and the best thing for her is sleep and fluids."

"So she's going to be out until morning?" Mo asks.

"Mo—"

"Think about it. Taking her out of the building now, when everyone's coming and going, is far riskier than leaving early in the morning, when everyone's asleep."

Chloe shakes her head again but slower this time. "I don't know, Mo. I've already gotten you in trouble, and if Kyle finds out—"

"He won't find out."

"Mo—"

"Clove, I'm telling you, he won't find out. Neither will Jerry." She makes a heroic effort not to let her eyes slide up toward the ceiling, where, one floor above and two doors down, her landlord lives.

She adjusts the towel so it covers the pup's exposed shoulder, pushes to her feet, picks up the tub of ice cream, and holds it toward Chloe. "Eat, rest, and in the morning, go to the van."

Chloe doesn't look fully convinced, but perhaps out of exhaustion or possibly hunger, she takes the carton from Mo, hoists herself onto the counter, grabs a spoon from the dish rack, and digs in.

Her eyes close with the first bite, and Mo smiles, glad they came to a resolution that doesn't involve Chloe sleeping with a stray dog in her van on the street.

"Does she have a name?" Mo asks.

"No tags," Chloe says around a mouthful of ice cream.

"Hmmm," Mo says as she considers it. She's always loved coming up with names. The dog is pretty, sleek, and refined looking with a cotton candy–pink nose, floppy ears, and long silver whiskers.

"Maybe Rudolph, on account of her nose?" Chloe suggests.

Mo frowns. While the dog's nose is her most defining feature, she's far too pretty for a boy's name. "How about Ruby?"

Chloe rolls her eyes but smiles. "Fine. Ruby."

The dog's cheek twitches, which Mo takes as a sign she approves.

She looks back at Chloe. "I guess this means you can't go out tonight?"

Chloe's brow furrows, and then her eyes pop open. "Your report! It came out! Crap! I can't believe I forgot. How'd it go?"

"Good. Great. Really good." Mo feels her cheeks grow warm.

"I knew you were going to kill it. Did CNN pick it up?"

"Yep. And the *Times* and the *Washington Post*."

"Wow, Mo, that's awesome. This officially makes you the reigning queen of truthdom."

Chloe looks at the dog . . . *Ruby* . . . then at the tub of ice cream, then back at Mo. And her face radiates genuine apology as she says, "Sorry, Mo, I wish I could . . ."

"It's okay," Mo says. "Haze should be home soon. Maybe she can go."

3
MO

Black Sands is a hipster bar a block from Mo's apartment that serves good beer and a famous smashed double-double cheeseburger. It's still early, only seven, but the tables and barstools are full, so Mo and Hazel carry their beers to the standing bar beside the window.

"To you," Hazel says, lifting her glass.

"To FactNews," Mo says, clinking her beer to Hazel's, happiness swelling her heart.

For five years, this has been her dream, to make her mark by building a media company known as a reliable source for frank, honest information. She thinks of her father smiling down and toasting her as well. After all, he was the one who encouraged her and believed in the idea enough to bankroll it.

"News with no agenda except to relay the facts. A bit of a throwback notion," he said, "but I like it."

A year and a half ago, a week after FactNews released its first story—a snapshot look at the growing wealth gap in America—he died unexpectedly from a brain aneurysm.

"So proud of you, Squirt," was the last thing he said to her, words that resound in her mind each time she walks through the doors of

FactNews and that motivate her to live up to them. He was a great man, a legend in the finance world, and she feels an enormous responsibility to carry on the Kaminski name with honor and continue his legacy as a pillar in the community.

"Mmmm," Hazel says. "This beer's delicious."

"It's the new Pliny," Mo says, taking a sip and rolling it around on her tongue.

It is very vibrant, rich in hops and remarkably dry—definitely unique and worthy of the hype around it. Russian River Brewing only makes a small batch of the pale ale each year, and only a handful of bars are able to get it. For three months, she's been scouting beer sites to see who this year's lucky recipients would be, and she was thrilled to find out Black Sands was one of them and that today was when they were getting their shipment. Each patron is allowed a single beer, and Mo's certain they'll be sold out before the night is over.

"It's fermented three times," Mo says. "That's what makes it so smooth."

"Triple the hop," Hazel says and does three little hops on her stool, her dark curls hopping with her.

"Ale yeah!" Mo responds, lifting her glass.

"Don't worry, be hoppy," Hazel shoots back, and both of them laugh.

Mo's glad to be sharing this moment with Hazel, the person who's been with her from the start.

"Nothing but the truth," Mo said five years ago.

They were in their dorm room, a week after finals their first year. Hazel was reading, and Mo was looking at the ceiling, her mind turning.

"Huh?" Hazel said.

Mo turned her head to look at her. "News that's not editorial," she said, the idea still forming, flittering like a trapped moth in her mind.

When she was sixteen, the RV she and ten others were riding in went over the side of a mountain during a blizzard. Two people died, and she barely survived. Choices were made that cost people dearly. But after, when the story was told, different versions of what had happened during their survival emerged that distorted the facts. Heroes were being vilified, and villains were being revered, so Mo made it her mission to uncover the truth, a notion she became obsessed with.

"Only the facts," she went on, "but told in a fun, engaging way. Reliable and unbiased so people can form their own opinions about it."

"I like it," Hazel said. "The meat of the bull with none of the bleep."

For months, Mo thought that was going to be the company's tagline, until her dad suggested she come up with something a bit more dignified. Kyle was the one who came up with *NEWS!—new, entertaining, worthwhile, and scintillating.*

And now, here they are, five years later, the two of them celebrating what that fledgling idea has become.

"Ready for some remarkable nonsense?" Hazel says, setting down her beer, a thin foam mustache on her lip.

"Hit me," Mo says.

"Did you know . . ." Hazel stops to build the suspense, her right brow arching high and her lips curled in a toothless smirk.

Mo double arches her eyebrows.

"Superman's vegetarian?" Hazel blurts, her dark eyes going wide as if it's the most earth-shattering revelation in the world.

Mo matches her incredulousness. "No way! The man of steel only eats vegetables?"

"And grains and dairy," Hazel says, returning to nonchalance and taking another sip of her beer.

"And you know this how?" Mo asks. "Have you secretly been dating Superman?"

Hazel wrinkles her nose. "Too hulky for my taste."

"Right. All those bulging muscles, definitely a turnoff."

"I'm more an Amadeus Cho fan," Hazel says.

Mo has no idea who Amadeus Cho is but imagines he's some geeky scientist superhero, which would definitely be more Hazel's type.

"Comic-Con just released an encyclopedia on superheroes," Hazel says. "And it turns out Superman's never eaten meat. His senses are sharper than a human's, so he's aware of life auras, making him highly attuned to the emotions of all living creatures, which would make eating meat very disturbing, like he would be feeling the animal as he was chewing on it."

"Wow. Yeah. I could see how that could be disturbing."

"I know, right? Of course, it brings up the whole debate of whether Superman needs to eat at all. I mean, he's Superman, and when he lived on Krypton, he derived his strength from the Krypton sun. But on earth, maybe it's different."

"I hope he eats," Mo says, as she believes food to be one of the greatest pleasures in life.

Hazel sweeps an imaginary curl from her eyes, a habit she has when she's thinking. "I figure he must. He needs to refuel somehow."

"To Superman enjoying a good meal," Mo says, lifting her glass.

"And Lois Lane," Hazel says, ever the romantic.

As they clink glasses, Mo makes a silent wish for Hazel to meet her own Superman or Amadeus whoever, hoping somewhere in the world, there is some extraordinary, big-brained superhero who just happens to be searching for his extraordinary, big-brained muse.

"Take off your coat," Mo suggests, determined to help make it happen.

Before they left the apartment, Mo found Hazel standing in front of her full-length mirror, frowning. She was wearing a black dress with no waist and beige ballet flats with gold buckles—an outfit better suited for a grandmother heading to a funeral in the old country than a twenty-four-year-old heading to a bar in San Francisco. Mo hurried away and returned a minute later with a cream sweater and suede camel bootees.

"Wear your shredded jeans," she said, holding them toward Hazel.

A few minutes later, Hazel walked into the living room, looking great, and Mo said, "Wowzah!" which was a mistake. Hazel's pale skin went crimson as she quickly shrugged on her oversize parka and zipped it to her chin—Hazel more a blend-into-the-wallpaper than "wowzah" kind of girl.

"Come on, Haze," Mo encourages when Hazel still hasn't moved, her eyes darting self-consciously around the room. "You look great. Trust me."

Hazel looks at Mo uncertainly, and Mo feels how hard this is. Hazel's shyness is as much a part of her as the deep dimple on her chin.

"Fine," she says and, in a great leap of faith, shrugs off the parka.

Mo takes it from her and hangs it on the hook beneath the bar, outwardly showing nothing as inside she cheers. Hazel looks great, her curve appeal on full display and the cream of the sweater setting off her best feature, her wild mane of black curls that Mo swears is a result of her fabulous mind, like the follicles are supercharged and can't be contained.

"Mo?"

Mo turns to see a tall guy with sandy-gold hair shaved tight on the sides and left long on top. He is around her age, and she recognizes him but doesn't know from where.

"Allen," he says, helping her out. "Sigma Nu."

Allen. She knew his brother, James, more, but both used to be at her sorority a lot. James was in her year and dated one of the girls a year below.

Allen gives a large, toothy grin as he rakes her over with his eyes. "Wow. You look great." A vague memory surfaces, a hazy recollection of him hitting on her at a party.

"This is Hazel," Mo says.

Hazel gives a shy smile and lifts her hand, and Allen glances at her with surprise. "Hey, I know you," he says.

"We had a class together," Hazel manages, her skin pinkening. "Innovation and Entrepreneurship."

"That's right. You killed it with your idea for that phone case."

Hazel's blush deepens, and Mo smiles to herself at the reaction. While she remembers Allen as annoying, Hazel seems smitten, and she thinks this could work. Allen is just the sort of assertive a girl like Hazel needs to compensate for her debilitating shyness.

"And your group did those cool new customized earbuds," Hazel says.

Mo believes this is the longest conversation Hazel's ever had with a guy in a bar, and her hope grows. If Allen can talk geek, Hazel will be in her zone.

"Yeah. I think one of the guys is actually still trying to pursue it," Allen says and offers another toothy grin before turning back to Mo. "We have a couple extra seats at our table if you want to join us?" He nods toward the community table a few feet away.

"Sure, that would be great," Mo says before Hazel can freak out and say no.

Allen grabs their beers, and Mo quickly hops from her stool and grabs both their jackets so Hazel can't put hers back on.

She scopes out the situation. There are four open stools, three in a row on one side of the table, and a single one kitty-corner across from them. Mo heads for the single and is about to sit down when her phone buzzes. She looks down, and her heart leaps when she sees the screen lit up with Kyle's name.

She lifts her face to see Hazel looking at her with a horrified, imploring expression that says, *Please don't leave me*. Mo ignores it. She'll be fine. Allen's a yapper. All Hazel needs to do is sit there and listen.

Handing Hazel her parka, she says, "I'll be right back."

She hurries for the door, passing Allen on the way. His back is turned as he watches something on the television above the bar. He's tall and well built, athletic looking. Not too shabby. Hazel could do worse.

"Hey, babe," she says when she's outside, the frigid air whipping her hair and sending an arctic chill down her spine.

Pulling on her jacket, she races around the corner to get out of the wind as familiar, irrational fear takes over her mind. It's probably no colder than fifty at the moment, but she and cold do not get along. People make fun of how much she overdresses for the weather, but of course, they didn't nearly freeze to death when they were sixteen.

"Hey, yourself," Kyle says, his voice warm like honey from a summer hive and making her suddenly not cold in the least. "So according to FactNews, women have finally wised up and realized dogs trump men when it comes to relationships. Should I be concerned?"

"You are a dog, remember?"

"Woof!" he barks.

She presses the phone to her ear and closes her eyes, pretending he's beside her instead of thousands of miles away.

"Dumb as a dog," he says.

"And twice as loyal," she answers back.

"Proud of you, Ace."

Another swell of pride as she thinks again about the story and what it means for her and the business.

"Your dad is smiling," he says, which is the perfect thing to say. While Kyle isn't schmaltzy, his love blazes like the sun, rising steadfast each day, there even when he's on the other side of the world.

"I have an interview with Jake Tapper tomorrow."

"Wow. That's big."

"Yeah. I'm nervous, but Clove said she'd rehearse with me." She feels a small pang of guilt about the dog but pushes it away.

When she and Hazel left the apartment, Chloe was asleep on the couch with Ruby curled on the floor beside her. Chloe's half-eaten plate of brussels sprouts was on the coffee table, and the fork was dangling from her hand, like she'd fallen asleep midbite.

"Chloe will make Jake Tapper seem tame," Kyle says.

"Exactly. If I can survive an interview with Clove, I can survive anything."

A group of three drunk guys wanders past, loud and laughing.

"Where are you?" Kyle asks.

"Black Sands. Haze and I decided to get a drink to celebrate. And"—she pauses for dramatic effect—"I think she might have met someone."

"Really? Haze? She actually *talked* to a guy?"

"She's talking to him now," Mo says proudly, hoping it's true, that Hazel is actually having a conversation with Allen and not just sitting tongue-tied and red faced beside him.

"That's awesome," Kyle says. He's always been a big fan of Hazel's.

"I should probably get back in there, make sure she's not rambling on about Python code—"

"Or Mars colonization," Kyle says, a smile in his voice. "Remember the first time I met her and she was all jazzed about intergalactic space stations, convinced they were going to be the real estate of the future?"

"Her and Elon Musk. I bought stock."

"So did I," Kyle says. "After all, how wrong could two of the smartest people in the world be?"

She laughs and holds the phone tighter to her ear, listening to him breathe. "I miss you."

"Three months," he says, and she closes her eyes, praying for it to be true, for life to stay the course and continue as it is for three short months, until Kyle's tour is over and he comes home for good.

They talk a few more minutes about everything and nothing, neither of them wanting the moment to end, until finally she says, "I hate it, but I really need to go." The line pulses, and then with a deep breath, she says, "Stay safe."

"Stay you," he answers back. "Don't change a thing."

Remaining where she is, she closes her eyes and, phone held to her heart, repeats her plea to the heavens to watch over him; then she tucks the phone in her pocket and returns inside.

"Hey," she says to a girl at the table. "Where'd they go?" She thumbs her hand at the two empty stools where Hazel and Allen were. Hazel's beer glass is empty, and Allen's is half-full.

"They left a few minutes ago," the girl says. Then with a wry smile she adds, "Looks like someone's getting lucky."

Mo tilts her head and looks again at the empty seats. Hazel's not the type of girl to "get lucky," especially with a guy she just met. She probably just got uncomfortable and decided to go home. Mo bristles with irritation, miffed that Hazel couldn't manage to hang a few minutes without her. She looks at her own Pliny, sitting half-empty on the table, peeved she didn't get to finish it.

4
CHLOE

Chloe startles awake at the sound of a key in the door and barking. Disoriented, she spins to sit up on the couch and sees a black dog charging toward the door.

"Mo! Stop!" she cries as she lunges to get hold of the dog's collar, snagging it just as the door opens. The dog's head snaps around, eyes wild, and her teeth sink into Chloe's forearm. Chloe's hand snaps open, and Mo yanks the door closed, missing the dog's nose by an inch.

The dog barks and snarls and howls.

Then she stops.

Eyes skittering, she looks back at Chloe, then again at the door, then once more at Chloe before slumping to the carpet with a whimper and dropping her head between her paws, clearly remorseful for what she's done.

"It's okay," Chloe says, inching toward her, angry at herself—first, for not bringing the dog to the van like she should have; second, for falling asleep and missing giving the dog her second sedative; and third, for not having the foresight to realize that what just happened could happen.

She strokes the dog's back, and the dog whimpers again.

"Clove, you okay?" Mo asks through the wood.

The dog belly crawls forward, then drops her face to the floor again.

"I'm fine," Chloe says. "You just startled her. You can come in; just come in slow."

Mo inches the door open, and the dog looks up guiltily. Mo squats and holds out her hand for the dog to sniff. "It's okay. Sorry I scared you."

The dog edges closer and sets her head on Mo's feet, and Mo plops onto her butt and scratches her behind the ears.

"Think Jerry heard that?" Chloe asks, guilt strangling her.

"I think the entire block heard that," Mo says, going for levity but missing the mark, and Chloe's guilt grows.

Three months ago, when Chloe found herself abandoned by her eight-year boyfriend and broke, Mo insisted she move in with her and Hazel. And the way Chloe has repaid her is with two warning notices from the landlord about them breaking the rules of their lease.

Mo turns to the dog, and in a baby voice, she coos, "That's okay. We'll talk to the big mean landlord and make everything all right."

"I'll talk to him," Chloe says. "I'll tell him we just showed up, and you told us to leave. Which is exactly what we're doing."

Mo looks up, and her mouth opens to say something, but then she stops. She nods toward Chloe's arm. "You're bleeding."

Chloe follows her eyes to see a single small puncture wound half-way down her forearm and a thin trickle of blood leaking from it.

"Crap," she says, while thinking, *Crap, crap, crap!* This day just keeps getting worse. A puncture wound from a stray means a trip to the ER to get it flushed and to get a dose of antibiotics, which means hundreds of dollars she can't afford.

"You should wait a few hours before you go to the hospital," Mo says, knowing the routine. "It's going to be crazy busy right now. Rest, then go. I'll watch the dog."

Chloe shakes her head the entire time she's talking.

"Clove, you need to get your arm taken care of, and you can't take the dog with you."

"I'll leave her in the van."

Mo sets her gaze firmly on Chloe. "No. You'll leave her here. She already barked. Like I said, I'll talk to Jerry in the morning, and it will be fine." She stands and pats her leg as she walks toward her room. "Come on, girl," she coos, and the dog obediently pushes to her feet and follows.

"Mo—"

Mo turns. "Clove, stop. I'll tell Jerry it was an emergency, or I'll lie and say I have no idea what he's talking about." She gives her trademark Mo smile, her Caribbean-blue eyes wide and her pink rosebud lips curled up sweetly, the expression she uses to give the illusion of an angel incapable of deceit, which in itself is a complete farce, as Mo is one of the most accomplished liars Chloe knows. "Get some rest. Ruby and I will be fine." The dog moons up at her. "Won't we, girl?"

Mo and the dog continue on, and Chloe sighs heavily and drops her face to her hands, unable to believe the mess she's made of her life. Only three months ago, things were going so well—a boyfriend, a job, money in the bank. But she supposes she knows better than anyone how quickly things can change.

"Hey," she says, lifting her face and stopping Mo just as she's opening her door. "Where's Haze?"

Mo tilts her head. "What do you mean? She's here. Isn't she?"

"Didn't you two go out together?"

"We did. We went to Black Sands. But then Kyle called, so I went outside to talk to him, and when I went back in, she was gone. I thought she came home."

"Nope. Just me and the dog."

Mo pulls out her phone and absently says, "I introduced her to this guy—"

"Haze met a guy?" Chloe says, her misery lightening at the thought.

"No text," Mo says, frowning at the screen.

"Is he cute? Actually, who cares. Is he nice?"

"He's a guy I knew in college," Mo says absently, still staring at her phone, her thumbs pecking out a message. "I don't know him well."

"But he was into Haze? And they were talking? *She* was talking? What were they talking about? Subatomic particles? Singularity? Nanotechnology?" She giggles, trying to imagine it. "Was he smart? He must be. And they had stuff in common?" Chloe realizes she's babbling, something she does when she's tired or excited—or in this case both.

Mo nods absently, her attention still on her phone. "Her Find My Friends is off."

"Haze hates that app. So do I."

"I'm going to call her." She dials, waits, hangs up. "No answer."

"That means she's *busy*," Chloe trills, her insides lit up. "Hopefully *very* busy." She giggles again.

"Don't you think she would have texted to tell me she was leaving?"

"It's Haze."

For someone as smart as Hazel, she's one of the most absentminded people Chloe knows, her brain constantly working in overdrive and operating on an entirely different frequency, which makes things like turning off ovens, closing doors, and texting when she's going to be late or not going to show secondary and often forgotten.

Mo continues to stare at her phone as if it's a Magic 8-Ball that's going to mystically give her the answer.

"Mo, Haze is a big girl," Chloe says. "She knows what she's doing."

"You think?"

Chloe rolls her eyes. "Yes. This is big. Finally, she's going to get the monkey off her back."

A month ago, Hazel turned twenty-four and, after a few too many beers, confessed to Chloe that being a virgin at twenty-four was no longer virtuous and more like an albatross of embarrassment around her neck. It was a horrible conversation. Hazel was starting to believe she might never meet someone. Chloe assured her she would, but inside, she wondered. At twenty-four, Hazel had yet to even kiss a guy.

"So you think she's okay?" Mo asks.

"I think she's more than okay. I think this is exactly what she wanted."

5
MO

It's one in the morning, but Mo can't sleep, her mind preoccupied with her interview with Jake Tapper. She was really hoping to rehearse with Chloe, but then Ruby bit her, and now she's at the hospital. Mo heard her leave around midnight. Even in the wee hours on a weeknight, the emergency room can be busy, so she's not surprised she's not back.

After pulling herself from bed, she shuffles to the kitchen. Ruby traipses after her. Chloe removed the bandages from the dog's head, and there's now a bald patch over the dog's left eye and a swatch of glue covering a row of six neat black stitches.

"Poor thing," she says as she opens the fridge. "Should we see if there's something to eat?" Ruby sits very close as Mo shifts the cooked brussels sprouts, hoping the food fairy magically delivered something delicious to munch on between this afternoon and now.

"Somehow, brussels sprouts aren't what I'm craving."

Ruby tilts her head as if truly interested, and Mo can tell she still feels bad for what happened earlier.

"It's okay," she says, closing the fridge and squatting to the dog's level. "It was only a moment in time, and now, sweet girl, it's over. Behind you. Just like your tail."

Ruby limply wags the aforementioned appendage, and Mo feels a pang of guilt, knowing tomorrow Chloe will be taking her to the shelter. "Sorry," she says, standing. "No pets allowed. It's the rule."

She tries not to think about the barking incident from earlier and how upset Kyle's going to be if they get evicted. He loves this apartment. It took them months to find it, and for two years, he's spent every minute he's been home working to make it theirs—painting; wallpapering; replacing knobs, handles, and fixtures. And now it's perfect, each room exactly how they want it.

"It will work out," she says as she fills a glass with water. "I'll smooth things over with Jerry, and it will be fine."

Ruby listens, ears perked and her pretty face tilted. A very sweet dog.

"Sorry," she says again, feeling terrible. "Someone's going to take one look at you and fall in love instantly. You'll see. You're going to find a wonderful home. How could you not? You're beautiful, sweet, smart. They'd be nuts not to want you."

Mo wishes the pep talk were working, but it only makes her feel worse. The dog *is* beautiful, sweet, and smart, and she doesn't deserve any of this.

She heads back to her room and, before climbing into bed, grabs her phone to text Chloe to see how it's going, and that's when she sees the message: Come get me.

She looks at the time stamp: 12:44. She looks at the clock: 1:12.

Her thumbs fumble over the screen, messing up twice before she manages to click on Hazel's number.

"Haze?"

Incoherent sobs shock Mo's system like a cattle prod, an instant rush of panic through her veins as she realizes something is happening that she doesn't want to be happening.

"Haze, where are you?"

A snivel followed by a hiccup, then nothing.

"Haze? Haze, are you there?"

The phone pinned to her ear, she pulls off her pajama bottoms to replace them with jeans.

"Haze?"

"Please come get me," Hazel says, the words broken with her distress.

"I'm trying," Mo says, pulling on her shoes. "But I don't know where you are."

Another pause, like the connection's been lost, though she knows Hazel's still there.

"Turn on Find My Friends," Mo says. "Can you do that?"

She hears muffled movement.

"I did it," Hazel says.

"Okay. Hang tight. I'm on my way."

6

CHLOE

"Raped?" Chloe says, the word pitching high before breaking in two, not registering, then slamming into her brain with a clang.

Mo nods, her bottom lip sucked in as her nose flares with her breaths, working hard to hold it together.

They are in the emergency room waiting area. Chloe was discharged a few minutes earlier and walked from the exam bays to find Mo and Ruby sitting beside the door. She thought they were there for her. She wishes, now, that were the case.

Ruby wears the seizure-alert dog vest Chloe keeps in the front closet that allows her to bring her patients places they wouldn't otherwise be allowed. The dog nuzzles against Chloe's leg, and though they've known each other only a day, already Chloe feels a bond developing between them, which is not a good thing. As soon as the dog gets her strength back, she needs to go to the shelter; Chloe is in no position to care for her.

"Where was she?" Chloe asks as she kneels and scratches Ruby's neck. The dog leans into it, her weight heavy on Chloe's shins.

"A liquor store in the Tenderloin," Mo says.

"The Tenderloin?" Chloe's hair bristles. The large, derelict wedge of the city is not a place most would enter voluntarily, especially at night. "Why would Hazel go into the TL?"

Mo furrows her brow, then shakes her head. "She didn't *go* there. It's where *he* dumped her. After."

"Dumped?" Chloe repeats, trying to make sense of it. "Wait. Back up. That's not where it happened?"

Mo's head lolls back and forth, and she wraps her arms around herself, her body trembling likely both from emotions and the cold that blows in each time the emergency room doors open. She is dressed in only a sweatshirt and jeans, surprising for Mo, who notoriously over-dresses for the cold.

"Allen raped her," she mutters, her voice hiccuping as she loses the battle and tears leak from her eyes.

"Allen? Who's Allen?" Chloe says, and then, realizing the answer, "Oh. From the bar. Your friend."

"He's not my friend."

Ruby leaves Chloe to nuzzle against Mo, and Mo crouches and buries her face in the dog's fur, muffling her sobs.

"Should we call the police?" Chloe asks, her heart hurting for Hazel and for Mo.

"I already did. They're on their way."

As if the words conjured him, the doors open, and a squat man in a uniform walks through. His dark hair is buzzed, and his jacket is a size too small, showing off gym-swelled muscles.

Hitching his thumbs in his gun belt, he says, "Maureen Kaminski?"

Mo wipes her eyes and stands. "Yes," she says as Ruby hunches and growls.

Chloe takes her leash and leads her to a row of chairs on the other side of the room.

"Officer Gretzky," the man says, his voice deep and gravelly like he's smoked a pack a day since he was twelve.

"Thank you for coming," Mo says.

He sizes her up. "You've been examined?"

Mo rears back. "*Me?* No. It wasn't *me*."

"Not you?"

She shakes her head, her blonde hair swaying. "It happened to my friend. She's still inside." She nods toward the doors that lead to the exam bays.

"Okay." He pivots toward them.

"She's not ready to report it," Mo says, stopping him. He turns back. "At the moment, she's confused and not sure what's happened. She was drugged."

Chloe's blood goes cold as she realizes what Mo is saying. Hazel was roofied. Allen put something in her drink, then took advantage of her.

The officer frowns. *"Confused?"* he says, a deep frown forming and impatience bleeding from his stance, like he's put out being here.

"But I was there," Mo says. "And I know who did it."

"You were there when your friend was raped?"

"No. Of course not. But I was there when he drugged her."

Chloe looks at Ruby and shakes her head. Chloe grew up with a mom who was a lawyer, and it doesn't take Clarence Darrow to know this isn't going well.

"You saw someone drug your friend?" he says aggressively.

"I was at the bar when it happened," Mo says in a deliberate, measured voice. "And I know the man who put the drug in her drink. He carried our beers from where we were sitting and turned his back before he set them down. His name is Allen Redding—"

"Stop," the officer says, holding up his hand. "Look, while I get that you *think* you know what happened, you don't. You're not the victim, and unless you actually witnessed something of use, like the guy actually putting something in your friend's drink, none of the rest matters."

"My friend was drugged and raped," Mo says, her voice losing some of its cool. "I think *that* matters."

"Yes. And if that's the case, then *she's* the one who needs to report it."

"That *is* the case. But she can't. She's drugged out of her mind on GHB."

Chloe stiffens at the mention of GHB. She happens to know a lot about the drug, having learned about it in veterinary school. It's an antianxiety medicine often prescribed to pets for stress. Ten times more potent than Valium, it's the most common drug used in date rapes because of its ability to render a victim helpless while leaving them awake.

The officer shrugs, and the small gesture pitches Chloe over the edge, her blood going hot, done with the officer and his uncaring, tetchy attitude.

"Look," he says, "I get you're pissed and want to get back at this guy, but the fact is you're trying to report a rape that didn't happen to you and that the victim isn't calling a rape and which she can't entirely remember. Was she drinking?"

"She had a beer, but—"

"So that's a yes?" he says accusingly.

Chloe, having heard enough, stands. She leads Ruby out the door and into the main lobby. They stop by the gift shop, then at the Starbucks cart beside the entrance.

When she returns, the officer is saying, "Fine, you want me to file a report, that's what I'll do. It's a waste of time, but it's the taxpayers' dollars, not mine."

"Cappuccino?" Chloe asks brightly, holding one of the two Starbucks cups toward Mo.

Mo furrows her brow and cocks her head. Mo is a tea girl, has been since they were teenagers. Chloe holds her eyes, and Mo's right dimple twitches. "No, thanks. It'll keep me up."

"Oh, right," Chloe says. She looks at the cappuccino, then at the officer. "Officer?" she asks, extending the cup toward him.

The officer runs his eyes over her, pausing on the inch-long scar on her forehead before continuing down to stop on her severed pinkie, which holds the cup. *Doberman,* she thinks with a shudder, and it takes all her restraint not to fold the pinkie out of view.

"Thanks," he says, his hand purposely grazing the stump as he takes it.

Chloe turns to Mo. "I'll run home and grab some clothes for Haze."

"Thanks," Mo says, sounding completely done in.

"Look," the officer says after taking a sip of his cappuccino, his attitude softening slightly with the gift, "I get you're upset, but if you want my advice, in the future, I suggest you girls learn to keep a better eye on your drinks."

He takes another long pull as Chloe smiles and nods along.

7
MO

The last thing Officer Gretzky said before leaving was, "Call if she changes her mind about being raped." Like it was a choice Hazel was making—deciding to be raped or not.

Mo drops her face in her hands, unable to believe this is happening . . . has happened. She can't get her head around it, like time has reversed, hurtled back eight years—different place, different trauma, same feeling of despair.

The doors to the outside open as a nurse leaves for the night, and Mo shivers as a gust of wind blows in. Hazel still has her jacket, and she is cold, a state that causes extreme stress no matter how much she tells herself she's not in danger.

She rubs her arms for warmth, hating herself. When she realized Hazel wasn't at the apartment, she knew something wasn't right. There was no way Hazel would go off with a guy she'd just met. Why didn't she listen to her gut?

Find My Friends led her to a liquor store in the Tenderloin, a place called Emperor Liquor. The owner had seen Hazel through the window, staggering unsteadily down the sidewalk with no coat, and he'd ushered her inside. *A good man.* Mo is often surprised by the kindness of strangers—people willing to go the extra mile for another, sometimes even sacrificing a great deal to help.

Eight years ago, Kyle—when he was only nineteen and someone she'd known less than a day—saved her along with six others when he bravely hiked into a blizzard to get help after the accident. He walked away not expecting a thing, not even a thank-you. She often wonders about that, if she's as good a person as he is. She knows she is generous, but it's easy to give when you have a lot. True evidence of one's humanity is when giving comes at a cost. The one time she was tested, she failed, and it left doubt of her goodness etched on her soul.

When she and Ruby got to the liquor store, Hazel was sitting on a stool beside the register, her head bent and her eyes focused on the scarred linoleum floor. She didn't look up, didn't seem to realize Mo was there. She wore a worn leather jacket, her parka nowhere in sight.

Ruby stepped close and sniffed her knee, her tail swishing with recognition of a person she knew, and Hazel swung her head toward the dog in a slow, languid way that made Mo realize something was wrong beyond whatever trauma had occurred. Her pupils were small, constricted so they barely existed, and her normally ivory face was white like it had been drained of blood.

"I came to take you home," Mo said, her heart scatter-firing as she tried to figure out what had happened. She thought maybe it was shock but quickly realized that wasn't it when Hazel said, "Mo? What are you doing here?" like she had no recollection of their conversation from twenty minutes before.

Mo wrapped her arm around Hazel's shoulders to help her up, but the leather jacket was large, and she slipped from Mo's grip. Hazel caught herself on the stool, and that's when Mo saw it, a patch of maroon on the cracked brown vinyl.

Sickness rose in her throat, and her knees went weak. "Oh," she said.

Hazel looked with her as the store owner looked away, his eyes sliding to the floor. Hazel didn't react. As she turned back, her chin dropped again to her chest, and then she tilted her head and said, "His jacket." Pulling from Mo's hold, she shrugged off the leather jacket and held it toward the store owner. *"Mamnoon,"* she said with shocking clarity, then slumped back to the dazed state of the moment before.

Mo also thanked the man, then led Hazel outside. It was cold, and Hazel shivered, so Mo peeled off her North Face jacket and draped it over her shoulders.

When they got in the Uber, Mo asked the driver to take them to the emergency room. Hazel said nothing, but a few minutes later, when they pulled in front of the entrance, she said, "No," and shook her head hard, her eyes fixed on the red **EMERGENCY** letters.

"Haze, we have to."

Hazel shook her head harder.

Mo felt tears threatening and swallowed them back. "Haze, you could be hurt." It took all her willpower not to look at the dark patch on Hazel's jeans. "And something's not right."

Though Hazel continued to shake her head, when Mo got out and opened Hazel's door, obediently she climbed out and followed. It was odd. Normally, Hazel was very strong willed, bullheaded to the point of frustration, but it was as if her free will had been turned way down or her brain wasn't quite firing on all cylinders.

The admitting nurse, a statue of a woman with a shock of white hair and piercing blue eyes, took one look at Hazel and asked, "Do you know what she's on?"

"On?" Mo parroted, looking from the nurse to Hazel and back again, and only then did it occur to her that Hazel was on some sort of drug.

"Haze?" Mo said. "Did you take something? Did Allen give you something?" It was the first time Mo had thought of Allen as having something to do with what had happened.

Hazel's head lolled up toward Mo. "He gave me your beer."

"Let's get her inside," the nurse said with some urgency, causing Mo to grow concerned.

Another nurse showed up almost immediately and took Hazel's blood pressure, pulse, and temperature. And a few minutes after that, the doctor appeared.

"Hazel, do you know why you're here?" she asked. The woman was old and tough. Her steel-gray hair was bundled tight on her head, and there was a tight pinch to her mouth that said, *Don't mess with me.*

Hazel's head lolled in a circle before stopping at five o'clock, her eyes on the floor.

"Do you know how you got here?"

Head sway.

"Do you have any idea what drug you've taken?"

No response at all.

"What's the last thing you remember?"

Hazel looked at Mo. "Can we go? I want to go home."

"Soon," the doctor said. "First, let's make sure you're okay."

Hazel's head dropped again so she was looking at the floor.

"Hazel, I'm going to have a nurse draw some blood. Your blood pressure's low, and so is your temperature."

"Will she be okay?" Mo asked, worried by the doctor's intensity.

The doctor ignored her. "Hazel, do you remember anything that happened tonight?"

"I want to go home," Hazel repeated.

"I know," the doctor said with remarkable tenderness. "Hang in there, kiddo. This will all be over soon." She patted Hazel on the knee and turned toward the door.

"Doctor," Mo said, hurrying after her. Keeping her voice low, she asked, "What about a rape kit? That's why we're here. I think she was raped."

The doctor sighed heavily and glanced at Hazel, then back at Mo. "She has no idea why she's here. At some point, she might figure it out, but at the moment, she's still heavily under the influence of whatever she's on, and until she tells me otherwise, it's not my place to speculate on what has or hasn't happened."

"But—"

The doctor held up her hand, gnarled and spotted, a simple gold band on the third finger. "If she was unknowingly given something, then assaulted, which seems possible given her current state, it will be up to her to figure that out."

"Unknowingly given something?"

"Roofied," the doctor said, a word that sent a jolt to Mo's spine as she realized what she was saying, that Allen had drugged Hazel's drink, then raped her.

"We need to do a rape kit," Mo pleaded, her pulse pounding. Allen had done this, and Mo was the one who'd left Hazel alone with him.

"When Hazel figures out what has happened, she will need to come to terms with that and deal with it," the doctor said calmly. "My job is to make sure she's well enough to do that."

"But—"

"Look, if you want to call the police and report what you know, have at it, but as far as Hazel goes"—she threw a look over her shoulder at Hazel, who was sitting slumped and slack jawed on the edge of the exam table—"at the moment, she's not going to be a part of it. These things are personal, and how they are processed is up to the individual. My job is to figure out what she's on and make sure she recovers from it. That's all."

She marched past, and Mo returned to the exam table. She reached for Hazel's hand, but Hazel pulled it away, clearly angry even through her daze. "Go away," she said and folded her arms across her chest.

So Mo returned to the waiting area with Ruby, sat in the chair closest to the exam rooms, and waited.

Half an hour later, the nurse came out and let her know Hazel had GHB in her system, a common date rape drug. They were giving her activated charcoal to absorb it, along with IV fluids to keep her hydrated and to help stabilize her blood pressure.

When the nurse left, Mo called the police. And a lot of good that did. Officer Gretzky was condescending, rude, and completely unhelpful.

She hugs herself tighter and rocks in the chair, shivering with the cold and her rage. *Rape.* The word causes spider chills across her skin. All girls grow up with a certain amount of dread at the thought, but for Mo it has always felt abstract—one of those sordid things that happens in dark alleys and seedy neighborhoods, not something that happens to someone she loves after a night of beers at their local bar to celebrate something wonderful.

How could she have not seen it? Recognized the danger?

She takes out her phone and pulls up Allen's Instagram. He looks so normal. His profile picture is a shot of him grinning the same toothy grin he gave when he greeted them.

She scrolls through his feed. He doesn't post much, but a girl named Ashley and another named Meg have tagged him dozens of times. Most of the posts are of them at concerts, parties, and clubs.

She switches to Facebook. His cover photo shows him and a group of friends standing on a rock in the mountains with backpacks. He drives a BMW and likes basketball—the Lakers—and football—the Rams. His brother, James, is in some of the photos. They look alike, except James looks nicer. There's a graduation photo that shows his parents, a handsome couple, the mom blonde and the dad bald. His profile says he works as an account executive for a local tech company called Bit-Works.

The door to the exam rooms opens, and a nurse Mo doesn't recognize pokes her head out. "You can come back now."

Mo shoves her phone in the pouch of her sweatshirt and follows her to Hazel's exam bay.

Hazel is now in a hospital gown and is sitting back in the bed with the head cranked up, looking like a proper patient. An ID bracelet is on her wrist, and a pulse monitor is clipped to her finger. She turns her head slowly to look at Mo, her pupils still small but with more recognition than was there before.

"Hey," Mo says, stepping toward her but then stopping when Hazel recoils. "Chloe's bringing you some clothes from home. As soon as she gets here, we can go."

Hazel looks at her hands on top of the blanket and doesn't answer. Unsure what else to say, Mo stands quiet. She wants to apologize, beg for forgiveness, but knows now is not the time. She wants to ask what she can do but knows the answer is nothing.

After what seems like an eternity but which is probably no more than a few minutes, Hazel repeats what she said earlier: "He gave me your beer."

"Yeah, okay," Mo says, only realizing the significance a few seconds later. *He gave me your beer.* Allen grabbed both their beers, and when Mo walked past to take the call from Kyle, he was still holding them, the handles fisted in one hand. Hers was slightly more full than Hazel's and had her lipstick on the rim. The beer Allen drugged was meant for *her.* *She* was the one he intended to rape.

8
CHLOE

The knock comes less than ten minutes after they arrive home. It's nearly six in the morning, and Chloe's so tired she can't see straight. In the last two days, she's slept less than four hours, and all she wants is to curl up in her bed and not wake up until dinnertime. But that's not possible. She and Ruby can't stay here. They need to go to the van. She only came back to get the wagon and her vet bag.

Ruby tilts her head, turns toward the sound, then goes into full-fledged guard dog mode, barking and howling and yapping up a storm, waking up everyone on their floor, in the building, possibly in the entire neighborhood. Chloe drops the water jug she was filling and shushes her, but it's no use. Dogs who care about their people bark. She hurries to the living room and, holding Ruby by the collar, opens the door, prepared to be facing Jerry the landlord and already rehearsing the plea she will make to keep Mo from being evicted. Instead, she finds herself looking at the officer from the hospital.

"What the hell did you put in my coffee?" he growls, his voice even gravellier than before.

Ruby lunges and snaps, but Chloe holds her tight. "Your coffee?" she says innocently, as if she has no idea what he's talking about.

He looks terrible, and she's amazed how quickly his appearance has come apart—his short, spiky hair matted with sweat, his eyes bloodshot, and his mouth pinched in a tight slash of anger.

"What's going on?" Mo asks, walking from Hazel's room. "Oh," she says. "Officer Gretzky. Do you have news about Allen?" she asks hopefully.

"Who the hell is Allen?"

Mo opens her mouth to answer but decides against it, her eyes sliding from the officer to Chloe and then back again. "Would you like to come in?" she asks with the same fake innocence Chloe used a moment before.

"Crap!" he exclaims and nearly pushes Chloe aside as he bursts into the apartment. "Bathroom?"

Chloe points down the hall, and he hobble-races past her. Both she and Mo watch, and when the door closes, Mo turns, her lips pursed, going for a stern look of reproach but failing miserably when the officer swears, and she nearly chokes on her giggle.

"What did you do?" she hisses.

"Just gave him a little Ex-Lax to help him relax, though it doesn't seem to be working. He seems pretty wound up."

Mo shakes her head, and Chloe smirks. It's not exactly GHB, but it gets the point across. Chloe's always felt there's too little justice in the world when it comes to jerks like Gretzky and that a little intentional karmic intervention once in a while helps balance things out.

More cussing through the wood makes it impossible not to laugh, and when it passes, Chloe asks, "How's Haze?"

Mo looks at the floor. "Not good. Still acting weird."

"It's the GHB. It's going to take some time to wear off."

"I should have gone after her."

"How? She didn't answer your texts. She didn't have Find My Friends on."

"I don't know," Mo mumbles. "I feel like I could have done something."

Chloe's about to say something more when the door to the bathroom opens and Gretzky stomps toward them. "I should arrest you," he says, wagging his stubby finger at her.

Ruby's hackles lift, and she growls with her teeth bared. Chloe holds her tight and is about to answer, but Mo gets there first. "Arrest her?" she says. "For what? Did you *see* her put something in your coffee?"

He glares, but trying to intimidate Mo is a complete waste of time.

"If you want my advice"—she offers her most engaging smile, the one that shows all her pearly whites—"in the future, I suggest you learn to keep a better eye on your drinks."

Gretzky glares, his eyes narrowed in on Mo before he turns them on Chloe. "This isn't over," he snarls.

Chloe shrugs like it's no big deal. And though she knows she shouldn't, as the idea is truly terrible and certain only to make things worse, as he walks past, she winks.

He whirls, his face red as boiled ham, but he's already past the threshold, so calmly she closes the door.

"Bitch," he snarls through the wood.

Chloe looks down at Ruby. "It's okay, girl. I'm sure he meant it as a compliment."

"You probably shouldn't have done that," Mo says.

"I did it for Haze."

"He's not the one who raped her."

"He's the one who didn't give a damn she got raped."

9
MO

"Dog? What dog?" Mo asks innocently.

Jerry narrows his eyes, possibly his nicest feature, golden brown and wide set over a hawkish nose and thin lips. She opens the door wider to illustrate it's only her in her pajamas in the apartment.

"Our television was on. Could that have been what you heard?"

Mo has always been an excellent liar, which isn't a trait she's necessarily proud of but is one that comes in handy at times like this. After Officer Gretzky left, Chloe and Ruby did the same. Nothing Mo said would convince Chloe otherwise, which turned out to be a good thing—no evidence, no crime. She smiles sweetly at Jerry.

"There was barking," Jerry says, his brow crunched deep over his eyes. "Last night, and again early this morning. Felicia heard it as well."

Felicia is a middle-aged woman who never leaves her apartment. She has some sort of job that allows her to work from home and seemingly no social life. Mostly she's sweet—delivering homemade gingerbread loaves at Christmas and always happy to pick up the mail if Mo needs it. But she's also the first one to tattle on her neighbors over any infraction of the building's rules.

"She must have been mistaken," Mo says, barely containing a yawn. Jerry's knock woke her almost exactly three hours after she went to sleep, and unlike Chloe, Mo's a girl who needs a solid eight hours of shut-eye to function.

"What about your roommate? The one with the short hair?"

"Not here."

She watches his eyes flick side to side as he tries to come up with something else to say. Finally, with no great epiphany, he mumbles, "No pets. We're clear on that?"

"Crystal."

"Fine." With one last glance into the apartment, he pivots and walks away.

Mo closes the door and slides down the wood to the floor, then drops her head to her knees as the reality of what happened last night plows into her.

Hazel was raped.

She stares at the crisscross pattern of the parquet floor, studying the grain of each wedge of wood and thinking of everything that went into creating it—each storm and gust of wind an influence on how the tree grew, slow and steady, until the day it was felled and all that stopped.

It was supposed to be me.

The knot in her stomach tightens—familiar—the same guilt she felt the day she lived and her best friend, Finn, died, when her first shameful reaction was relief. "We do not control our reactions," her mom said when she confessed the awful truth. They were at the hospital, where Mo was recovering from frostbite, her fingers and toes in danger of infection. "Only our actions."

Tears threaten as Mo thinks of all the actions that led to what happened last night: her selfish desire to go out even though Hazel really wanted to stay home; her choice to take Kyle's call and leave Hazel alone with Allen; the inaction of not looking for her when she realized Hazel hadn't come home.

The wake-up chime of her phone goes off in her room, and with a shuddering sigh, she pushes to her feet. On her way to the bathroom to get ready, she stops at Hazel's room. The sign on the door reads, THINK LIKE A PROTON, ALWAYS POSITIVE.

She knocks lightly.

Nothing.

"Haze?" She rests her forehead on the wood. "I need to go to work. I have my interview today." Mentioning the interview with Jake Tapper seems wrong. Going to work seems wrong. Leaving Hazel alone definitely feels wrong. But what choice is there? Hazel doesn't want her around; she's made that clear. At the hospital, she continued to tell her to go away. When they got in the van, she climbed to the far back so she was as far from Mo as possible. When they got home, she refused to let Mo help her.

"I'll be back this afternoon. Do you need anything?" She sets her hand on the door, torn between staying and leaving. Finally, she says, "Chloe's in the van if you need her. She said she'll be back later this morning after she takes Ruby to the shelter."

Mo continues on, thinking how quickly everything has come apart. *Snap*, like a pretzel or a twig, she thinks as she steps under the hot stream of water in the shower.

In the mountains, eight years ago, it was a pop, actually three of them . . . *pop, pop, pop* . . . as the rivets that held the guardrail gave way and the camper she and ten other people were in plunged over the side of a mountain. Last night, it was the buzz of her phone . . . *buzz, buzz, buzz*.

"Don't touch me," Hazel said when Mo reached out to help her from the exam table, the words thick but the sentiment razor sharp—hate and blame radiating.

The doctor explained Hazel's anger could be a result of the GHB. It messes with a person's emotions and can stay in the system for days, sometimes weeks. She said not to worry if Hazel wasn't acting like herself. She will probably be anxious and moody and might suffer posttraumatic stress episodes. The hangover will be brutal. She will be nauseous and confused and have a screaming headache that Advil and Tylenol won't help. She should not be left alone for long periods, and she should not drive. When she is feeling better, she should talk to someone, a professional who deals with these sorts of things.

Mo steps from the shower and dries herself off. Hazel's not going to talk to someone. She is an intensely private person and would never go to a psychiatrist. It's possible she might never admit what happened to anyone at all.

She pulls on her clothes and only realizes she didn't rinse the conditioner from her hair when she goes to brush it. After undressing, she gets in the shower again and focuses more carefully on the tasks in front of her—clothes, makeup, hair, Uber to the office.

She walks into the Market Street high-rise that's been home to FactNews since she started the company two years ago. Usually, walking into the building lifts her spirit like a jolt of caffeine. Her dad worked in a building similar to this, and each time she enters its gleaming lobby, she feels like she is carrying on in his footsteps.

"Hey, Mo," Esther says when Mo steps off the elevator. Tall, lean, and mostly sweet but with a heavy dose of sass, Esther played first-string basketball for NYU until she blew out her shoulder and decided to hang up her high-tops. "You're late."

"Yeah. Sorry," Mo says, going for perky but not sure she's pulling it off.

"The phone's been ringing off the hook. This story is on fiii-re." She smiles a great big grin with lots of teeth, which was the reason Mo hired her—anyone with that great a smile is someone you definitely want on your team.

"Thanks, E. That's great."

"You okay?"

"Yeah. Uh-huh. Fine."

"Thought you'd be happier."

"I am," Mo lies. "I've just got a lot on my mind."

"Yeah. No kidding. Jake Tapper. Mmm, mmm. If that man grew a foot and hit the weight room, I might have a crush."

Mo manages a laugh. Esther is over six feet and ripped, and she likes her men the same.

Mo continues toward the newsroom but detours before she gets there into the only private space on the floor, the conference room. Leaning against the door, she closes her eyes as her pulse throbs and her eyes well with fresh tears.

Pull it together, before everything falls apart, she orders, but telling herself that only makes it worse. She understands this is the biggest story in the company's history, the break they've been working toward, and that in half an hour she has the most important interview of her life. She knows she needs to focus, put on her game face, and nail it. But all she can think about is Hazel.

A knock on the door startles her.

"Mo?" Esther says through the wood.

"Yeah. Here," she says stupidly, sounding like a ten-year-old answering roll call in gym class.

"CNN's on the line," Esther says. "They need to run a sound check."

"Yeah, okay. Just give me a second."

Closing her eyes again, she takes three deep breaths. As she exhales the final one, her phone buzzes with a text. Pulling it from her pocket, she sees a message from Kyle: Have a great interview. I know you're going to kill it. xoxo

Strange, she thinks as she stares at the words, that he doesn't know what's happened. This thing that is so catastrophic and big and that has thrown her life completely off kilter, Kyle is entirely unaware of, his life exactly as it was yesterday when they talked.

At some point she will need to tell him, but at the moment, it's all she can do not to fall apart. She texts back a thumbs-up and two red hearts.

"Mo?" Esther says. "They're waiting."

"Yeah. Okay." Straightening her sweater and her expression, she reaches for the door, but before her hand touches the lever, she stops. Pulling out her phone again, she dials from memory.

"Agent Fitzpatrick," Fitz answers.

"Hey, Fitz," Mo says, the words cracking.

"Mo? Everything okay?"

"No."

10
CHLOE

Chloe was supposed to take Ruby to the shelter. She promised Mo that was what she was going to do, and she told herself it was what she needed to do. She cannot keep this dog. She has no way of taking care of her.

The problem is, when she woke up after falling asleep in the back of the van, the dog was curled against her, shivering. Typically, dogs do better than humans when it comes to cold, but the pup is so depleted she has no reserves. Chloe tried to get her to eat, but she just stared forlornly at the bowl, then went back to snuggling against Chloe for warmth.

Dogs are devoted creatures, the best of them so committed to their families that abandonment can devastate them to the point that they shut down, emotionally and physically. Sometimes, that suffering manifests itself as anorexia, a debilitating condition in which, no matter how hungry, a dog is unable to eat.

If Chloe takes her to the shelter, they will undoubtedly put her down. Shelters simply don't have the resources to deal with traumatized animals in distress. Ruby's only hope is for Chloe to get her eating.

Chloe leans her head back against the panels of the van. The vet she worked for before Eric, her loser boyfriend of eight years, decided to take off to "find himself" warned her: "We're not superheroes, kid. All we can do is our best. But at some point you need to realize there's simply no way to save them all."

He was the kindest person she knew, but he never took home a stray. And this was why. Chloe can't take care of this dog. She can't even take care of herself. Her stomach growls ravenously as if to prove it. She hasn't eaten since the half plate of brussels sprouts she had last night.

Her phone buzzes, and she looks at the cracked screen to see a message from Hazel: R u nearby?

The van is parked in the lot of a supermarket half a block from the apartment.

Yeah. On my way.

Chloe looks down at Ruby, and she looks back with intelligent, curious eyes that say, *Where to, boss?* And Chloe knows she's done for. She could no more bring this dog to the shelter than cut off her own foot.

"Sorry, girl, but I'm going to need to knock you out again," she says and pulls a syringe from her vet bag along with another bag of IV fluids she can't afford.

As soon as the dog is hooked up and asleep, she places her in the wagon and covers her with a towel. As she walks toward the apartment, she prays Jerry's not around. But as soon as she walks through the doors, she knows the jig is up. Felicia, Mo's nosy neighbor, walks around the corner from where the mailboxes are.

She looks at Chloe, then down at the wagon. "I knew I heard a dog."

11
MO

Mo drops her elbows to the conference table and her face to her hands. She bombed the interview. She started out off balance and never quite found her footing. She could tell Jake Tapper was disappointed, and she doubts he'll invite her back.

In the last minute, she redeemed herself slightly with an anecdote about people and dogs: "I actually don't agree with a lot of this," she said with a flick of her hand to the chart with the *BOOM* graphic on the screen. "The doom and gloom of it. I know what the data shows and that it's real, but I also believe things are going to change and that the trend is going to turn around."

"Why's that?" Jake Tapper asked.

"Because you, Jake, like most of us, are a lot like a dog." She smiled wide, and Jake tilted his head, which made him indeed look a bit canine. "All any of us really want is to belong to something more than ourselves and to feel safe and loved. So while, at the moment, things might look a bit bleak in the 'happily ever after' department, I think it's only temporary and that, ultimately, the pendulum is going to swing back and we will figure out new ways to navigate the world as it continues to evolve and discover all sorts of ways to love and be a family." She smiled wide again, then barked, and Jake barked back his approval, which made her feel a little better about things.

She pulls off her false eyelashes, packs up her laptop, and, with a deep sigh, walks from the conference room.

"Good job," Esther says brightly. "Woof!"

"Woof!" Mo musters back, hoping that single sound bite might be enough to get the story some traction, *#Woof, #WeAreDogs*. She'll work on a few more hashtags during the day and send them to their social media person. "I have a meeting. I'll be back this afternoon."

"You're leaving?" Esther says. She holds up a stack of message notes. "You just got here."

"Yeah. I know. And I'll be back. Hold down the fort."

Mo flees before Esther can ask any more questions. In the two years since Mo started the company, she's rarely not first in the office or last to leave. All those long days put in to get to this moment, the day FactNews became a legit player in the news game, a moment that, until last night, seemed incredibly important.

Her phone buzzes as she steps from the building, the frigid wind whipping and making her wish she had her North Face jacket, which Hazel still has.

The bark was good.

She runs her thumb over Kyle's words, wondering if he noticed how off she was. Probably not. Kyle's not perceptive that way—straightforward and earnest, he takes things at face value, a quality she loves.

More texts pop up from friends, associates, her mom. She emojis back smiley faces, hearts, and thumbs-ups, then turns off the phone and shoves it in her pocket as she continues on to Ritual Roasters, her favorite coffee shop in the city.

Fitz is already seated at a table beside the window, and just seeing him brings enormous comfort. She can't say exactly why, except Fitz is that sort of person, the kind you can count on no matter what, and who, once he's your friend, will always be on your side.

"Hey," he says, standing and offering his trademark crooked smile, always slightly higher on the right. "Earl Grey, one sugar?"

"Please," she says as she shudders away the cold.

He hurries away, and she looks through the window at the city, people bustling around with their shoulders hitched against the wind, happily going about their lives. Yesterday, she was one of them. She had lunch with their media designer at Tadich Grill. He was excited about tickets he'd scored to see Beyoncé. She was excited about the report. It all seemed so wonderful.

Fitz sets her tea in front of her, along with a cinnamon twist. Her stomach rumbles, and she realizes she hasn't eaten anything since the ice cream she had yesterday afternoon.

"You looked hungry," Fitz says with a shrug, his thin shoulders not quite filling out his dark charcoal suit. He sits down with his own coffee—black, dark roast—a simple guy with simple tastes.

"How's chasing bad guys going?" she asks.

"I've hung up my holster."

"Really?" She's genuinely surprised. For as long as she's known Fitz, his dream has been to be a field agent with the FBI, an opportunity he got less than two years ago.

"Turns out I'm better behind a desk."

"Probably true," Mo says. Fitz is definitely more Poindexter than G.I. Joe.

"It seems I have a soft spot for criminals when I actually meet them."

"Oh no. That's not good."

"Nope. Definitely a problem."

Mo smiles, imagining Fitz confronting a drug smuggler and ending up in a conversation with him to figure out where his problems began.

"So you're back to using your diabolical mind to take them down anonymously?"

"Exactly." He grins. "I really would make a good mob boss." He attempts to screw his mouth into a surly scowl, which looks ridiculous on his white-bread, boyish face.

"Absolutely," Mo says. "No one would ever suspect you."

He sets his coffee in front of him, and his face turns serious.

"That bad?" she asks.

"Definitely not good."

"Allen has a record?"

"Worse," Fitz says. "He doesn't." He lifts his phone and reads: "Allen Clayton Redding. Twenty-six. One sibling. A younger brother, James Tyler Redding. Allen was born in Thousand Oaks, California. He works as an account executive for a company called Bit-Works and is squeaky clean except for a few speeding tickets."

He sets down the phone.

"But?" Mo says.

"But . . . ," Fitz says, "it's what's between the lines that's disturbing. The first thing I noticed was from his senior year in high school."

"High school?" Mo asks as her mind calculates. Allen is two years older than she is, so Fitz is talking eight years ago.

"He transferred to a different school," Fitz says.

"Okay. So?"

"Three months before graduation."

Mo doesn't see the significance.

"It seemed odd," Fitz goes on. "His whole life he attended the same public school system, and in high school, he ran track and was good. But then suddenly, right before his final season, he transfers to a new school where he's ineligible to run."

Mo's nose for news twitches, and she nods in appreciation of how good Fitz is at his job.

"So I called the school," Fitz says, "and the principal gives me the standard line about not being able to share information about a student. But then, without prodding, she goes on to say she remembered Allen transferring *right after prom*. She emphasized the words like she was trying to tell me something. So I did some digging, searched through social media posts from that time, and found out the girl Allen took to prom ended up in the hospital that night."

Mo's eyes get wide, and Fitz nods as he confirms it. "GHB poisoning. The girl nearly OD'd and needed to have her stomach pumped."

"He started doing this *eight* years ago?" Mo says, her blood going cold at the thought.

"That's what it looks like."

"But he doesn't have a record? How? How is that possible?"

"I called the girl's mom, and she said they did go to the police, but Allen denied having anything to do with it. Which made it his word against the daughter's, and since the daughter couldn't remember most of what happened, the police decided they didn't have enough to make a case."

"So that was it—he just got away with it?"

"Not entirely. It seems the students had no problem deciding who to believe, which was the reason he transferred."

"But no charges . . . and no record?"

"It gets worse," Fitz says. "When he was at Berkeley, there were two separate sexual assault investigations at his fraternity. Both involved victims who had been roofied with GHB."

"At Sigma Nu?"

Fitz looks at his phone. "Yeah. Sigma Nu. There was no mention of Allen, but he was kicked out of the house shortly after the second investigation started, which makes me think he might have been involved."

"And what happened?"

"Nothing. The inquiries were dropped due to lack of 'credible'"—he makes quote marks in the air—"'evidence.'"

"So what you're saying is Allen's been doing this for over eight years, to who knows how many women, and despite several of the victims coming forward, not a single accusation has stuck?"

Fitz blows out a hard breath. "It's tough to nail these guys. The drug makes the victims pretty much useless as witnesses because their testimony is deemed unreliable, so the cases rarely go forward. Sorry, Mo. I know this isn't what you wanted to hear."

She shakes her head, unable to believe this is what she's left with. "So it's going to just keep happening?"

"Unless someone stops him, I'm afraid so."

12
CHLOE

Chloe walks into the apartment to find Hazel sitting on the couch, her feet planted on the floor and her eyes fixed on the wall in front of her. She is still in the sweats she wore home from the hospital, her hair unwashed, and Chloe conceals her wince at the idea she hasn't showered, knowing it means Allen Redding's stench is still on her.

"Hey," she says, and Hazel turns, her eyes spiraling in and out before focusing.

"Oh. It's you."

She seems surprised, as if she doesn't remember that she was the one who texted and asked Chloe to come home, and Chloe realizes she might still be under the effects of the GHB. She looks both better and worse than she did last night. Her eyes have returned to normal, the pupils no longer constricted and dazed, but they are laced with such sadness it's hard to look at her.

Chloe leaves the wagon beside the door and takes a seat in the armchair across from her.

"How does it work?" Hazel asks.

"How does what work?"

"GHB."

"Oh," Chloe says, not really surprised this is what Hazel's thinking about.

Eight years ago, after she survived the accident that killed her brother and sister, she became obsessed with cold and what it does to you, possessed with an intense need to understand it, mistakenly believing that if somehow she could decipher the source of what happened, she'd have some sort of control over it. Which of course was foolish, like thinking that if you know you will drown without oxygen, it will no longer be true.

"It's a disinhibitor," Chloe says, working to recall what her pharmacology text said about the drug. "Which means it slows down your brain activity, making you less excitable, which is why it helps with stress."

Hazel nods. "Dulls you?" she says, half statement, half question, her eyes on the wall again. "But not enough to knock you out?"

"When I use it on animals, they stay conscious," Chloe says. "It's like heavy-duty Valium."

She looks at Ruby, conked out in the wagon, and the thought crosses her mind that perhaps she should try it, thinking a small dose could mellow Ruby out enough to get her eating.

"I thought you were taking her to the shelter?" Hazel says, then sees Chloe's sheepish expression and adds, "Couldn't do it?"

"I'm planning on taking her tomorrow."

The corner of Hazel's mouth twitches with almost the hint of a smile. "I'm glad. I like this dog."

"I just need to get her eating. Speaking of which, I'm starving. Are you hungry?"

Hazel shakes her head. "My stomach hurts."

Chloe's throat tightens, unsure if the cramping is from the physical effects of the rape or the drugs, both ideas upsetting. She looks from Hazel to Ruby and back again, two tender souls done in by their innocent trust and the harsh cruelty of the world.

"How do you get it?" Hazel says. "GHB? Is it a prescription?"

"It is, but it's also pretty easy to make. The clinical name is gamma-hydroxybutyrate, but it's just a fancy way of saying butoxyethanol and—"

"Right," Hazel says, deciphering the base elements easily. "So he made it himself?"

"Probably."

Hazel is about to say something else when a knock at the door interrupts, startling Ruby and sending her toppling drunkenly from the wagon.

"That would be Jerry," Chloe says.

"Uh-oh. Looks like someone's got some 'splaining to do," Hazel says, doing her Desi Arnaz impersonation but without its usual panache.

Chloe takes hold of Ruby and opens the door to see the landlord, red faced and furious.

"Get out!" he says without preamble. "I did not rent this apartment to you. You are not on the lease. And there are *no pets* allowed in this building."

Ruby growls as Chloe nods; everything he said is correct.

"I just came to get my things," she says. "I'm sorry. This has nothing to do with Mo . . . Maureen. She doesn't even know I'm here."

"You have one hour," he says. "If you're not gone by then, I evict Maureen and Hazel as well." He motions with his chin over her shoulder, and Chloe glances back to see Hazel backed in the corner beside the couch, a stricken look on her face that Chloe takes a moment to recognize as fear. Hazel, who only yesterday would walk boldly around the city not worried about a thing, is afraid to get within a dozen feet of their blustering, harmless landlord.

Chloe turns back. "I promise," she says. "You won't see me again."

13
MO

Mo knows this is a very bad idea. It's something Chloe might do, and Mo would tell her it was a very bad idea. Yet she continues on, propelled by anger so great it feels as if her organs have grown too large for her body and are going to explode.

The offices for Bit-Works are located a few blocks from her own office, sprawled across two floors of a modern glass-and-steel building on Mission Street. The elevator shoots up so smoothly she isn't sure she is moving until the doors open at the eleventh floor and she steps into a travertine lobby, where a black-haired pixie with bright-pink lips greets her. "Can I help you?"

"I'd like to speak with Allen Redding."

She sizes Mo up. "Do you have an appointment?"

"I'm an old friend."

"Your name?"

"Maureen Kaminski." As she says it, she wonders if Allen will recognize the name. Most people only know her as Mo, a nickname given to her as a toddler.

The office is warm, so she takes off her wool coat and drapes it over her arm as she steps into the waiting area. Floor-to-ceiling windows look out over the Bay Bridge, and she admires the view before sitting on the black leather couch. An array of magazines is neatly fanned on top of a glass-and-chrome table: *Forbes*, *Wired*, *PC World*.

"Would you like some water?" the receptionist asks, a clip to her voice as she assesses Mo again now that her coat is off.

"No, thank you," Mo says, offering her most engaging smile, the one that says, *I mean you no harm.*

With a curt nod, the woman pivots away, and Mo thinks she might have feelings for Allen. Poor thing.

"Mo!"

The jovial greeting surprises her, until she realizes the man walking toward her isn't Allen but his brother, James. He opens his arms wide as if to hug her.

"James," she says, standing but keeping her distance.

His arms drop. "Al's in a meeting?" It comes out a question, his head tilting right.

"I'll wait."

"Perhaps I can help you," he says, the tone still upbeat but taut, like his vocal cords are strained. And that's when she sees it, the flit of his eyes as he struggles to maintain his smile.

You know, she thinks.

Keeping herself very still, all of her on fire, she says, "This is between me and your brother."

His weight shifts, and she watches as his eyes move to the table with the magazines, then the window, then the floor.

She keeps her gaze steady, merciless in its quiet accusation.

"It might be a while," he says finally.

"That's fine. I have nothing more important to do."

With a nod almost of defeat, he pivots and shuffles away.

Mo sighs and sits back on the couch and drops her face to her hands. *Even the good are bad,* she thinks. Would she do that, lie about something so big for someone she loved? *No,* she thinks, immediately followed by, *Yes*. If asked under oath if Chloe had spiked Officer Gretzky's coffee, she would say no. Of course, that was a case of the runs, not rape. But what if Chloe did do something worse, hurt someone? Would she still lie to protect her? She shakes her head. She wouldn't. Or she doesn't think she would. How could she live with herself if she did?

It's less than a minute before Allen appears, stopping a foot in front of her.

"Mo," he says brightly. "Twice in two days—must be my lucky week."

She considers how to respond. Originally, she thought she was going to confront him about what he did, but she's quite certain, looking at him now, that he will only deny it.

"Do you really think you will continue to get away with it?" she says instead, surprised at the steadiness of her voice.

"Get away with what?" he asks, his small eyes dancing as if he's enjoying himself.

"With drugging and raping women?" Mo says plainly, his lunacy stilling her, like a mountain watching a cyclone. She sees now he is off his rocker and can't believe she didn't realize it last night.

"I have *no idea* what you're talking about," he says, his voice pitching high on "no idea," letting her know he knows perfectly well what she's talking about and is relishing it.

The receptionist has stopped shuffling papers, and two coworkers, a man and a woman, have paused on their way to the elevator and now watch.

Feeling emboldened by the audience, Mo says, "No idea? Really? You have no idea how your prom date from high school ended up in the hospital and nearly died from GHB poisoning? Or about the two women who pressed sexual assault charges against you when you were in college after being drugged and raped by you? Or about my friend last night, who I introduced you to at Black Sands, who you then roofied and raped?"

A shadow passes over Allen's features, and Mo knows she's hit her mark, surprising him with her knowledge.

"None of that rings a bell?"

No longer glib, he says, "Not sure where you're getting your information, but you might want to check your facts. My prom date was my girlfriend. We'd been together for years. And she never went to the hospital for any sort of poisoning. And there have never been any sexual assault charges against me."

He's right about the second part. Charges were never filed.

"As for your friend," Allen goes on, "we had a very nice time last night, and I don't recall her complaining." He looks over and smiles at the male coworker. To the man's credit, he doesn't smile back.

Allen returns his attention to Mo. "Anything else?"

Eyes steady on his and her voice steely calm, she says, "You may think you have this figured out and that you can keep doing what you've been doing—drugging women, raping them, destroying their lives— but I'm here to tell you that you can't. Your day of reckoning is coming, and if it's the last thing I do, I promise I am going to make certain you get what's coming to you."

14
CHLOE

Chloe has an emergency house call. Mrs. Linden in Nob Hill. Her cat is vomiting. Chloe's certain it's nothing. Cats vomit. It's simply part of who they are. But she's grateful for the money it will give her.

She takes Ruby for a quick walk around the block, then frowns when they get back to the van and she sees the back right rear tire low again. Replacing her back tires will cost $300 she doesn't have.

She sighs as she climbs into the driver's seat. For working as hard as she has to get to this place in her life, she's amazed how little she has to show for it. She's broke, worse than broke, in-debt-and-drowning-fast kind of broke.

"One day at a time," she says to Ruby, who sits tall in the passenger seat, raring to go. She looks at Chloe and tilts her head, truly interested and concerned.

Chloe cranks up the indie-rock station that's become her new favorite and punches Mrs. Linden's address into her phone. The van fills with a haunting new song full of stirring drones that sound like they come from a hurdy-gurdy—a wonderful instrument that makes you want to seek it out just to hear the sound that inspired such an interesting name.

She is listening intently, trying to decide if the song is happy or sad, when her side mirror fills with flashing red and blue lights. With a groan, she pulls to the side of the road, hoping she can talk the officer out of giving her a fix-it ticket that will force her to get her tires replaced immediately and that will cost her the headache of needing to go to the precinct to prove that it's done.

She cranks down the window.

"License and registration," the cop says, and her face snaps around at the voice.

"License and registration," Officer Gretzky repeats in his unique gravel.

"Are you kidding?" she says, her blood growing warm.

"Nope. Definitely no joke," he says, his beady eyes glinting.

"This is harassment."

"Please step from the car."

"Why?"

"Because I said."

15
MO

"I told you spiking his coffee was a bad idea," Mo says as she lets them into the apartment.

Ruby lopes in ahead and collapses beside the couch. Luckily, Mo was home when Chloe called, and she was able to race down the street to get the dog before Officer Gretzky carted Chloe away.

Mo offered to move the van so it wasn't parked illegally, but instead, Officer Gretzky had the van impounded, relish in his voice as he did it.

This is what retaliation gets you: a pissed-off cop on a power trip. Mo sighs out heavily and drops her purse on the table beside the door.

"Guy can't take a joke," Chloe says like it's no big deal, but Mo hears her stress.

Bail cost $1,000, and getting Chloe's van out of impound will cost another $150. Plus, Chloe lost the fee she would have gotten for helping the woman with her sick cat, making her net loss for the night close to $1,300. Thirteen hundred dollars that Chloe, a girl living on brussels sprouts, doesn't have. All for giving a guy diarrhea.

"Disorderly conduct and contempt of cop, are you kidding?" Chloe says, continuing into the kitchen. She is wearing her "work" outfit, conservative by Chloe standards but still rocking major funk—cargo pants held up by a military belt; a leather bomber jacket, circa WWI; a frayed white tank beneath it; and brass-buckled Mary Jane Doc Martens emblazoned with dragons and stars. "Gretzky deserves more than the runs; he deserves to have *his* butt thrown in jail . . . along with Allen."

Mo is completely done in, from her hair to her toes. Between what happened last night and then today at Allen's office and then again tonight with Officer Gretzky, she just wants to crawl into bed and sleep until the world rights itself and stops spinning off its axis.

"What are you doing?" she asks as she watches Chloe spooning cooked brussels sprouts into a Tupperware container.

"Ruby and I can't stay here," she says. "Remember?"

"So where are you going to go? The van's been impounded."

Chloe shrugs noncommittally. "I don't know. We'll figure it out."

Mo yanks the bowl of brussels sprouts from her hand and puts it back in the fridge, then does the same with the Tupperware tub. "You're staying here. Both of you. Jerry can just deal with it."

"Mo—"

"No!" Mo says. What she really wants to say is, *Too much.* All of it too much. *Enough.* "You're staying here. End of discussion."

"Fine," Chloe huffs, clearly because there's no other choice. Her parents and sister are in Orange County, eight hours away, and Mo and Hazel are her only friends in the city. "But in the morning, we're leaving."

"We'll talk about tomorrow tomorrow," Mo says. "I'm going to bed."

On the way to her room, she knocks on Hazel's door. "Haze, we're home."

Silence.

"Haze?"

Nothing.

A lump forms in her throat. Hazel's made it clear she blames Mo for what happened. And she's right. Mo left her in the bar and didn't look for her when she discovered she was gone. So many mistakes made so quickly, confounding, when each step of the way she's tried so hard to do what's right.

16
CHLOE

It's later than Chloe hoped. Nearly nine. She wanted to be at the impound lot when it opened at eight to get the van, but exhaustion got the better of her, and she slept through her alarm. She pulls her bowl of cooked brussels sprouts from the fridge and sautés them in a pan with a couple of eggs, her head fuzzy from lack of sleep and food.

Ruby lies at her feet, looking as done in as Chloe feels. The clinical term is the *letdown effect*. During acute stress, the body releases hormones and adrenaline, which protect you against pain and fatigue, but once the pressure is lifted, those same chemicals drop, your dopamine levels get knocked down, and your system crashes. And that's exactly how Chloe feels, like she's crashed into a wall and been shattered into a million pieces.

She still can't believe she was arrested. *Her!* For "contempt of cop"! Not that she doesn't have enormous contempt for Gretzky. She does. But not to any criminal extent. She flips the eggs with too much force, and a brussels sprout flies from the pan. Ruby watches it land, pushes to her feet, and goes over to examine it. She sniffs the morsel, then returns to flop again at Chloe's feet, obviously hungry but not able to eat.

"It's okay," Chloe says and reaches down to pet her. "We're good. Sadness doesn't last forever." It's something a shrink told her a long time ago. At the time, Chloe didn't believe her. At the time, she didn't believe anything anyone who was trying to help told her. But it turned out she was right. Impossible as it seems, even the worst grief eventually dulls, and life replaces it. Small moments of brightness that were impossible at first breaking through, little nothings that seem insignificant, until one day, you're sitting there, going about your business, and you realize you almost have to work to remember your sorrow. Though her sister and brother are never far from her thoughts, she thinks of them less often these days and rarely with sadness.

Mo bailed her out before she made it through processing, so she never saw the inside of a jail cell, but her fingerprints and mug shots are now on file, and in a month, she will need to appear in front of a judge to defend herself against the charges. Which means telling her mom what happened in order to enlist her help. The thought causes her skin to flame, and she wonders if she should just plead guilty to avoid the humiliation.

With a heavy sigh, she slides the scramble onto a plate and carries it to the living room so she can eat while Ruby gets another dose of IV fluids. She tries not to think of the cost, but it is impossible. Each IV bag is around twenty dollars, and the sedative is about the same. At two infusions a day, Chloe is losing money faster than she's earning it, and she's not sure how much longer she will be able to keep it up.

She sets her plate on the coffee table. "Time for breakfast," she says to Ruby. The dog looks sorry for the trouble she's causing. "It's not your fault," Chloe says. "You just put your trust in the wrong person." She thinks of Eric as she says it.

Grabbing the scruff behind Ruby's neck, she injects the sedative. Ruby's still looking at her when she slumps to the floor and closes her eyes.

Chloe hooks up the IV and returns to the couch to eat her own breakfast. She's about to take her first bite when there's a knock at the door. Ruby stirs but thankfully doesn't wake.

She looks through the peephole to see two men in suits.

"Can I help you?" she asks through the wood.

"Maureen Kaminski?"

"No. I'm her roommate."

The one on the right, who is distinctly shorter than the one on the left, pulls something from the inside breast pocket of his suit jacket and holds it toward the peephole, some sort of ID. "We're with the San Francisco Police Department, and we'd like to speak with Maureen Kaminski."

A nervous current buzzes Chloe's spine as she opens the door. Bad things happen in threes: Hazel was raped, Chloe was arrested, and now two men from the SF police are here to talk to Mo.

"I'm Detective Halling," the shorter one says. "And this is Detective Wallace."

She was right about the size difference, though it's not because Detective Halling is short but instead because Detective Wallace is exceptionally tall.

"Would you like to come in?" Chloe asks and opens the door wider.

They step inside, and Detective Halling glances at Ruby, then away, while Detective Wallace's gaze sticks on the IV in her paw before looking at the stitches on her head, and a shadow of sympathy crosses his face.

"She's a stray," Chloe says. "And she's not eating." She doesn't know why she tells them this, perhaps for the delay or more likely because she's nervous. "I'm a vet, and I'm trying to save her."

Detective Wallace nods, a dog lover. Detective Halling could care less, his eyes roaming the room. "Nice place."

Chloe nods. Almost everyone has a similar reaction when they first walk into the apartment; the north-facing windows have a commanding view of the city, and Mo and Kyle did an amazing job refurbishing it, so it is modern and chic.

Grabbing her cooling breakfast from the coffee table, she carries it to the kitchen before continuing to Mo's room and rapping on the door. "Mo."

Music blasts behind the wood. When Mo is stressed, she rocks out to horrible pop songs from the eighties that make Chloe cringe.

"Mo!" she says louder.

A second later, the door opens. Mo is in black leggings and a sports bra, and Chloe realizes she was working out. Chloe jerks her head toward the men in the living room. "There are two detectives here to talk to you."

"Really?" Mo says, sounding excited. "Because of what happened to Haze? Hang on, I just need to change."

Chloe doesn't think that's why they're here, but Mo disappears before Chloe can respond.

Chloe returns to the living room. "Can I get you something to drink?" she asks. "Water? Coffee?" She hopes they don't say coffee. She's the only one in the apartment who drinks coffee, and she is down to her last scoop.

"No. Thank you," Detective Wallace answers politely, while Detective Halling shakes his head with annoyed impatience, and Chloe decides she only likes half this pair, the taller, politer, dog-loving half.

Several minutes awkwardly tick by before Mo appears. She's dressed in jeans and a button-down blue blouse, and her blonde hair is brushed and her makeup applied.

"Hello," she says brightly. "I'm Mo . . . Maureen."

The detectives introduce themselves, and Mo gestures to the couch, then sits in the armchair across from them. Chloe leans against the archway to the kitchen.

"I assume you're here about Allen," Mo says, and Chloe watches as Detective Halling's right cheek twitches and as Detective Wallace leans in, causing her nervous feeling to grow.

"You know that's why we're here?" Detective Halling asks. "When was the last time you saw Mr. Redding?"

"Saw him?" Mo asks.

Halling nods, his attention tight on Mo, while Wallace's dark eyes wander, examining the details around them as if taking an inventory.

At Black Sands, two nights ago, Chloe thinks when Mo still hasn't answered.

"What's this about?" Mo says instead.

"Did you see him yesterday?" Halling asks.

No.

"Yes," Mo says, and Chloe nearly falls off the wall.

You saw Allen yesterday? Where? Why?

"I went to his office."

You what?

Mo glances at Chloe, perhaps hearing her silent rant, then quickly looks away. "He raped a friend of mine, and I wanted to confront him about it."

Chloe barely stops her groan from escaping.

"So you went there to confront him?" Halling asks.

"I did. I was angry and upset."

"And what did he do when you confronted him?"

"He denied it. Said it never happened."

"And what did you do then?"

"Nothing. I left."

"Did you threaten him?"

Mo opens her mouth to answer, but Chloe gets there first, launching herself off the wall as she says, "This interview is over."

Halling looks up as if just remembering she is there, and his eyes narrow to slits in clear unhappiness with her interruption. "Just a few more questions," he says.

"What's this about?" Mo repeats.

Halling turns back. "Where were you last night?"

"Mo, don't answer," Chloe says, her pulse pounding.

"Between the hours of eleven and three in the morning?" Halling persists.

"Unless you intend to arrest her," Chloe says, surprised how much she sounds like her mom, "I'm going to need to ask you to leave."

"Arrest me?" Mo says, her voice pitching high. "For what?"

"Did you see Mr. Redding after you left his office?" Halling asks.

Mo is shaking her head before Chloe can tell her again not to answer.

"Leave! Now!" Chloe orders, marching to the door and opening it.

Wallace stands, and reluctantly, Halling follows. He holds Mo's eyes a full five seconds before reaching into his pocket and pulling out a business card that he sets on the table. "We'll be in touch."

They walk out, and Chloe closes the door behind them.

"What was that?" Mo asks.

Chloe whirls. "You went to Allen's office? Why? What could you possibly have thought that would accomplish?"

Mo drops her eyes to the floor. "I don't know. It was stupid."

"Ugh!" Chloe screams. "And you threatened him? Were there people there when you threatened him?"

Mo half nods. "It wasn't a real threat, more like a karma's-a-witch-and-this-is-going-to-come-back-to-bite-you kind of threat."

"Ugh!" Chloe says again and runs her hand through her hair.

"That's why they were here? Because I threatened him?"

Chloe's brain is on fire. "I doubt it," she says. "Something must have happened after you threatened him."

Mo's eyes pulse once, and her skin loses some of its pink. "Which is why they were asking where I was last night." She pulls out her phone and, using her lightning-fast thumbs, pecks at it. "Oh no," she says, her head shaking.

"What?"

She holds out the phone for Chloe to see. The headline at the top of the screen reads: Bit-Works Executive Found Drugged and Beaten in the Tenderloin.

Mo turns the phone back. "It says Allen was found unresponsive on the corner of Turk and Hyde a little before two this morning." She looks up. "Clove, that's like a block from the liquor store where I found Haze."

The awful buzz in Chloe's veins intensifies until it feels like her whole body is vibrating. "When you filed the report with Gretzky, did you tell him where you found Haze?" she asks, praying the answer is no.

"Of course," Mo says. "It was important." She looks again at her phone, then back at Chloe. "But they can't possibly think I had something to do with this. I would never . . . I could never . . ." Her voice quakes, and Chloe feels how close she is to losing it.

"Does it say if he's okay?" Chloe asks.

Mo's eyes flick side to side as she reads the rest of the article. "It says he was taken to UCSF Medical Center, where it was determined he had GHB in his system, making the police suspect the crime was premeditated and intentional. He's in critical condition and currently unresponsive."

"He's in a coma?"

"Sounds like it." She looks up, her blue eyes brimming with tears. "GHB, the Tenderloin. I don't know, Clove." Her eyes slide to Hazel's door. "Do you really think it's a coincidence?"

17
MO

Mo lies back on her bed and stares at the fan turning slowly over her head, unable to believe how quickly things have come apart. Allen's in a coma, beaten to within an inch of his life in what appears to be a copy-cat crime of what he did to Hazel. But the detectives don't know about Hazel because Hazel didn't report the rape. Mo did. Heeding the ER doctor's stern admonishment about Hazel needing to process and deal with what had happened in her own time and on her own terms, Mo left Hazel's name out of it. So now the detectives, instead of looking at Hazel as a suspect or anyone else, are looking at Mo, who very stupidly made things worse by going to Allen's office and confronting him.

The whole thing is ridiculous. Yes, she threatened Allen, but it wasn't a threat on his life. She could never drug someone and leave them in the Tenderloin.

"Hey," Chloe says, poking her head in the room.

"Hey," Mo says, sitting up and swinging her legs off the bed.

"I talked to my mom."

"And?"

"And she said you should be fine."

"Should?" Mo says. "Not exactly the reassurance I was hoping for."

"What they have isn't enough to make a case. My mom said it was a fishing expedition, meant to rattle you and see what might come out of it."

"Well, it worked. I am officially rattled." Mo drops her elbows to her knees and her face to her hands. "I need to tell you something," she mumbles.

"Okay?"

"I did something stupid."

"More stupid than going to Allen's office and threatening him in front of his coworkers?"

Mo peeks through her fingers, and Chloe crosses her arms and frowns, her posture and expression so much like her mom's it's like Mo is looking at Mrs. Miller.

"I might have posted something on Instagram," Mo says, blood flooding her face so she's certain she's pink as a flamingo.

"You posted something?" Chloe's frown deepens.

Mo closes her fingers over her eyes again, unable to look at Chloe as she confesses the mortifying cherry on top of her incredibly foolish banana split day. "A photo of Allen with a really bad caption."

Chloe waits, but Mo can't bring herself to say it out loud. On the elevator ride down from Allen's office, Mo was so furious she felt like her veins were going to rupture with her rage, so she pulled out her phone, found a photo of Allen grinning, and posted it on Instagram with the caption *Do you know this rapist?* As soon as she got in the Uber, she realized how much trouble it could lead to and deleted it, but it was up long enough for two girls from her sorority to share it on their own pages. And by the time she got to her office, it had been reposted dozens of times and was blowing up with hundreds of comments and thousands of reactions.

"Tell me you're kidding," Chloe says, and Mo peeks again through her fingers to see Chloe glaring at her phone. "You posted this? What the hell were you thinking?"

Mo shakes her head. She wasn't thinking, her mind red with rage at the idea of Allen getting away with what he'd done and continuing to get away with it for who knew how long.

"Do you know how many times this has been shared?" Chloe asks.

Mo groans and falls back to the bed. She doesn't want to know. She stopped checking when she realized it had gone viral and there was nothing she could do about it.

"Over three hundred times," Chloe says.

Mo pulls her pillow over her face. Some of the comments she saw were about Allen, but most were about guys like Allen—personal, horrible stories all similar to Hazel's—nights that started in good fun and ended in rape.

"Well, at least you're not the only suspect," Chloe says. "Some of these responses call Allen out specifically."

Mo pulls the pillow off her face. "I'm not a suspect at all," she says. "I was home last night. You were with me."

Chloe doesn't answer, causing Mo to open her eyes and push up on her elbows.

"After we got home, I went out," Chloe says, "for the cat appointment. Remember? I asked you to watch Ruby."

Mo furrows her brow as the vague recollection of Chloe waking her last night returns. Though it had only been a little after eight when they'd gotten home from Mo bailing Chloe out of jail, Mo had immediately gone to bed, completely done in from the miserable day.

Chloe knocked, then poked her head in and said something about her client paying for an Uber so Chloe could still check on her sick cat. She asked if it would be okay if Ruby hung in her room until she got back. Mo mumbled yes, and the door closed. Ruby licked Mo's elbow, and Mo fell back asleep.

"Fine," Mo says. "Haze was here. She can vouch for me."

"Right," Chloe says. "She knows you were here?"

Mo starts to nod, then stops. On her way to bed, she knocked on Hazel's door to tell her she was home. Hazel didn't answer, and Mo thought nothing of it. Hazel hadn't spoken to her since they'd returned from the hospital.

Pushing from the bed, she walks past Chloe and knocks on Hazel's door. "Haze?"

No answer.

She knocks harder.

"Did you see her last night?" Chloe asks.

"She was in the kitchen when you called me to get Ruby," Mo says.

"And when you got home?"

Mo looks back at the door, a sense of dread growing. With a deep breath, she reaches for the handle, then steps into the room.

18
CHLOE

A shiver like déjà vu shudders Chloe's body as she looks at Hazel's neatly made bed, the niggle of intuition she never doubts telling her something is wrong. While the rest of Hazel's room is a war zone—the floor barely visible beneath the strewed papers, clothes, and debris—her bed looks like it belongs in a Macy's catalog, the corners of the comforter draped in perfect triangles and the pillows fluffed and karate chopped in the middle. *Arranged* is the word that comes to mind, the stark neatness unsettling against the mayhem around it.

Chloe's not a big believer in coincidence. The notion of cause and effect has always proved much more probable than random happenstance. Pull a thread; things unravel. Kick a rock; create an avalanche. The night that Chloe went into that alley to help Ruby, a chain of events was set in motion that sent Mo, Hazel, and herself tumbling forward, their fates entwining despite the seeming separateness of their individual misfortunes.

"Did she tell you she was leaving?" she asks as she follows Mo inside. The next question rolls off her tongue before Mo has had time to answer the first: "So she was here when you left but gone when we got home?"

Mo's face is very pale as she nods, her eyes fixed on the disturbing bed. Chloe continues toward the side table, drawn to a book left open on the nightstand. Beside the book is a photo of Hazel with her parents—serious-looking people, her father solemn and intelligent looking, her mother pint size and not quite looking at the camera. Burning beside it is a seven-day religious prayer candle with the Blessed Virgin painted on it, melted vanilla wax half an inch thick pooled around the wick and lightly perfuming the air.

Chloe blows out the flame.

"That's weird," Mo says, causing Chloe to turn.

"Don't touch that!" Chloe yelps. But it's too late. Mo's fingers are already closed around the blue can.

"What?" Mo says. "It's only paint thinner. I thought Haze hated painting."

Two months ago, Hazel signed up for an online painting class and made it through two sessions before declaring it the most brain-numbing hobby in the world.

Chloe makes a heroic effort not to react, the paint thinner glowing toxically in Mo's hand. "Maybe she was using it to get out a stain," she says, surprised how legit it sounds.

"Haze?" Mo says almost with a smile.

She's right, of course; Hazel is the last person to care about stains, tears, or general dishevelment.

With a shrug, Mo sets the can down and nods toward the book in Chloe's hand. "What's that?"

Chloe lifts it for Mo to see: *The Tongues of Toil and Other Poems*, by William Francis Barnard. "It was open to a poem called 'Two Powers,'" Chloe says. "And Hazel underlined part of it."

Mo steps closer and looks over Chloe's shoulder as Chloe reads aloud:

> The power of wrong
> Is iron strong;

Is the power of right, then, weak?
The power of right
Is a greater might
Than thou can'st think or speak.

The last three lines are double scored, and Chloe rereads them silently.

The power of right
Is a greater might
Than thou can'st think or speak.

"What's it mean?" Mo asks.

Chloe shakes her head. But between the poem, the candle, the creepily made bed, and the paint thinner, it doesn't take Sherlock Holmes to know something is happening . . . has happened—clues like bread crumbs deliberately left for them to find.

"Maybe she's trying to work things out," Chloe says, not sharing her true suspicion, which is that Hazel is on a mission of either vengeance, self-destruction, or both. She forces herself not to look at the paint thinner, also known as butoxyethanol. When Mo is not around, she will get rid of it, the book of poetry as well. No good can come from any of this. "Do you know where she might have gone?"

Mo shakes her head, her chin on her chest, very close to losing it.

"No call or text?" Chloe asks.

Mo pulls out her phone, scans through what look like dozens of messages, then shakes her head. She swipes the screen, taps a different app, and tilts her head.

"What?" Chloe asks.

Mo holds the phone toward her. The screen is open to Find My Friends and shows Hazel's face on a map.

Chloe peers closer. "What's she doing in Oregon?"

"I have absolutely no idea."

19
MO

Mo stares at the small, round circle, a shy, smiling Hazel staring back. Mo shot the photo, one of a dozen she took before Hazel finally agreed her smile didn't look stupid.

"Text her," Chloe says.

Mo's thumbs fly over the screen. Heyooo. Wondering where you are?

She stares so hard as she waits for a reply that the screen blurs. She's still staring when a knock on the front door causes both her and Chloe to jump.

Chloe leaps forward and snatches the paint thinner off the desk.

"What are you doing?" Mo asks, watching as Chloe shoves it, along with the book of poetry, in Hazel's bottom desk drawer.

"Nothing," Chloe says, closing the drawer and marching past.

Mo follows, preparing herself to talk to the detectives again, certain they've come back with more questions. Instead, she looks past Chloe to see a young woman with ink-black hair to her waist and wide, round glasses.

The woman pushes the glasses up on the bridge of her nose. "Hello. I'm looking for Mo, Mo Kaminski."

Chloe opens the door wider, and Mo steps closer. She doesn't recognize the woman, and the woman doesn't seem to immediately recognize her. "Are you Mo?"

"I am."

Her eyes drop. "I saw your post."

"Oh," Mo says, and her first instinct is to push Chloe aside and shut the door. Already, life is spiraling out of control, and the last thing she needs is to deal with whatever this woman has come to lay at her feet, which, based on her expression, is not going to be good.

"Would you like to come in?" Mo asks, painting on a smile.

Ruby, who is curled on the dog bed beside the couch, senses something and stirs from her sedated sleep to look up groggily.

Chloe hurries over to soothe her. "Shhh."

Ruby sniffs the air, decides the intruder's okay, wags her tail sluggishly, then plops her head back to the floor.

Mo gestures to the couch, and tentatively the woman steps inside and sits on the edge. She twines her hands together on her lap and looks at the expanse of windows. "Your apartment is beautiful."

"Thank you," Mo says.

The woman casts her eyes at the coffee table. "I'm sorry to bother you."

Everything about her feels like an apology, the way her shoulders curve forward, her small voice, the drabness of her clothes, as if she is constantly repentant for taking up too much space.

"No bother," Mo says, while silently wishing for the hundredth time she hadn't made that post.

"I'm . . . or I was . . . a Delta Gamma."

"Once a DG, always a DG," Mo says brightly, feeling very phony. She left the sorority after her junior year and couldn't have cared less about it.

The woman takes a long time before continuing, her hands twisting and her mouth skewed to the side, as if trying to figure out what to say or working up the nerve to say it.

Mo waits, knowing from experience that sometimes people just need a little space. While the girl is plain, she is not unpretty, her skin porcelain, her hair a sleek curtain of black, and her lips full.

"Would you like something to drink?" Chloe offers. "Water? Coffee? By the way, I'm Chloe."

"Kora," the woman says. "Water would be lovely."

Lovely. The word strikes a nerve. Mo's mom says "lovely." It's not a word that gets used a lot, though Mo thinks it should. Only *lovely* people use the word *lovely*.

Chloe pivots for the kitchen, and Ruby drunkenly pushes to her feet to follow.

"Is she okay?" Kora asks, watching her.

"She's having trouble eating. Chloe's been giving her IV fluids to help. She's a vet."

"Wow. A vet. That's cool. I thought about becoming a vet." She shakes her head as she says it.

"What was your major?"

"Biology. I was deciding between medical research and veterinary school." Shrug. "I suppose Starbucks barista is close." The right corner of her mouth lifts in a self-deprecating grin, which makes Mo think of Hazel. Though the two look nothing alike, there's something similar that makes Mo very uncomfortable.

"Someday, I might go back," Kora says, shaking her head again, a disconcerting habit she has, as if she's simultaneously denying every word she says.

"Here you go," Chloe says, holding out a glass of water.

Kora takes a sip.

Chloe sits on the macramé pouf Mo's mom sent last Christmas, and Ruby sits beside her.

"A lot of people responded to your post," Kora says, then politely takes a coaster before setting her glass on the table.

"I'm sorry if it upset you," Mo says.

Kora shakes her head. "The opposite."

Mo looks at her curiously. She hasn't read even a fraction of the responses, but almost all the ones she did read were awful.

"I can't believe how many others there are," Kora says.

And though Mo was expecting it, the words still strike like a blow, the knowledge that this "lovely" woman was also a victim.

"Allen?" she asks.

Kora's mouth skews hard to the side as she offers the smallest nod. "I don't know why this is so hard. It was such a long time ago."

"Grief has its own watch," Mo says, repeating the words her psychiatrist said to her eight years ago, when she was struggling to come to terms with the accident and Finn's and Oz's deaths. "We can't rush it, and we can't stop it. It needs to run its course, and all we can do is allow it to carry us to its end."

Kora tilts her head as if considering it, and again Mo is reminded of Hazel, both of them thoughtful and contemplative.

Lifting her face, she says, "But what if it never ends?"

It was the exact thought Mo had when she was given the advice. She just wanted things to go back to the way they had been, which was of course impossible, so then what she wanted was for the watch to tick faster so she could move past it. Back or forward. But no matter how hard she wished it, her sorrow took its own sweet time, moving in ebbs and tides that felt endless and forever.

"You'll get there," Chloe says, causing Kora to look her way, and Mo watches as their eyes connect and some common understanding passes between them.

Kora nods, then reaches up to sluice a loose strand of hair behind her ear, and that's when Mo sees it, a jagged pink scar peeking from the cuff of her sweater.

Chloe sees it as well and goes very still.

Kora, noticing, brings her hand down quickly and tugs the sleeve down, the edge gripped in her hand. "I'm getting better," she says, shame radiating.

Mo's heart pounds, her mind filled with thoughts of Hazel.

"I came here," Kora says, "because when it happened to me, I thought I'd gone crazy."

It's exactly what Hazel struggled with in the hospital. She thought she'd lost her mind, which seemed as distressing to her as what had happened.

"I didn't know what was real and what wasn't," Kora goes on, "and I no longer trusted my own thoughts." She stares at the sweater sleeve clutched in her grip, the disturbing scar beneath it. "I remembered bits and pieces, but there were gaps, and the parts I did remember didn't make sense." Her head shakes and shakes and shakes as Mo's blood pumps wildly.

"He said I liked it," she rasps so quietly it's barely a breath, "and I remember nodding . . . I think I even smiled." Her chin drops to her chest, so far that Mo is looking at the razor-straight part in her hair. "Why would I do that?"

Mo wants to tell her it was the GHB. It had to be. That's how it works. But she's certain Kora already knows this and that the knowledge doesn't help.

Kora pushes her glasses up on her nose and lifts her face, her brown eyes magnified by the lenses. "When I saw your post, all I could think about was how I didn't want you to go through that, to think somehow you caused it or were in some way to blame."

Me! Mo's insides go cold. *You think* I *was the one who was raped?*

Kora's still talking, but Mo's no longer listening, unable to hear past the whooshing in her ears. *How many people who saw that post think* I *was the one he raped?*

"Mo?" Chloe says.

"Huh?" She looks up to see Chloe frowning. "Kora was asking if that's how you felt." There's warning in her eyes, her unhappy expression making it clear that she knows what Mo's hung up on and that she needs to move past it. "Were you also charmed by Allen?"

Mo looks from Chloe to Kora, her mind on fire, every neuron screaming at her to clear up the misunderstanding and set the record straight. She wasn't raped, and horrible as it is, especially with Kora sitting across from her, she doesn't want people thinking she was. She opens her mouth to tell Kora she's mistaken, but when Kora tilts her head, her lashes fluttering like a scared doe's, what she says instead is, "Yes. I was definitely fooled."

20
CHLOE

Chloe walks with Ruby from the apartment, the paint thinner and poetry book in a bag over her shoulder and Kora on her mind. Trauma either weakens you or makes you stronger. Chloe hopes the latter is true for her, but there are days she's unsure.

A shudder, not from the cold, lifts her head, and she scans the street around her.

Since the accident, she's become highly attuned to people looking at her. The perception is called *gaze detection*, and she imagines anyone with a visible disfigurement—like missing fingers and toes—is high on the acuity spectrum.

She sees the car on the second pass, a black, macho muscle car parked a hundred yards down the street that runs perpendicular to their building. A tree beside it reflects off the windshield, but she's able to see through it well enough to make out the distinctive short, cropped hair and stocky build of the person behind the wheel—Gretzky.

You've got to be kidding! It was a case of the runs, not murder!

She picks up her pace, and Ruby trots alongside to keep up. Poke a bear, and this is what you get—a pissed-off, omnivorous grizzly looking to feast on the flesh of whatever it was that poked him.

Instead of dumping the paint thinner and poetry book in the dumpster behind her building, she continues two blocks farther to throw them in the trash inside a McDonald's before continuing out the opposite door. She circles back so she is on the street behind where Gretzky was parked, relieved when she looks down the street to see he is gone.

Her phone buzzes, causing her to jump.

"Hey," she says to Mo. "I was just going to order an Uber to go to the impound yard."

"Change of plans," Mo says. "I'm coming with you."

"Why?"

"Haze is in trouble."

"You talked to her?"

"No. But I know why she's driving north."

21
MO

The conversation Mo and Hazel had was over five years ago, and she had almost forgotten about it. But the moment Kora left, Mo's phone buzzed. It was Hazel responding to her text: Decided to go home to see my kin.

A white lie or a white truth? Either way, if not for Kora's visit, Mo wouldn't have thought anything of the word *kin* in place of *parents* or *family*. But the pink scar on Kora's wrist brought new meaning to everything.

The conversation took place on the fourteenth day of their Camino de Santiago pilgrimage, the summer of their first year of college. The sun was setting, and they were past the point of exhilaration about the adventure and into the slogging-through-it phase of the journey, deep in the Meseta, an endless trail of dirt and gravel without any trees or landmarks to tell them they were getting any closer to their destination.

"What's your highest-ranked bucket-list place?" Hazel asked.

"Bucket-list place?" Mo responded.

"The one place you absolutely have to go."

Walking dozens of miles a day made you think about things like that, especially in the Meseta. Mo supposed that was what made it a pilgrimage. Already, after only two weeks, she was letting go of certain ideas and embracing new ones.

"The single place," she said, thinking about it. Growing up with her dad, who'd loved to travel, Mo had already been to every continent and over forty countries, all of them amazing. But she sensed what Hazel was asking was different. "I'm not sure I know," she said finally, thinking of Kyle and feeling like it would have to be someplace they experienced together, and that it might be someplace cold, a test to prove she had finally conquered her fear. "How about you?"

"Snoqualmie Falls," Hazel said without hesitation, her expression dreamy, letting Mo know she'd been thinking about it for some time.

"In Washington?"

"The mountain was named for my great-great-great-grandfather," she said. "Mount Si."

"His name was Si?"

"His name was actually Josiah, but everyone knew him as Si."

"That's cool."

"Yep. He left his home and family back East in search of gold, and when he reached Mount Si, he took one look at the falls and declared he'd found it. He settled and never left. Eventually his family joined him, and the mountain became his—Mount Si."

"I love that," Mo said, a sucker for anything romantic.

"I figure it must be a pretty special place."

"You've never been?"

"Nope."

"Why not? It's not that far from San Francisco."

Hazel looked off toward the horizon—dry, endless desert hazy in the fading sun—then looked back at Mo and, the dreamy smile still in place, said, "Don't want to ruin it. The waterfall's not just any place; it's *the* place, the final stop on the journey when there's nothing left to see."

And now, five short years later, Hazel was driving straight toward it.

"I think we should stop for dinner," Chloe says, startling her from the memory.

"Huh? Yeah. Sounds good." Mo sits up from where she was half dozing on the back bench of the van. Ruby is in the passenger seat, her head out the window and her tongue flapping in the wind.

She rubs her eyes, and her stomach rumbles, and she realizes she's starving. They've been on the road since eleven, and she hasn't eaten since breakfast.

Chloe takes the next exit as Mo pulls up the Diners, Drive-Ins, and Dives app on her phone to see if there are any great hole-in-the-wall restaurants nearby.

"Ooh. Best pad thai in Oregon is only a few blocks away," she says.

"There's a motel," Chloe says, ignoring her, and Mo realizes that when she said they should stop for dinner, her concern was for Ruby, not them. The poor dog isn't doing well, and Mo knows Chloe is worried. She's still not eating, and while she is still loving and sweet, her vivaciousness has definitely dimmed.

Chloe parks beside the office of the Carnival Motel, and Mo hops out and hurries toward the office before Chloe has put the van in park. Already, Chloe made a huge deal over Mo paying to get the van out of impound and then paying for two new back tires.

"I'll pay you back," she said almost ferociously when Mo handed the mechanic her credit card. "I'm just a little short at the moment."

Mo nodded uncommittedly but then turned and said, "Though, honestly, Clove, we're doing this for Haze, and I'm the one asking you to do it, and you're losing out on work because of it, so I'd feel a whole lot better if you'd just let me pay."

"No."

And that was the end of the conversation. Though the whole thing is quite frankly irritating and entirely unnecessary. Chloe is living on brussels sprouts and driving around on bald tires, while Mo has more money than she knows what to do with. Since her dad passed, she is horrendously rich, a fact that she's still coming to terms with and that, at some point, she is going to need to deal with. Her father said often, "With great wealth comes great responsibility and a hell of a lot of headaches and grief." Well, it should also come with the perk of being able to help a friend who's fallen on hard times.

She walks into the motel office, and a thin guy with long sandy hair and a guitar on his lap sets the instrument down and stands. "Evening," he says with a wide smile that makes Mo like him instantly.

"I'd like a room."

"How many nights?"

Her mouth skews to the side. She thinks only one, but strangely, Hazel's Find My Friends icon hasn't moved since this morning. It's still at the Hilton in downtown Bend. Which is odd but also a relief. Mo was worried they wouldn't be able to catch up with her.

The original plan was to track Hazel down and talk to her, but then Chloe brought up the very good point that they're only going to get one shot at this. As soon as Hazel realizes her Find My Friends is on, the jig will be up, and they won't be able to find her again. Which means it might be best to hang back and try to figure out her plan before confronting her.

"How about we take it day by day?" the clerk says, and Mo realizes she's been standing with a perplexed look on her face for at least a minute. "Lucky for you, Elizabeth's been held up at Windsor, something about her corgis chewing on the royal carpet. So the Jungle Suite happens to be available." He says it completely straight faced, which makes the joke funnier than it is, and Mo giggles loudly, the release like a great burst of oxygen to her lungs.

"Name's Hunter," he says, handing her a key. "I'll be here if you need anything."

22
CHLOE

"No way!" Chloe says, her backpack on one shoulder and her vet bag on the other. Ruby bounds past and gives a yip and a small leap, matching Chloe's excitement. "This is awesome!"

Mo smiles wide as she walks in behind them. "Best room in the house. It's where Queen Elizabeth stays when she visits."

"The queen has mighty fine taste," Chloe says, sloughing her vet bag to the faux-tiger rug.

Every inch of wall is papered in a print of jungle leaves. The ceiling is painted with vines. The two queen beds are dressed in zebra stripes. And the bedside lamps are made from smiling pink flamingos with pink shades laced with feathers.

"Great for 'lion' around," Mo says and makes lion claws in front of her face. "I'm going to grab us dinner while you get Ruby hooked up."

"Let me know how much I owe you," Chloe says as she tosses her the key for the van.

Mo frowns, but Chloe doesn't care. Already she's living in Mo's apartment rent-free, and now she owes her money for bail, the impound fees, and her back tires. She's not going to have her paying for her meals as well.

When the door closes, Chloe plops onto her butt beside Ruby and pulls a can of dog food from the vet bag. She spoons half of it onto a paper plate and slides it in front of her. Ruby sniffs at it but doesn't take a bite.

"It's okay, girl," Chloe says, petting her head. "You're okay. We've still got time."

As she pulls out a syringe to sedate her, she hopes it's true. She's not sure how long it's been since Ruby's eaten, but she knows it's been long enough that her body is starting to show signs of shutting down—her eyes jaundiced and her fur thinning.

Ruby settles easily from the drugs, and Chloe continues to pet her even after the IV is set up, her thoughts wandering from her worry for Ruby to her worry for Hazel and back again. When Mo first explained her suspicion of why Hazel was driving north and that they needed to go after her, Chloe's first instinct was to say no, mostly because she felt like she was already drowning and couldn't bear any more weight. Immediately, she straightened the thought, thinking how, eight years ago, it had been Mo who'd realized Chloe was in trouble and that, if not for her intervention, she might not be here to make the choice to help Hazel at all.

She's not entirely sure Mo's suspicions are right. It's a great leap to go from an icon moving north to the certainty that Hazel is traveling to the place of her forefathers to end her life. While it seemed to Chloe that Hazel was definitely affected by what happened, when they talked yesterday, she seemed okay, sad but processing it. The paint thinner and poem are disturbing, but again, they could simply be her way of working through it. They need to tread carefully. Chloe knows better than anyone that if you push too hard when someone doesn't want it, it could do more damage than good.

She looks at the IV dripping fluids into Ruby's worn-out body. "Sometimes, in our darkest moments," she says softly, "we need someone else to shine a light."

Leaning her head back against the bed, she closes her eyes as she continues to think about Hazel. She thinks about the poem she left for them to find, a cryptic message left by someone of extraordinary intelligence, and Chloe has a bad feeling they're missing its meaning entirely.

When the door opens, she startles and realizes she must have dozed off. She blinks her eyes to see Mo carrying a large brown bag with waves of deliciousness wafting off it.

"Yum," she says, pushing to her feet.

They eat straight from the containers, sitting on the beds, too hungry to worry about plates. Chloe uses chopsticks. Mo uses a fork.

"So good," Mo says around a mouthful of pad thai, then shovels another forkful into her mouth.

Chloe can only manage a nod as she devours a container of vegetable fried rice, the satisfaction of filling her belly with warm, delicious food occupying her mouth so wonderfully she doesn't want to talk.

When the last bite is gone, Chloe sets the container on the table with a burp.

Mo groans. "So full." She sets her hand on her stomach, which indeed looks a little round.

Her phone rings to the cheesy tune of "We Go Together," the ringtone for Kyle, and Chloe watches as Mo tenses, then ignores it.

"You're not going to get that?"

Normally, Mo snatches her phone on the first ring when it's Kyle.

Mo looks at the phone, then sheepishly at Chloe. "I haven't told him what's going on."

"Oh," Chloe says, purposely keeping her expression neutral, then busying herself with cleaning up their dinner.

Chloe likes Kyle. She might even say she loves him. After all, she owes him her life, as well as the lives of her mom, her dad, and Mo. But he's not a fan of hers and has made that clear for the past eight years—forgiveness for what she did is not on the table.

She gets it. After all, it's not like she accidently left a burner on that burned down the house, or didn't see the family cat in her side mirror when she backed out of the driveway. Eight years ago, on the night her family's RV plummeted over the side of a mountain, leaving her sister dead and her father gravely injured, she intentionally walked away, followed her boyfriend at the time away from the accident and into the snow, a mistake that cost her half a pinkie and three toes and likely cost her brother his life.

Meanwhile, Kyle, barely older than she was at the time, was a hero. A complete stranger who they had picked up on the side of the road who courageously and selflessly helped her family through the night and then, in the morning, hiked out with her mom for help. A lopsided relationship that chafes whenever they're near.

The phone pings that a voice mail's been left, and Mo sets the phone on the table, then swings herself around so she's sitting sideways on the bed.

"Now what?" she asks. "We're here."

Chloe's been thinking nonstop about how best to approach Hazel ever since they left the city. While she knows more about being on the edge than most, she feels no better equipped for talking someone back from it. The problem is, once someone's made the choice, it's pretty tough to change their mind. Her heart pounds as she thinks about the blind determination she had in the aftermath of the accident, certain that ending her life was what she wanted.

A light rap on the door interrupts her mental spinning, and she leaps up to answer it before whoever it is knocks again and causes Ruby to wake and start barking. Standing a foot away is a man around her age in a flannel shirt with rolled-up sleeves. His hair is long, and a wide smile fills his face.

"Hey," he says in surprise.

"Hey."

He glances at the scar on her forehead, and she brushes her bangs away with her left hand, flaunting her abbreviated pinkie. His smile remains easy as his gaze returns to her eyes, not affected in the least, which causes her breath to hitch slightly as she wonders if it's possible that she is encountering a rare but genuine working dog mutt.

"I forgot to give you the pool key," he says, lifting a gold key attached to a plastic circus-tent key ring.

"Oh. Okay. Thanks."

As she takes it, she purposely grazes her stump over his skin to test him, and he either doesn't notice or doesn't care, his posture and smile unchanged as he asks, "How do you like the Jungle Suite?"

Her cheeks spread wide. "Seriously awesome. Someone has some wicked, retro-kitsch style."

"That would be my mom." He beams, making Chloe like him that much more. "The woman doesn't do dull."

"Life's way too short for dull," Chloe says, surprised by how it sounds, like she is flirting, which she definitely is not. She is done with men. Permanently.

"Yeah, well, okay." He looks like he wants to say more but, unable to come up with anything, says, "Have a good night," then gives a two-finger salute and pivots.

Before he's taken a step, Chloe blurts, "Wait."

He turns back.

"Any chance you have a car?"

His left eyebrow lifts, and his eyes spark like a little boy looking for trouble just for the adventure of it. "I have a truck."

"That'll work. Mind if we borrow it?"

His smile twitches, and she thinks he is definitely going to say no. After all, who in their right mind would loan their truck to someone they've known less than two minutes? But without a blink of hesitation, he digs into the pocket of his jeans and pulls out a heavy ring of keys. After removing a Ford key, he holds it out and gives a nod toward the parking lot, where an old white pickup is parked. "She sticks a bit in reverse, but give the shifter a good tug and she'll drop."

"Thanks," Chloe says, and though he continues to look at her curiously, his brown eyes glinting in question, she doesn't add anything more.

With another two-finger salute, he turns and walks back toward the motel's office.

"Huh-hum," Mo says behind her, and Chloe realizes she's still standing in the doorway watching him.

She holds up the Ford key. "How do you feel about a stakeout?"

23
MO

"His name is Hunter," Mo says, a smile tickling her lips.

"Who?"

"Yeah, right," Mo says, glancing sideways from the passenger seat and smirking. "The motel guy . . . the guy you've been smiling about ever since he handed you the key to his truck . . . and maybe his heart."

Chloe rolls her eyes. "I met him for two seconds."

"Uh-huh." Mo smiles wider, and Chloe pretends to throw the coffee she's holding at her.

Mo winces like the wimp she is, then sticks her tongue out at Chloe. "He's cute, in a scruffy, Oregonian, outback sort of way. Just your type."

"Vance was cute. Eric was cute. I don't need cute."

Chloe's high school boyfriend, Vance, was actually hot, movie-star good looking. Eric was more brooding handsome. Neither was good enough for Chloe, and they proved it in extraordinarily hurtful ways. Vance led Chloe into the snow after the accident, then abandoned her to save himself. Eric took off to "find himself" and emptied their joint bank account on his way out of town. It's not fair. Chloe deserves better.

Mo is worried Chloe's lost her faith in love altogether, like a dog who's been kicked one too many times.

When they were little, Chloe was the greatest romantic of all time. Stunning from the moment she could walk with her oversize green eyes, smattering of freckles, and copper-penny hair, she had the sort of confidence only girls who never need to concern themselves with whether they're pretty possess. With the confidence of a warrior queen and the chutzpah of a diva, she was the girl on the playground boldly chasing after the boys to give them the cooties, believing any boy lucky to be caught by her.

Then the accident happened, and all that changed, as if, along with her toes and a piece of her pinkie, that part of her was lost as well. It's been heartbreaking to watch, knowing it's not Chloe but rather the men she's chosen to love.

"I think the fact that his radio was tuned to the same awful grunge you like to listen to is a sign," Mo says, believing Chloe just needs to find the right cootie catcher and having a good sense about Hunter. After all, he loaned them his truck without batting an eye. Who does that? Someone who's either crazy, stupid, or willing to take an extraordinary leap of faith, and her heart tells her Hunter is the latter . . . just like Chloe.

Chloe rolls her eyes again and turns up the music as if trying to drown Mo out, but her cheeks blush, revealing she might not be as done with men as she claims.

After another five minutes, Mo says, "This is sooo boring."

"Yeah, I thought a stakeout would be more fun."

They've been parked across the street from a small café a mile from Hazel's hotel for the past two hours, watching as Hazel ate a burger, then pulled out her journal and started to write.

It was brilliant of Chloe to borrow Hunter's truck, since the vet van is hardly inconspicuous with its bright-yellow paint and the giant black paw prints marching across it, but now that they're here, the plan seems like a complete waste of time, and she's not sure what they are hoping to accomplish.

"I should just go talk to her," Mo says for the fourth time.

Chloe shoots her a look that says, *Not yet*, and Mo sighs out heavily. Eight years ago, Chloe was in a similar place to where Hazel is now, so if anyone knows about a situation like this, it's her. The problem is Hazel looks so normal, so much like herself—plain, rumpled, distracted—her second-best friend in the world.

She has considered calling a suicide hotline. But there are two major problems with that. Number one, Mo is not certain Hazel is having thoughts of suicide. When she made the connection to Mount Si, she was sure, but taking a drive is hardly proof of intent to harm oneself. Number two, Hazel is the smartest person Mo knows, her intellect far beyond that of a normal person, so unless the counselor on the other end of the line is Dr. Maguire from *Good Will Hunting*, she knows any advice they offer is not going to work with Hazel. While they were waiting for the tires to be replaced on the van, she looked at the National Council for Mental Wellbeing's website and read the online steps for suicide prevention: talk to the person, ask about their feelings, offer reassurance, and encourage them to seek professional help. Hazel refuses to talk to her. And she would never seek professional help. So there you have it. Mo's gut is telling her Hazel is in trouble, and the only hope they have of helping her is some sort of intervention by her and Chloe that they haven't figured out.

Chloe glances at the dash for the time, and Mo knows she's thinking about Ruby. They had no choice but to leave her in the room. First off, she was sedated, and second, they were borrowing Hunter's truck, and it didn't seem right to bring along a drooling dog who might pee because she was drugged.

Though if Mo had to guess, she'd say the truck's had plenty of canine passengers. It's at least as old as Mo; the inside is red, and the seat is patched with duct tape. The outside is rusted white and has a bumper sticker that says, **I BELIEVE IN A BETTER WORLD WHERE CHICKENS CAN CROSS THE ROAD WITHOUT THEIR MOTIVES BEING QUESTIONED.** Chloe laughed out loud when she saw it, further proof that Hunter might be the perfect guy to break her out of her man ban.

"Maybe you should text her?" Chloe says.

"Fine." Mo pulls out her phone. "What should I say?"

"I don't know. Something random. Just to see how she responds."

Mo skews her mouth to the side. "Got it," she says, and her thumbs fly over the screen.

"What'd you write?"

"'What six-letter word starts with *T*, ends with *P*, and means *extreme summit*?'"

"Tiptop," Chloe says so fast Mo blinks. It took her half a day and filling in nearly every other word in Saturday's crossword puzzle to figure that out.

"She got it," Chloe says with a nod through the windshield.

Mo looks toward Hazel, who is now looking at her phone. She sets it back on the table.

"She's not going to answer?" Mo shrills in disbelief. "Are you kidding? She always answers." Mo's been asking Hazel for crossword help for years, and her responses are always almost instant.

Hazel leans forward and returns to writing, her face placid as a summer's day.

Before and after, Mo thinks, a lump forming.

For a long time after the accident, that's how she thought about things: *before . . .* and *after.* Her life cleaved in two, nothing from *before* the same as it had been, and everything *after* wonky and misaligned, like a shoe that had at one time fit but had been left out in the rain and now chafed and rubbed and felt all wrong.

Before, Hazel would always answer Mo's crossword conundrums. *After,* it no longer matters.

"We should go," Chloe says. "Whatever she's doing, she's not doing it tonight."

Mo nods, barely stopping herself from leaping from the truck and running to where Hazel is and saying something—begging forgiveness and pleading with Hazel to let her help, to allow her to make amends and set things right.

Chloe starts the truck and drives toward the motel.

A few minutes later, she says, "Tomorrow, we'll talk to her. Let's think about what we want to say, and in the morning, we'll go to her hotel and see if we can convince her to come home."

"I just want to tell her I love her," Mo says, the words cracking. "And that I'm sorry."

Chloe glances over and, for the dozenth time, says, "This isn't your fault."

Of course, she could say it a hundred times—a million—and it still wouldn't make a difference. The truth is Mo messed up. She left Hazel alone with Allen, and the result was catastrophic.

"What's he doing?" Chloe says, and Mo follows Chloe's nod through the windshield to see Hunter sitting outside their motel room, strumming his guitar and singing.

Chloe jams the truck into park and leaps from the cab. Mo follows.

Hunter smiles when he sees them and continues to strum and sing "Don't Worry, Be Happy." He winks and jerks his head toward the door. "There's a little dog I know, doesn't like to be alone. Don't worry, be happy . . ."

Chloe throws her head back and laughs, and Ruby, on hearing her, goes wild with yips and howls. Chloe unlocks the door, and Ruby bounds out to leap and jump around her, causing Mo to smile all the way to her toes, the scene so bright that, for a moment, she forgets her worry.

Hunter sets down his guitar and stands, and Ruby circles and bounces around him as well.

Mo steps toward them at the exact moment her phone rings, chiming with Kyle's ringtone. Her heart leaps before filling with dread. For two days, she's avoided his calls, texting excuses for why she can't answer and cravenly putting off telling him what's happened.

Knowing she can't put it off any longer, she swipes the answer bar and hurries around the side of the building to where she won't be heard. "Hey."

"How could you not have called?" he snaps, his anger like a lash. "What the hell is going on?"

24
CHLOE

Chloe is being smothered with dog kisses, Ruby's tail whipping around dangerously as Chloe fends her off with useless admonitions of "Okay. Enough. You're okay. I'm here now. Settle down."

The guy from the motel . . . Hunter . . . watches with a wide smile, clearly amused.

Finally, Ruby buries her head in Chloe's chest and stays there. Chloe plops to her butt on the concrete and strokes her fur.

Hunter returns to the plastic chair, sets his guitar on his lap, and picks at it absently. "Dog's a lot like me," he says, "doesn't like waking up alone." He gives a wry eyebrow lift, and Chloe laughs again. The guy's caused more giggles in the past ten minutes than she's had in the past three months, and it's crazy how good it feels.

He tips the chair back so it's on two legs and continues to pluck the strings, the melody almost familiar, no longer reggae but with a sort of tribal beat. Ruby leaves Chloe and plops down at his feet, her chocolate eyes mooning up at him.

"Looks like you've got an admirer," Chloe says, crossing her legs and leaning her elbows on her knees. "Traitor," she says to Ruby.

Hunter stops playing, sets the guitar aside, and picks up a white paper sack spotted with grease. He pulls out a bag of crinkly fries and holds it toward Chloe. "Want some?"

She takes a couple, and as he pulls the bag back, Ruby's eyes follow. He drops a fry on the sidewalk in front of her, and with no hesitation at all, Ruby laps it up as if it's the most natural thing in the world.

"Do that again!" Chloe yelps, causing Hunter to freeze, his handful of fries halfway to his mouth. "Please," she adds.

"First my truck, now my dinner. Very demanding." He drops the fries, and again, without missing a beat, Ruby gobbles them up.

Chloe's eyes fill with tears and then, in the next second, overflow, hot rivulets streaming down her cheeks.

"Wow, never had that reaction to feeding scraps to a dog," Hunter says and drops another bunch of fries to the ground. "You okay?"

Chloe blots the wetness as Ruby inches closer to Hunter on her belly, looking imploringly up for more.

"Fine," Hunter says with a soft chuckle and dumps the remainder of the bag in front of her. "I'm a sucker for beautiful women." His eyes flick to Chloe as he says it before quickly returning to Ruby.

"She hasn't been eating," Chloe explains, embarrassed by her tears. "She's a stray, and ever since I found her . . ." The words trail off, stuck behind the thick lump in her throat, and she realizes how worried she's been. "I thought she might never start."

"Homesick, are ya?" Hunter says with understanding and scratches Ruby behind the ear, then takes her jaw in his hand and examines the stitches. "And ran into some trouble along the way. I know what that's like, but you're in good hands now."

He releases her and tousles her head, and she likes it, her butt going in the air and her forepaws to the ground, challenging Hunter like she wants to play, and Chloe thinks whoever Ruby's previous caregiver was, it was probably a guy. Men tend to be different with dogs than women, more physical and rougher. It would never occur to her to scruff a dog's head like that.

Hunter paws at her, and she play bites his hand, a game of tag Hunter quickly wins, getting hold of her muzzle and clamping it shut. "Got you," he says before releasing it and sitting back in his chair. He pulls a chicken sandwich from the bag and generously shares it with Ruby, dropping pieces of meat at her feet between his own bites. "Mabel's cooking," he says. "If that doesn't get a dog eating, I don't know what will."

"Where's Mabel's?" Chloe says. "Is it still open?"

Hunter glances at his watch, an old Timex with a worn leather strap. "Should be. A few miles down on the left. Mind picking me up a sandwich while you're there? I seem to have lost my dinner." He holds up the empty, sagging bun.

Chloe laughs again, and Ruby gets jealous and sits up and plops her head on Hunter's lap.

"Actually, you need to come with us," Chloe says. "It might not be the chicken. I think it might be you."

25
MO

When Mo gets back to the room, Chloe and Ruby are gone. She's relieved. She needs a moment to collect herself. Her conversation with Kyle did not go well. She flops on her bed and stares at the ceiling.

News of her possible involvement in Allen's assault has spread, and Kyle found out about it through one of his bunkmates. It's all over Facebook and Instagram and has even been picked up by some of the local news stations—some calling her a hero, others labeling her a psychopath. Theories and narratives are being proffered by everyone from legit journalists to conspiracy theorists. And the stupid post she made about Allen is being shared everywhere.

It's awful, and she's been avoiding the frenzy as much as possible, staying off social media and not going near the news, believing it will blow over. After all, it's ludicrous. But she should have known, being the daughter of the late, great Ryan Kaminski, that no story is too small for the piranhas to feed on. She didn't even consider Kyle would find out that way. How foolish. As if news doesn't travel to Germany.

Her dad would be so upset. His whole life he guarded himself and his family against this sort of tabloid fodder. And in a matter of days, she's undone all that with her carelessness. She wishes he were still here.

It's the problem with losing someone. No matter how long they're gone, there are moments when the yearning for their counsel is so acute that the grief of the loss strikes anew like a fist. His death marked the end of her childhood. She no longer had his shoulder to lean on or his experience to guide her.

She squeezes her eyes shut, wishing she could turn back time and not go to Allen's office or, better yet, never go to Black Sands in the first place. So many mistakes. She presses her fingers to her eyes until spots appear.

The worst part is, like Kora, everyone is getting the story wrong, the world assuming she was the victim and that the vengeance she took was personal.

"Is it true?" Kyle asked, his voice breaking in two.

"No," Mo said.

She felt his enormous relief, a shudder she couldn't see but that resonated like an aftershock over the line.

"But the part about going to his office and threatening him is right?"

She held in her groan as she realized that part of the story had also gotten out.

"I went there to confront him," she said. "The victim was a friend. It was stupid."

She considered telling him it was Hazel, but after her conversation with Kora, she decided she needed to keep Hazel out of it, even with Kyle. The doctor at the hospital was right. Rape is personal, and each victim needs to deal with it in their own way. Hazel wouldn't want Kyle to know. She reveres him and has always looked up to him like a big brother.

Kyle's voice was measured as he asked, "But you had nothing to do with what happened to him?"

"Of course not," she said sharply.

He didn't answer, which made her angrier. She and Kyle rarely fought, and the few times they had, it was through harsh silences, not yelling.

"You can't just ignore this," he said finally. "You need to explain your side of things."

Ignore it. Was that what he thought she was doing?

"I am dealing with it," she seethed.

"Really?" he said. "It looks to me like you're running away."

And that was the straw that broke the proverbial camel's back. She ended the call, then turned off her phone entirely. She and Kyle had made a promise when he'd enlisted that they would not stalk each other. She wouldn't torture herself by obsessing about where he was—possibly in danger—and he would allow her the freedom to go about her life without wondering if he was watching.

Now, she is lying on the bed replaying every word of the awful conversation. Since his first deployment, they have never hung up without her saying, "Stay safe," and him responding, "Stay you. Don't change a thing."

Tears leak from her eyes as she prays he hears the sentiment across the miles. He has to stay safe. All of this needs to go away, and he needs to come home safe.

The door opens, and she pushes onto her elbows to see Ruby and Chloe walk into the room. Chloe closes the door and leans against it, a goofy grin on her face. Ruby walks a few steps farther and flops on the faux-tiger rug with a groan.

"What's up with you?" Mo asks, wiping the wetness from her cheeks.

"Nothing."

"So why are you grinning like that?"

"I'm not," Chloe says, straightening the expression before stumbling forward to fall facedown on the bed. She turns her face sideways, the grin back in place. "Ruby started eating."

"Really? That's great."

"You okay?"

Mo shakes her head and rolls onto her stomach so she's prone like Chloe, their faces two feet apart.

"I take it Kyle wasn't so keen on your newfound fame."

"Nope. Less than thrilled."

"Can't be easy for him, being a superhero and all."

Mo doesn't respond. The entire time she and Kyle have been together, she has walked an unsteady tightrope between him and Chloe, careful not to defend either too much for fear they'll think she's choosing sides. The two are simply too different to get along. Though her mom says it's the opposite, that it's actually a problem of them being too much alike, both proud and defiant, though they express it in different ways—Kyle believes in standing up for the rules, while Chloe is in favor of pushing back against them.

"Of course, you're the one they're calling a hero," Chloe goes on. "Did you know there's a meme of you in a cape with your foot pinning a beaten man on the ground?"

Mo groans and turns her face into the zebra quilt.

"The hashtags are *#VictimVengeance, #MoVersusEvil, #CoochieCrusader*."

Coochie Crusader! Mo pins her elbows against her ears, the nightmare growing worse by the minute. Through her muffled ears, she hears Chloe's phone ring.

"Hey, Mom," Chloe says, causing Mo to spin and sit up. "Whoa. Really? He woke up. That's great."

Mo's pulse quickens. Finally, some good news. If Allen woke up, he can tell the police she had nothing to do with what happened, and all this nonsense can go away.

"Huh?" Chloe says. "Why?"

Mo doesn't like the tone.

"What do you mean, they didn't say? Don't they need to tell you *why* they're searching our apartment?"

Searching the apartment? She swallows. *Hazel!*

"Yeah, she's here," Chloe says. "Do you want to talk to her?"

Mo holds her hand out for the phone, but Chloe keeps it pinned to her ear.

"No. We're in Oregon." She hesitates slightly before lying: "We decided to get away because of everything that was going on. Plus, I have that dog I told you about, so I needed to get out of the apartment."

Chloe listens a second longer. "Yeah, okay." She gives a small smile. "Love you too."

Setting down the phone, she looks at Mo. "Allen woke up."

"Yeah, I got that."

"And the police issued a search warrant for our apartment."

"Yeah, I got that too." She shakes her head. "I can't believe Haze did this."

Chloe tilts her head. "Haze? Haze didn't do it."

"What do you mean? Of course she did. Why else would they be searching our apartment? Allen woke up, and he pointed the finger at her."

Chloe's brow furrows, making a deep V in her forehead, and then she shakes her head. "No way. Haze is way too smart to do something so stupid."

Mo doesn't answer, but inside she's thinking, *Nothing to lose.* At the time Hazel did it, she didn't think it would matter if people figured out it was her.

"Maybe we should call her," Chloe says. "Let her know the apartment's being searched."

Mo pulls out her phone.

"Actually," Chloe says, "I should call her." Her eyes drop, letting Mo know she's aware how much Hazel hates her.

Chloe dials and, a few seconds later, hangs up. "It went straight to voice mail. She's probably asleep. I'll try again in the morning."

26
CHLOE

The call to Hazel never happened. This morning, as Chloe was about to dial, Mo stopped her. "She's not at the hotel," she said, then held out her phone. Find My Friends showed Hazel's icon just outside Spokane.

"Spokane?" Chloe said. "When did she drive to Spokane?"

It was six in the morning, the sun already risen. For Hazel to be in Spokane, she would have needed to have left the night before.

"Hmmm," Mo said, squinting at the screen. "That's weird. Mount Si is near Seattle, not Spokane." Then half a beat later, her eyes widened. "Oh."

"What?"

"It's another bucket-list place," Mo said. "Look where she stopped." She held the phone toward Chloe, and Chloe looked closer.

"Barking Goat Kitchen?" Chloe said, reading off the exact location.

"It's a restaurant we've both always wanted to go to."

"She drove to Spokane for a restaurant?"

"Not just any restaurant. Barking Goat. It's supposed to be amazing."

Chloe just stopped herself from rolling her eyes. Mo and food. The girl is lucky to have the metabolism she does for the way she loves to eat.

"We need to wait to talk to her," Chloe said, "until we're close enough to catch her in case she decides to bolt."

The problem was Spokane was more than six hours away from where they were, while Mount Si was only four hours from where Hazel was.

"We need to go," Mo said, figuring it out as well.

So they packed quickly and left, Chloe driving as fast as the van would go, which unfortunately wasn't very fast. Two hours into the drive, she relaxed when Mo said Hazel's icon had stopped at a hotel in Spokane, which they took to mean that Hazel intended to stay the night.

Now, it's close to noon, and with the stress ebbed, Chloe's mind has wandered, floating away from Hazel to drift to a place she repeatedly has told herself not to go: *Hunter.*

This is no time for such foolery, she tries, always liking that word, short for *tomfoolery,* which has always made her wonder who Tom was to have such a word named after him. She feels Finn smiling. Her sister also loved words—*hodgepodge, argle-bargle,* and *snollygoster* were among her favorites.

Well, Finn, this is some profound tomfoolery. Hunter lives in Oregon. I live in California. I barely know him. He doesn't know me at all.

She shakes her head, trying to clear away the thoughts, and realizes how tired she is, her mind veering this way and that.

And if he did know me, he'd lose interest immediately.

Finn frowns.

Seriously, it's one thing to overlook a shortened pinkie, but you've seen my feet.

Her toes curl inside her shoes.

For years, she has told herself her scars don't matter, that they are a part of her and, in their own way, beautiful for what they represent— life, survival, luck, Oz, Finn—everything that tragic day took but also gave her.

Most of the time she believes it, but there are moments when the insecure, vain girl of her youth emerges, and she's certain no one could love someone so marred. Worse than her hand, her feet are scarred and misshapen, the skin puckered and indented where the surgeon needed to dig out the deadened skin, two of the toes gone completely and a third shaved to a nub. She met Eric when she didn't care what anyone thought, and he quickly grew used to them, but she can't imagine any other man being so accepting.

It doesn't matter anyway. After all, Hunter is behind her, in the rearview mirror. She presses on the accelerator, urging the van to go faster, though it does no good, the van shuddering at sixty and staying there.

It's just that he was so funny. And cute. And a good kisser. But mostly funny. The night filled with laughter as he regaled her with stories too outrageous to be true but also too inventive not to have some basis that was real.

"God's honest truth," he said when the food was gone, each of them sipping on a milkshake—strawberry for her, chocolate for him.

Mabel's Chicken and Waffle Shop was closed, and they were on the patio, alone except for the two workers closing up inside and the billion stars above. The night was cool, and Hunter had given her a striped Baja jacket he kept stowed beneath the seat of his truck. Ruby was sleeping on the ground between them, full on Mabel's chicken and fries.

"You're telling me the school honestly thought your dad's name was Bruce Wayne?" Chloe said, her mouth stuck in what seemed like a permanent grin.

"For most of seventh grade," he said. He talked with his hands, which were larger than the rest of him, like they belonged to a much bigger man, and she found herself drawn to them, the fingertips calloused from playing guitar and the knuckles gnarled from what she guessed was a life of hard work.

"And they never made the connection to Batman?"

"Nope. Once, I even wrote a note that said, 'Holy bellyache, my son ate mulligatawny soup and came down with food poisoning!'" He penned the note in the air.

"Mulli-what?"

"Mulligatawny soup, Batman's favorite meal."

And that might have been the moment Chloe fell a little in love. She's always had a weakness for people who care about the minutiae of life, the small details that elevate the mundane to interesting.

She giggles, thinking about it. *Mulligatawny soup*: she has no idea what that is but would very much like to try it.

Mo looks over, her eyes bruised with worry, and Chloe straightens her thoughts. *Hazel,* she tells herself. That's what she needs to be thinking about.

But not ten seconds later, Hunter is back in her brain, grinning wide as he continued to weave his story. "The teacher asked me the next day if I was feeling better."

"She never figured it out?"

He gave an aw-shucks shrug. "She might have, eventually, but I think she had a soft spot for me."

"I bet she did," Chloe said, believing it.

Hunter has a mischievous charm Chloe imagines works well on lots of women, regardless of age. At first glance, he looks scruffy with his long hair and unshaven beard, but the moment he starts talking, his eyes take hold, sparking with laughter, and then his hands cast a spell, and after that, the disguise falls away. You realize his jaw is strong, his hips slender, and his shoulders broad, and that he is, in fact, very good looking but hiding it as if he doesn't want anyone to notice.

He slurped the last of his milkshake with a great sucking noise, his eyes squeezed tight in an effort to get every last bit. On his forearm was a crude tattoo—an *X* with a line through it—and Chloe found herself wondering what it meant. Her own tattoo, a small black swallow on her left shoulder, has little meaning except to remind her of the girl she was when she chose it—impulsive, brazen, and recklessly in love. Only after the accident did she realize how childish it was, a petty, defiant scribble against her mother with no real meaning at all.

"But the jig was up before the year ended," Hunter went on, setting his empty cup on the table. "You can only skip so much school when you're twelve before the adults wise up. The principal called my mom and asked her to come in."

"Uh-oh."

His smile spread. "You know what my mom said when he showed her the notes?"

Chloe shook her head, grabbed a leftover fry, and swept it through the ketchup, feeling like she was eating popcorn at a really suspenseful part of a movie.

"Cool as a cucumber, she said, 'Well, you know, the son of Batman has an awful lot of responsibilities.'"

"She got it right away!" Chloe exclaimed, loving his mom instantly.

"Oh yeah. My mom would never miss a reference to Bruce Wayne. He's her superhero crush. The best part was the principal still didn't get it. So my mom goes on to list all the things that would keep me from going to school: clean out the Batcave; wax the Batmobile; iron the capes." His love for his mom radiated, and Chloe found herself leaning in, then realized what she was doing and jerked herself back.

They drove back to the motel with Ruby between them, full on a night of Mabel's fries, shakes, and laughter. The radio was tuned to alternative rock, and Hunter drove with one hand on the wheel and the other tapping the beat on the open window, and though he looks nothing like her dad, as she sat beside him, Chloe felt a little like she did when she was a girl.

She climbed from the truck to find him standing beside the door, and with no warning at all, he lifted her chin and kissed her, his large hands sliding around her waist to pull her close, the sweet tang of chocolate and ketchup between them.

"I've been wanting to do that all night," he said when he pulled away, then pivoted and walked toward the office, leaving her off balance, an unsteady, goofy state she's been in ever since.

27
MO

"You kissed him?" Mo says, her heart doing a happy dance despite the weight of her worry.

At the moment, Hazel is safe, parked at a hotel in Spokane, and she and Chloe are on their way to Barking Goat Kitchen. Mo figures, since they need to eat, she might as well knock the restaurant off her bucket list as well.

"Why didn't you tell me?" she asks, looking at Chloe, who is blushing, her ivory skin betraying her poker-straight face.

"I am telling you," Chloe says.

Mo should have known something was up. The playlist for the drive was far less grungy than it had been on the way to Bend, and Chloe was tapping along, something Mo hasn't seen her do since she moved to the city three months ago.

"I didn't mean to," Chloe says, the dimple in her right cheek twitching.

"Your lips just happened to land on his?"

"Actually, his landed on mine," she says.

"Wow, that is seriously awesome. So you think you'll see him again?"

"I kind of have to. He has my dog."

"*Your* dog?" Mo asks with an eyebrow lift.

"Yeah. I think Ruby's a keeper."

"Wow. A guy and a dog."

"It was a kiss, not a proposal."

"Never know," Mo says. After all, she and Kyle fell in love almost instantly, and Hunter seems exceptional.

Chloe turns the radio louder as if trying to put an end to the thought and the conversation, but her mouth continues to twitch with the tug of a smile, so Mo knows it isn't working.

Less than a minute later, they see a sign for Elmer City, and Mo forgets all about Chloe's kiss and Hunter, her insides somersaulting as they turn onto a narrow two-lane road that cuts through a thick forest of pine.

"I can't believe I'm finally going to eat at Barking Goat Kitchen," she says.

"You know that sounds like the punch line to a joke."

"No joke." Mo leans forward, peering down the road, which feels like a deep tunnel of anticipation. Having lunch at Barking Goat Kitchen has been on her bucket list since she was a kid. She read about the restaurant in a magazine her father had in the lobby of his office. A local Laguna Beach architect, Jillian Kane, wrote the piece, an article about how all the senses integrate to create the architectural experience. The example she gave was a place called Barking Goat Kitchen. She said that though the building was nothing special—*an old house in the middle of a forest of evergreens*—the restaurant was remarkable for how you experienced it, the dappling light on the tables from the sun through the trees outside the windows, the smell of ancient cedar that permeated from the floor and joists, the sound of running water from the nearby river as she and her kids ate grilled catfish and deep-fried corn fritters that tasted like they'd jumped straight from the river and earth and onto their plates. *And a place derives its spirit from its inhabitants,* she wrote, *and finer people than Goat and the townspeople of Elmer City don't exist.*

Mo has followed posts about the restaurant ever since, travelers who sought it out as well as those who, like Jillian, stumbled upon it by some lucky turn of fortune. Each day, a different single meal is served, decided on by the owner and the seasons. And when the food runs out, so does the meal. Many people have posted how disappointed they were to have made the trip only to be turned away. Mo really hopes she and Chloe are not among them.

"Wow. Okay," Chloe says as they pull into a dirt parking lot in front of a two-story clapboard house with sagging windows that looks like it's straight out of *The Amityville Horror.*

Not what Mo was expecting, yet exactly the kind of wonderful for which she had been hoping. The porch bows in the middle as if gravity is pulling it down, the dormer windows on the second floor angle in like curious eyes, and the sign planted in the ground is so faded you have to squint to make out the goat behind the letters. A dozen people snake from the entrance, and the incredible smell of grease and bacon wafts in the air around them.

"Yum," Chloe says as they step from the van and hurry into line.

Mo prays the food lasts long enough for them to make it through the door, feeling like she's in line for an e-ticket culinary ride she might never have the chance to experience again.

"It smells delicious," Chloe says as a woman appears in the doorway. She counts the customers, takes two steps, and, with her hand, slices a line between a man and a woman who are clearly together.

Heads bow, people grumble, and the severed half shuffles away, everyone except the man who was with the woman, as well as Chloe and Mo.

"So that's it?" Chloe says with great disappointment. "We don't get to eat?"

Mo's heart sinks, the small ray of light in the horrible, dismal day snuffed out by the stroke of a hand.

The woman who was on the fortunate side of the line says to the man she's with, "Well, just because you didn't make it doesn't mean I shouldn't get to eat here."

Mo dislikes her instantly. She's pretty in the way of a person who spends an immense amount of time and energy on herself, her hair woven blonde, her makeup airbrushed, her teeth unnaturally white.

"Well, what am I supposed to do?" the man asks, his shoulders folded forward like he missed a final goal or struck out and lost a game. He's wiry thin, nerdy, and at the moment bewildered, not sure if he has the right to be upset or if this is normal in a relationship.

"There's a restaurant down the street. I'll meet you after," the woman says brightly, as if this is a wonderful solution.

"Witch," Chloe mumbles, and Mo worries the couple might hear her. Chloe's never been shy about offering her opinions.

"Yeah, okay," the man says and leans in to give the woman a kiss.

When he turns away, the woman wipes it from her lips, and Mo feels Chloe getting ready to say something else, but just as her mouth opens, her phone rings.

"Hey, Mom," she says, turning and taking a few steps toward the parking lot.

Mo's ears burn as she watches Chloe nodding.

"Yeah, she's here."

She listens for a beat.

"No. We left Bend this morning. There was this restaurant near Spokane Mo wanted to try." She chuckles. "Yeah. You know Mo when it comes to food."

Mo hates that Chloe is lying to her mom, but she's doing it for Hazel, and there's nobody better at keeping a secret than Chloe.

"He what?" Chloe yelps, and Mo watches as her eyes dart to Mo before quickly snapping away. "He's lying!"

Chloe shakes her head.

"The bastard's making it up. Mo had nothing to do with it."

Mo's blood goes cold. *Me? What?*

"Chloe?" she says, the word coming out a croak.

Chloe looks her way and again shakes her head.

"Mom, you know there's no way—" She stops. "Fine. Finish." She taps her foot as she listens and, after a long minute, says, "I don't care what they say they found—"

What they found? Who? The police? They found something?

"Yes. I know . . . I am listening . . . But I'm telling you . . . Mom, stop . . . I was with her . . . Yes, all night."

Mo touches Chloe's shoulder and shakes her head. She won't have Chloe lie for her, not about this. Chloe slides her chin out, and Mo glares, a standoff that, after several seconds, Mo wins.

"Actually, not all night," Chloe says, closing her eyes and lifting her face to the sky as she blows out a frustrated sigh. "I had an appointment. But Mo was asleep when I left and asleep when I got home. Trust me, Mom, it wasn't her. You know it wasn't."

Another long minute passes as Chloe listens, Mo's heart pounding. She was so certain it was over. She was worried for Hazel but no longer concerned for herself. She holds her hand out for the phone. "Let me talk to her."

Instead of handing it over, Chloe takes another step away and continues to listen. Finally, she says, "Yeah, okay, I'll tell her," and then, after a short pause, adds, "Love you too."

Blowing out a hard breath, she puts the phone in her pocket, then turns. "Allen said you were the one who drugged him."

"But I didn't?" Mo says, the words coming out a question.

"I know, but he's saying you did, which is why the police searched the apartment. They still haven't made the connection to Hazel. Neither has my mom. Which is why the next part is bad." She frowns hard, a deep furrow forming between her brows. "They found a measuring cup in the dishwasher with paint thinner residue on it and your fingerprints."

Mo tilts her head, not understanding. The morning they left to follow Hazel, she moved the measuring cup on the top rack of the dishwasher to fit her coffee mug. "What does that have to do with anything?"

"Paint thinner is one of the ingredients in homemade GHB."

"Huh?" Mo says, the words floating. "What?"

"It's how you make GHB."

Mo tilts her head, and then her vision goes red as she remembers Chloe's reaction to the paint thinner in Hazel's room. "You knew," she says.

Chloe nods.

"And you didn't tell me."

"I thought the less you knew about homemade GHB, the better."

Her emotions bounce around all over the place—panic, anger, hurt. "You knew Haze did this, and you didn't tell me?"

"I didn't know she did it," Chloe says. "And I still don't."

"How can you say that? Haze did this, and the police think it was me!"

Infuriatingly, Chloe shakes her head. "Think about it, Mo. It doesn't make sense."

"Of course it makes sense!"

"Mo, settle down."

"You settle down! I'm the one being accused of a crime I had nothing to do with."

"I really don't think Haze did this. Allen knows who Haze is. If she was the one who drugged him, he would have said it was her."

"No. He wouldn't. The guy's a lunatic, and he doesn't hate *her*. He hates *me*."

Chloe frowns. "Yes, I agree, he's probably doing this out of revenge, but I think if he knew his true assailant, he would have said who it was. I know what it looks like because of the paint thinner, but—"

"And because he was dumped in the Tenderloin. And because Haze left that twisted poem. And because she left the night Allen was assaulted. How much more evidence do you need?"

"But it's Haze," Chloe says. "Haze can barely stammer out her order at Subway. Can you really see her confronting Allen, drugging him, then somehow managing to get him to the Tenderloin?"

Mo can't, but somebody did it, and it wasn't her, and the only other person that makes sense is Hazel.

"It doesn't matter anyway," Chloe goes on.

"What are you talking about?"

"Regardless of who did it, Allen is saying it was you, so you're the one the police suspect."

Mo shakes her head. "That's ridiculous. I moved a stupid measuring cup in a dishwasher. Didn't they find the paint thinner in Haze's room?"

Chloe shakes her head. "I dumped it, along with the poetry book."

"You did?"

"I was worried what might happen if the detectives came back and found it."

"Oh," Mo says. "Good thinking. Too bad you didn't think to do the same with the measuring cup."

"Yeah, unfortunate." She blows out a breath. "I could tell the police the truth, tell them I saw the paint thinner in Haze's room and threw it away."

Mo shakes her head, imagining Chloe being dragged in as a coconspirator or as an aider and abettor or some other such thing. And most likely they wouldn't believe her. As Chloe said, Allen isn't saying it was Hazel; he's saying it was her.

Her emotions spill over, tears running down her cheeks, and Chloe wraps her arm around her shoulders and leads her to the steps to sit.

"How can they think I did this?" she mumbles.

"A series of very unfortunate events," Chloe says. "The good news is you're innocent. My mom is emailing the name of a lawyer—"

Mo's face snaps up. "She's not representing me?"

Mrs. Miller is the best attorney on the planet, and she loves Mo like a daughter.

"She can't," Chloe says, eyes on her feet, which are swishing back and forth in front of her. "Conflict of interest. I live in the same apartment where the evidence was found. She said any good lawyer will paint me as a possible suspect, and she can't represent both of us."

Mo cries harder, all of it too much.

"She said she knows someone good," Chloe goes on. "An old friend. My mom let the detectives know you're out of town, so they're giving you until Friday to turn yourself in."

Friday? Mo tries to think what day it is. The rape happened Thursday. She went to Allen's office Friday, and he was assaulted that night. The detectives showed up the next morning, followed by Kora. Then she and Chloe drove to Bend and stayed at the motel. And this morning, they drove here. *Sunday. Today is Sunday.*

She has five days before she needs to turn herself in.

"I need to talk to Haze," she says, realizing it's the only way. Hazel needs to come clean and explain that the measuring cup with the paint thinner was hers.

The door behind them opens, and she turns to see the woman who earlier divided the line behind them. She nods toward the restaurant.

"Really?" Mo says. "We can eat here?"

The woman gives a half grunt that sounds more like "uh" than "nuh" and returns inside.

"See, look at that," Chloe says. "Things are already looking up."

Mo blots her eyes with the heels of her hands. "Either that, or this is God's way of offering a last meal."

28
CHLOE

As soon as they cross the threshold, it's like they've walked into an oven filled with bacon, bread, and potatoes. The hostess gestures to two seats at a table of four. The other two occupants are a couple of men in their sixties, grizzly as bears and intent on their meals. Nothing in the room matches—not a single chair, table, plate, or cup. There are old woven carpets on the floor and glass-shaded lamps attached to the walls. The server station is fashioned from a credenza that looks like it belongs in a palace, and beside it is an old green Igloo ice chest that holds longneck bottles of beer.

"I feel like I'm in an Agatha Christie novel," Mo whispers.

"Or a time machine. It's like this place has time traveled back and forth for a century."

The customers are as mismatched as the decor. The locals are easy to spot, faded and comfortable as the furniture. The tourists are brighter and higher strung. The girl who ditched her date sits beside a very old man with a face of white whiskers. He looks annoyed as she prattles on about the food, her hands with her long nails gesticulating wildly. He looks up occasionally, squinting as if an alien invader has interrupted his lunch, then returns his attention to his food.

Chloe is pulling out her chair when her sixth sense buzzes, and she looks up in time to catch a glimpse of a middle-aged man in the pass-through window, his gaze darting away as hers finds his—striking eyes the exact green of Finn's set in deeply weathered skin. She shakes off the feeling—premonition, warning, guidance, strength—which is rare these days. Her sister's spirit's been gone a long time. Yet every once in a while, she feels it, the soft glow of something that remains.

Her butt has barely hit the chair when a plate is set down in front of her by a woman, slight as a girl but at least two generations older. Three round gold balls, roasted potatoes, and collard greens with bacon. It's followed by another plate with two rosemary-flecked buttermilk biscuits and some sort of special butter.

"Salt-cod fritters!" Mo exclaims. "So many people have posted about these." She cuts into one of the balls with her fork, and steam rises from the center, releasing the sharp brine of salt and fish.

Chloe pops a bite of potato in her mouth. "Oh, that's good," she mumbles around it.

"Careful," the grizzlier of their two fellow diners says, "get used to Paul's cooking, and you might never want to eat anywhere else again."

Both she and Mo nod in agreement as they continue to eat, the experience dulling the shock of her mother's call.

"Can I have your bacon?" Mo asks.

Chloe forks the pork bits she picked from her greens onto Mo's plate, then slathers a biscuit with butter and bites into it. "Yum. What is that?" She points to the butter, which definitely is not butter but something far more heavenly, sweet like honey but thicker and tangier.

"Maple butter," the man on her right says.

"Dang, the owner should bottle and sell that," Chloe says. "He'd be rich."

The man chuckles. "Don't think Paul cares much about being rich." He stands and tips an imaginary hat. "You ladies have a nice day." He plucks a ten from his wallet and sets it on the table. The other man does the same.

"Ten dollars?" Chloe hisses when they're gone. "Are you kidding? This meal is only ten dollars?"

"I'm good with this being my last meal," Mo says, forking another bite of salt-cod fritter into her mouth. She says it as a joke, but Chloe feels her worry.

"We'll figure it out," Chloe says, her own stress returning.

Mo is right to be worried. Chloe's mom, who is the coolest person Chloe knows in a crisis, was more than a little concerned. Which is, quite frankly, terrifying. "It's not good, Bug," her mom said. "Allen is saying it was her. And there's hard evidence to back him up. This is going to be tough to beat." She didn't say impossible, but "tough" to her mom is almost the same as impossible for most. And her mom won't be Mo's attorney. It will be someone else. Someone likely not as good and who won't care as much.

The server whisks away their empty plates. "Ten each," she says as she goes.

"Lunch is on me," Chloe announces, beaming that she can actually offer to pay for something. She plucks the last remaining twenty from her pocket and lays it on the table.

"I've got the tip," Mo says, matching the twenty with another.

"Nice tip," Chloe says, as the gratuity is generous even by Mo standards.

"My guess is our lunches were meant for the staff," Mo says. "And someone took pity on us because of my pathetic sobbing on the stoop."

Chloe glances toward the pass-through window and again catches a glimpse of the man with the remarkable eyes. *A good man,* she thinks, someone moved by another's tears and willing to give something of themselves to help. Rare, but not extinct, and she thinks of Hunter and how he was singing to Ruby outside their motel room last night to calm her, then how he gave the dog his dinner. This morning, as they were leaving, he walked from the office. He was freshly showered and wore a Nirvana T-shirt, as if somehow knowing the band was one of her favorites.

"Hey," he said, hands shoved deep in his jean pockets, looking almost as nervous as she felt. "You're leaving?"

Ruby jumped and circled, clearly excited to see him.

"Family emergency," she mumbled, the kiss blazing bright in her mind. "We need to go to Spokane."

Hunter squatted down and scratched Ruby behind her ears, then slap-played with her as his eyes repeatedly glanced up at Chloe. She pretended not to notice, her focus on Ruby, as if she were the most fascinating dog in the world.

"Hmmm," he said, pawing Ruby's mouth. "Means you'll be coming back this way."

Her cheeks flamed despite the early-morning chill. "Might be."

"Then maybe," he said, "it would be best if you leave Ruby with me." He stood, catching Chloe's eyes before she could look away. "You know, considering she likes Mabel's cooking so much."

"She does like her chicken," she said, a flittering in her chest that was terrifying.

Ruby planted herself beside Hunter as if weighing in on the decision. Hunter stepped toward Chloe, and she thought he might kiss her again, but then Mo stepped from the room.

"Mo," a voice says, waking Chloe from the thought.

She turns toward it, then blinks several times, certain her mind is playing tricks.

"Kyle?" Mo says, confirming Chloe's not imagining it.

A dozen feet away, silhouetted in the light through the entrance, is the man who saved her life and who has hated her ever since. He takes a step, and Mo runs at him. He opens his arms, and she buries her face against his chest. He wears his army fatigues. A white band with a red-cross insignia on the sleeve signifies he's a medic.

"What are you doing here?" Mo mumbles into his shirt.

"I could ask you the same thing," he says as he bends down to kiss the top of her head.

Mo sniffles, and then she is sobbing, ugly, hiccuping tears as all the bravado she mustered dissolves with the relief of being in the arms of the man she loves. Chloe's throat swells closed as she watches, jealous all the way to her toes.

Since Mo and Kyle met, they have had *that* kind of love, the kind fairy tales and love sonnets are made of. And when they are together, they morph into a single being of incredible mushy devotion that makes you want to both puke and applaud at once.

"Trouble," Kyle says quietly. "Little *t* or capital *T*, you are my trouble, and whatever this is, we're in it together."

And Chloe loses it, blinking back tears, and she notices the hostess pressing her knuckles to her eyes as well.

Mo takes his hand and pulls him outside.

"Wow," the hostess says.

"Yeah, wow," Chloe says, stepping beside her.

"For you." She holds out two brown bags. "Dessert."

Chloe takes the offering and carries it outside. She looks left toward the road that looks like it leads to town, then right toward a path that looks like it leads to a river. She chooses right.

Finn was an ocean girl, drawn to the sea like their dad. Chloe's mom and Chloe's older sister, Aubrey, prefer cities. And Oz was like Chloe and needed the earth—mountains and trees, running water and musty green moss. The forest calls to her.

As she walks past the restaurant, a strange language drifts through the open window to the kitchen, and the melodic rise and fall makes her think of the man with the extraordinary eyes.

29
MO

Kyle holds her hand as they walk, and Mo keeps glancing over to make sure he's real.

He stops, takes her face in his hands, and kisses her to prove it, his lips lingering—the kiss of a soldier gone a long time, the familiar taste of coffee and cinnamon on his tongue. It always stuns her when he returns, the change in him, and the time it takes for him to acclimate to being home—the shadow in his features and his neediness, like he's greedy or starved or both.

"How?" she says again.

"It's called a plane."

"I mean, how did you get the time off?"

"I requested emergency leave, and Greg understood." Quietly he adds, "He saw the news."

Greg is Kyle's commanding officer and also his best friend—a straight-shooting, no-nonsense sort of man who would take a bullet for his country or a friend but wouldn't bend the rules for either. She feels her cheeks burn at the thought of him knowing the accusations against her and for the embarrassment it must have brought Kyle.

"Good thing I checked your location before I left the airport, or I'd be in Oregon right now." There's a question in his voice she ignores.

"Why don't we get some food?" she says. "You must be hungry."

As her mom likes to say, things always look brighter on a full belly. Plus, she needs time to process that he's here and to figure out how much to tell him now that he is. His appearance was so sudden, and now things are so much worse. While last night his confidence in her innocence was certain, she's not sure how unwavering it will remain once he hears the latest turn of events.

If she tells him everything, including the part about Hazel and the paint thinner, she knows what his reaction will be. He will want to go to the police and tell them the truth, not caring that Chloe thinks Hazel is innocent or about the fragile state Hazel's in.

"Food would be good," he says, taking her hand again and giving a stay of execution.

They continue into Elmer City, a tiny village barely worthy of being called a town, let alone a city. Less than half a block long, it has a post office, a bank, a gas station, a church, and a general store with a small diner attached. They take one of the two tables outside, and a middle-aged man with the stitched name of Fred on his red apron steps from the store to hand them a couple of menus.

Kyle waves them away. "A burger and fries and two lemonades."

Fred has kind eyes, and again Mo thinks of the article by the architect: *A place derives its spirit from its inhabitants, and finer people than Goat and the townspeople of Elmer City don't exist.* And she wonders if Jillian Kane and Fred might have crossed paths.

"So?" Kyle says when Fred is gone.

"I can't believe you're here," she says evasively, then takes his hand and runs her thumb over the rough skin of his knuckles.

He lifts her fingers to his lips, the stubble of his beard grazing her skin, and his eyes rise to look deep into hers, seafoam green with flecks of blue, like she's looking into a lagoon.

When they first met, she was only sixteen and he was nineteen, a boy on the cusp of being a man—all of him sinewy and gold. Now, eight years later, the boy is gone and he is nothing but man—a shadow of bronze always on his chin, his body filled out, and his features, smooth in college, roughened and his skin chiseled with small scars and laugh lines that will someday turn into deep creases from a lifetime of smiles.

"How about you start at the beginning?" he says, setting their hands back on the table.

The beginning? And again, Mo feels the break between before and after like a fault line in her life. *Wednesday was before.* She was happy and bebopping along. FactNews was on the precipice of its big break. Kyle was finishing his tour and in three months would be returning home forever. In her head, she was planning their wedding and daydreaming about houses and babies. *After.* Thursday, Hazel was raped. And now, because of that, Mo is the prime suspect in an assault investigation against her assailant, and she is sitting at a café in a small town outside Spokane, across from the man she loves, faced with the choice of lying to him in order to protect Hazel or telling him the truth, knowing it will put him in the impossible situation of either keeping her secret or betraying her and going to the police, thinking it will save her.

"Mo?" he says, his brows pinched together.

She pulls her hand from his and looks down at the table. "You already know. The police think I had something to do with what happened, but I didn't."

"Yeah, that part I got. What I don't get is why you're here"—he sweeps the scene with his hand—"or why you went to that guy's office and made that post. It's so unlike you."

He's right, of course. Normally, she is very deliberate, her actions carefully considered before she makes them, like a chess match.

"I don't know," she says honestly. "I just sort of lost it. I found out Allen had been drugging and sexually assaulting girls for years and getting away with it. And I knew he was going to get away with it again, and I couldn't stand the thought of that. It was stupid. I had no idea it would blow up the way it did."

Fred interrupts. "Here you go," he says, setting down their lemonades.

"Thank you," she and Kyle say together. People make fun of them for the quirk, their politeness in sync—"thank yous" and "excuse mes" and "bless yous" always in harmony. Normally, it makes them smile. Today, it only serves as a sharp reminder of their bond.

She takes a sip of her lemonade. "There's more," she says.

Kyle sets his glass down.

"Allen woke up."

"He's out of the coma?"

She nods.

"That's great."

Her head reverses direction.

"It's not great?"

She blows out a breath. "Try not to freak out."

He doesn't answer but looks on the verge of doing just that, his muscles bunched and his lemonade gripped so tight she's afraid the glass might shatter.

"When the police interviewed him, he said I was the one who drugged him."

Silence.

"I wasn't," she says. "He only said it to get back at me because I made that post."

"He said it was you?"

"He did, and the police believe him."

"Allen said *you* drugged him?"

Her heart pounds, and she knows she should tell him the rest, all of it—about Hazel and the paint thinner and the poem and the measuring cup—but warnings blare in her head, telling her it would be a mistake.

"They issued a warrant for my arrest," she says. "And I have until Friday to turn myself in."

When a minute passes and he still hasn't responded, she says, "He's lying. I didn't have anything to do with it."

It's very slight, almost imperceptible, the exhale slow and deliberate through his nose as he says, "Obviously." But she knows, even as he says it, he's wondering if she's lying and if maybe, in fact, she did.

30
CHLOE

Chloe sits on a boulder beside the river, kicks off her Doc Martens, and sticks her feet in the water. She looks at her abbreviated toes beneath the surface, the glistening crystal-clear stream making them almost pretty. Several doctors have suggested prosthetics, but she's not interested; her scars are as much a part of her as the unmarred pieces that remain. Everyone has a history, and if there's one thing she's sure of, it's that the only way forward is to come to terms with the path you walked to get where you are.

She opens one of the bags the hostess handed her as she left the restaurant and pulls out a bite-size chocolate macaroon, the sweet surprise adding another thin layer of satisfaction to the moment— fleeting, considering the circumstances, but not taken for granted. She bites into it and thinks of her brother, knowing he would have given up all his worldly possessions in an innocent trade for the two bags of chocolate.

For you, Oz, she thinks, silently toasting him with the bit that remains and imagining him smiling. *Happy moment,* she thinks, reminding herself even the best memories can turn to pain if you're not careful, and Oz wouldn't want that. He liked when the people around him were happy. Unlike Finn, she never feels the presence of her brother within her, though she often finds herself living her life in honor of him. It's part of why she became a vet and definitely why she chose to specialize in dogs.

She lies back on the rock, and as she looks up at the sky through the trees, two words come to mind: *green* and *peaceful*. She takes a deep breath of the verdant air and holds it in her lungs, then releases it and smiles as she thinks about Kyle showing up the way he did. Like a superhero.

Kyle the hero. Mo the angel. Chloe the screwup. Vance the loser. Bob the villain—none of the labels from that single moment are entirely fitting, and yet they have stuck: self-fulfilling prophecies as much as inherent truth. And she often wonders who each of them might have become had the accident not happened, had they simply gone to dinner as they were supposed to and spent the next two days skiing.

Though that's not fair to Kyle. His love for Mo is real, and the heroism he showed eight years ago is as much a part of him as the aqua green of his eyes. Her mom as well. And her dad. Even her brother. All of them heroes. Everyone in her family except for her.

She closes her eyes and tries to push the thought away. *Always forward, never back*—it's something her dad said to her once when either he was struggling or she was—*It's okay to remember, baby, but regret's a waste of the time we have left.* Like her, he barely survived, so he understands feeling like you're living on borrowed time.

Her mind turns to the new evidence against Mo, and a hard knot forms in her gut with how damning it is. *Bad luck,* she thinks. So much of destiny turns out to be based on that, rotten twists of fortune that neither money nor love nor faith can protect you from. Hazel was simply in the wrong place at the wrong time. Mo threatened Allen on the wrong day. One choice this way or that, and everything would be different. But it's not. This is how it turned out. So this is where they are.

The sun's warmth soaks her lids, and her mind drifts, the words of the poem Hazel left playing in her mind:

> The power of wrong
> Is iron strong;
> Is the power of right, then, weak?
> The power of right
> Is a greater might
> Than thou can'st think or speak.

"Afternoon."

Her eyes snap open to see the man from the restaurant, his body silhouetted against the afternoon sky and his remarkable eyes shadowed by a baseball cap. In his right hand is a fishing rod; in the other, a tackle box.

"Fishing might help," he says. "More often than not, when you stop thinking, that's when the answer comes to you." He smiles a broken grin. "Or at the very least, you get dinner."

"But you only have one pole?" Chloe says as she pushes to her feet, the idea of watching a line bob in the water already comforting.

"I'm meeting my sous chef, and he always brings extra gear."

Sous chef. She smiles at the highbrow term coming from such an unpretentious mouth. The guy wears cutoff jeans so loose on his narrow hips they look in danger of falling down. His once-black T-shirt is mottled gray with a few bleach stains. And his arms are riddled with poorly executed tattoos that speak to a life lived in the moment and most of those seconds spent not giving a damn.

"Paul," he says as Chloe pulls on her shoes.

"Chloe," she says. "You own the restaurant?"

"More like it owns me," he says. "But yeah, she's mine."

He walks with a limp, and though she'd guess him to be in his forties, his life's been harder than that. The hair that sticks out from beneath his baseball cap is dirt brown and wavy, his skin earth colored, and in his features, she sees remnants of the hostess and the woman who served them, and she realizes he's Native American.

They reach another outcropping, a few large boulders perched above a pool of water with barely a current. Standing on a rock upstream is a man around Chloe's age dressed nearly identically to Paul, except his shirt advertises a surf shop and his shorts are better fitting.

"Hawk, meet Chloe," Paul says.

Hawk glances over, tilts his head, then straightens it. "I know you."

He has straight brown hair to his chin and a remarkably beautiful face Chloe's certain she would remember.

"I don't think so. I'm not from around here."

"Neither am I." The right side of his mouth twitches before settling back to neutral. "Gear's in the shade. Help yourself."

"I'll get you baited up," Paul says.

"I've got it," Chloe says. "My dad fishes."

He smiles in appreciation and walks toward the bank. Chloe chooses a rod from the two leaning against a tree, digs a worm from the bait cup, and spears it onto the hook. *Sorry, little fellow. Hierarchy of life. It sucks to be a worm.*

She walks left of Hawk and Paul, positioning herself downstream and far enough away so as not to encroach on their spots.

Her nerves prickle with a bit of apprehension about her rusty skills, and she nearly cheers when she casts her line and it soars in a perfect arc to the middle of the river. Feeling Hawk's eyes, she glances sideways, and he gives a small nod before returning his attention to his own line.

She watches her bob bouncing in the current, and as Paul said, magically, it lulls her worries away. A pair of Canada geese floats by, and she watches them with a sigh: *love* . . . or at least a partner to go through life with. And she thinks how much she would like that, to have someone to float on a current with and see where it takes them.

Her line catches, snapping her attention back and sending a jolt of adrenaline through her veins. The rod bends, and she cranks the reel to pull it in, a sick thrill running through her at the prospect of having caught something.

While she loves animals and cherishes life, her dad is the captain of a fishing charter boat, and she grew up with an appreciation for the abundance of the ocean and the natural bounty it offers. She doesn't eat ocean mammals or octopus and recently gave up crab and lobster, but when she can afford it, she loves every other kind of seafood—shrimp, clams, mussels, halibut, salmon, cod. And fresh trout and bass from a river are definitely among her favorites.

"Ease off," Paul says, appearing beside her. "Give her a bit of line, then pull her back, then do it again. Let her fight."

Chloe does as he says and feels better for what she's doing because of it. "A good death," her dad likes to say. "It's all any of us can really hope for, a life well lived and a noble goodbye." She knows he's thinking of Oz when he says it. Her brother died a hero, and he lived the best life he knew how.

The line quivers as the fish continues to fight, surging forward, then relenting when it grows tired before surging again, until finally, after many minutes, the fight drains and Chloe feels its surrender. She pulls the glistening fish from the water, a silver trout at least ten inches long.

Paul's grin spreads wide as he pulls the hook from its gasping mouth and whispers words in a language Chloe doesn't understand before setting it in the tall grass to die in the shade.

"Good to know at least one of us will be eating tonight," he says.

Hawk looks over. "Speak for yourself, *squebay*. I've already caught my bellyful."

Something in the taunt is familiar, and Chloe tilts her head to look at him again. A vague recollection tickles her brain, though Hawk is a name she's certain she would remember. She's about to ask him where he's from when her phone pings with a new text. She pulls it from her pocket, expecting a message from her mom or Mo. Instead, it's a number she doesn't recognize.

Ruby and I got matching pedicures from my mom.

The photo above the words shows two outstretched black paws beside a guy's foot with matching purple nails.

Her spit of laughter causes Paul and Hawk to look over and smile.

31
MO

They are in a rented room over the general store, naked and entwined in each other's arms. Mo texted Chloe to ask if she wanted to join them for dinner, and thankfully . . . and surprisingly . . . she said she already had dinner plans. She also assured her she was keeping an eye on Hazel and not to worry.

Mo's emotions are all over the place—love, worry, sadness, fear, and an odd repulsion she cannot shake. While she was not the one Allen raped, the entire time Kyle made love to her, she could not stop thinking of Kora and Hazel and what they endured at Allen's hands.

"I missed you," Kyle says, leaning over to kiss her shoulder, seemingly oblivious to her strange mood.

"Mmmm," she says in a low purr as her mind continues to spin. While she is overwhelmed he is here and that he dropped everything to be by her side, she's also quite anxious for him to leave. Having him here complicates an already-impossible situation, and she feels like she's walking a tightrope over an inferno. It's one thing to be evasive over the phone when someone is thousands of miles away, and something else entirely when they are right here in front of you and looking at you like you are the moon and the earth and the stars.

In an hour, he will want to make love again. Always when he returns, his amorousness is nearly insatiable. They barely made it through the door before he was undressing her and backing her into the bed.

He flops onto his stomach and drapes his arm over her hips, and it's all she can do not to shove the appendage away, agitation running through her she cannot explain. She likes things neat. She likes things orderly. And her life is falling apart.

"You okay?" Kyle asks sleepily.

"Uh-huh," she lies. "I'm just going to brush my teeth."

She slides from beneath him and hurries to the bathroom. After closing the door, she slides down the wood to the floor, pulls a towel from the rod, wraps it around herself, then drops her head to her knees.

She can't believe this is happening. How could Allen have said it was her? It makes no sense. Yes, the post she made was awful, and she's certain it pissed him off, but enough to lie to the police? Her eyes flick behind her lids, a feeling that she's missing something niggling at the edges of her brain. She thinks of his expression when he greeted her at his office, glib, almost happy, as if he was glad she was there.

Spider willies crawl over her skin. *Hate,* she thinks. Even before that moment, he hated her. But why? In college, she barely knew him. She tries to think back to that time. Vaguely, she recalls a party and him hitting on her, then keeping at it even after she said she had a boyfriend. The memory is far away, not important . . . or at least, she didn't think so at the time.

She might have been drunk, and she might have needed to push him away. Then James was there. "Hey, Al, how about we get you a drink?"

"Mo, give me a chance. I like you."

Her blood pumped wildly. "Not if you were the last man on earth," she hissed, wiping her arms where he had touched her and giving a visible shudder.

But to hold a grudge for so long over something so small? That's insane. But then Allen is insane. He's proved that.

He gave me your *beer.* Hazel's words replay in her overwrought brain. Allen saw Mo at Black Sands, and his intention was to exact payback for her insult all those years ago. But then Kyle called, leaving Hazel in the crosshairs of a long-standing grudge that had nothing to do with her.

One of the stories FactNews reported on a few months ago was the psychological effects of rejection. The report revealed that it's one of the most traumatic and damaging experiences a person can go through, affecting everything from your physical well-being to your IQ to your ability to reason, the pain greater than physical pain and much longer lasting. The reason is that people can recall it in detail, the injury able to be replayed again and again, which can cause intense surges in anger and aggression. It's been proved to be a greater predictor of violence than drugs, poverty, or gang membership.

"Lonely out here," Kyle says from the other room.

"Just a sec," she says, her head spinning with the revelation of how deep Allen's hate goes. Shakily, she pushes to her feet, and since her suitcase is still in the van, she opens Kyle's Dopp kit to use his toothpaste. Beneath the tube is a baggie. Curious, she pulls it out, and her eyes go wide as she realizes what it is. Beneath the plastic is a black velvet ring box.

Quickly, she returns it to where it was, arranging it so it's concealed as tears form in her eyes. Marrying Kyle is all she's ever wanted, is still all she wants, so why, suddenly, does seeing that box make everything feel so wrong?

32
CHLOE

They are sitting on the porch of Barking Goat Kitchen, Paul softly playing harmonica as Chloe rocks on a porch swing and looks out at the million stars in the clear night sky, their bellies full with the trout they caught in the river and potatoes pulled from the garden behind the restaurant.

Hawk left straight after dinner. He was right about them having met. She was surprised to learn they'd both grown up in Laguna Beach and that, when she was in kindergarten, he was the third-grade bully who had tried to take the book she was reading. At the time, he went by his given name of Drew.

They both ended up in the principal's office. She had a skinned knee, and he had a chunk of hair missing. The principal asked what had happened, and they both said, "Nothing." Hawk said he'd never forgotten that, then cast his eyes at the table and apologized for the person he had been. She'd never heard anyone do that—apologize not for something they'd done but for being the sort of person who would do such a thing.

She doesn't know why she didn't tell the principal the truth, some sense that Drew would be hurt by it more than she would by keeping it to herself. Her dad smirked and tousled her hair when he picked her up. Her dad didn't like snitches, and he believed in standing up for things when necessary, no explanation needed. Her mom didn't live by that philosophy. She wanted to know what had happened, and when Chloe wouldn't tell her, she sent her to her room and told her not to come out until she was ready to explain. Chloe stayed there two days, until finally her dad decided he'd had enough and got in a blowout fight with her mom, forcing her to let Chloe out. Her mom fumed for a week.

Chloe loves her dad more than any person on the planet, but she knows now that her mom was right. Without her mom's firm hand, Chloe would have for certain ended up on a wayward path. Even in kindergarten, she was defiant and rebellious to the point of recklessness, and the only thing that kept her on the straight and narrow was the unrelenting, constant correcting of her mom, the unspoken threat of *I love you, but I will not let that love interfere with my opinion of you.* To this day, Chloe cares a great deal what her mom thinks.

She takes another long pull of her beer, her fifth of the night and more than she's drunk since the three days she spent drunk after Eric left. She tells herself to stop, but the buzz blurs the edges, and at the moment, blurry's a whole lot better than clear.

"Do you believe in an eye for an eye?" she asks when Paul stops playing to take a sip of his own beer. Paul is laid-back cool and deeply mellow, exactly the kind of guy you can ask something like that to, and not only will he not be surprised, but it will almost be as if he were expecting it, like people ask him his opinion on the universe all the time.

He takes a moment before answering, polishing his harmonica on his shorts, his head tilted slightly to the left and his thick lips set in a line.

"I suppose it depends," he says finally, sitting back and putting the harmonica in the pocket of his hoodie, which advertises Jim Beam. "The woman who first owned this place used to say, 'Throw me to the wolves, and I'll return leading the pack.'"

"That was Goat?" Chloe asks.

Mo told her the restaurant originally belonged to a Native American woman who had learned to cook as a servant for a French family that had lived in the house. No one knows what happened to the family, but Goat continued cooking after they were gone, and people started paying to eat her food.

"It was," Paul says, his eyes sparking with love and respect. "She was the fiercest, most loyal woman I know, and she lived her life by those words. She didn't blink an eye when it came to hurting those who deserved it but then made up for it with kindness toward those who deserved better. I'd say that was a fair trade, though I'm sure others might have had a different opinion of it."

Chloe picks at the label of her beer, watching the silver bits float like glittery snowflakes to the porch, her thoughts again on the poem Hazel left about right and wrong, wondering if what happened to Allen—a direct retaliation that was a mirror of what he'd done to someone else—would change him, and if it did, if it would make him better or worse.

Paul pulls out his harmonica again and begins to play a slow, sorrowful song that sounds like longing, and she closes her eyes and lets the notes take root in her heart as she thinks of Hazel and the trouble she's in. Long minutes pass, the breeze lifting the hair on her arms as crickets and frogs sing along with Paul's mournful playing.

When the song ends, she asks, "How did Hawk come to live with you?" curious how a boy from Southern California, who started out so mean spirited as a child, could turn into such a gentlehearted man living in the backwoods of Washington.

Paul gives a soft smile. "A little like how you ended up here. He and his mom and sister were just passing through. We ended up having a meal, and it turned into them staying on for a bit. His mom worked a few months at the restaurant." He picks up his Coors. "This place calls to certain people. Hawk was one of them, so when he graduated high school, he came back."

Chloe believes it. It's been months since her lungs have felt so full, as if the air contains more oxygen or the sky has more space. This is exactly the sort of place she'd like to settle someday, surrounded by nature, where the pace of life matches the serenity of the world around it.

"You know," Paul goes on, "my ma used to say worries are like river stones, the burden easier shared, each person taking a rock until the largest dams are reduced to only pebbles."

Chloe tucks her feet beneath her, wishing it were that easy—share her burdens and lighten the load. But to tell anyone the truth would be to make them complicit in the deceit and would endanger Hazel.

"And some burdens," Chloe says with a sigh, "when shared, only make the world heavier for everyone."

Paul nods and doesn't argue, and she knows he's a man who understands secrets. He stretches his arms over his head and pushes to his feet. "You can stay in the room beside the kitchen."

"I can stay in my van."

He ignores her. "Toilet sticks, so hold it down when you flush."

She opens her mouth to protest again, but he's already turned and is walking inside.

She collects the empty beer bottles and throws them in the trash, the five beers she had making the task more challenging than it should be.

The room beside the kitchen is no larger than a Ping-Pong table, with a single bed along the far wall and a red futon wedged between it and the bathroom. She kicks off her shoes and flops on the mattress at the exact moment her phone pings. She rolls onto her back and holds the screen over her face, moving it in and out until the words coalesce into focus: It's taken three months but I realize I've made the worst mistake of my life. I love u with all that I am and I want to come home. Yours til butter flies . . . Eric

33
MO

The text is silent, but Mo feels the vibration. She slips from the bed, silent so as not to wake Kyle, and carries her phone to the bathroom.

The burned hand teaches best

She doesn't recognize the number, but a bad feeling creeps down her spine. The words she knows. They were spoken by Gandalf to Pippin in *The Two Towers*. Whoever is texting knows she is a fan of J. R. R. Tolkien.

Who is this? she texts back.

Three pulsing dots appear, letting her know whoever's on the other side is typing.

U think u r clever so here is a riddle: This thing all things devours—birds beasts trees flowers—gnaws iron—bites steel—grinds hard stones to meal—slays king—ruins town—and beats high mountain down.

Time. It's the final answer Bilbo Baggins needs to come up with to escape the underground lair of Gollum in *The Hobbit*.

Time, she texts.

That is what I am offering

Allen? Her heart pounds. *Time?* Because she only has until Friday? Time because she might go to jail . . . prison?

Hand trembling, she types: What do you want?

More pulsing dots.

"Ace, everything okay?" Kyle asks from the other room, causing her heart to jump.

"Yeah, good," she manages, staring so hard at the pixels they blur. "Be out in a minute."

Right the wrong and I will allow u to continue on

Her thumbs fly over the screen: What wrong?

The response is instant. Tell the world u wanted it

34
CHLOE

Purple-painted toenails.

Ruby leaping and barking on the bank of the river. Chasing gray geese floating downstream.

A jail cell with a cot. Inside looking out. Then outside looking in.

Eric. His hand reaching. Her falling.

Chloe startles awake, heart pounding, and her eyes blink rapidly, not knowing where she is. A red futon, a small room. *Barking Goat Kitchen.* She swallows, rubs her knuckles hard against her chest.

Her throat is dry, and her head pounds. Beer hangover, the kind that makes your ears feel like they're stuffed with cotton and your stomach like it's churning with fermenting yeast.

Trying not to move too quickly for fear of rupturing her brain, she reaches for her phone to see if Eric responded to the reply she sent last night: Need time to think. She had originally added: Yours til ice skates. But then erased it.

She runs her thumb over his plea for forgiveness, and tears form. For eight years, she loved him, devoted herself to making a life together. Then he left. And now, he wants to come back. Does a single misstep erase all the rest? Or is being able to forgive a test of true love?

She thinks of what is going on with Mo and how Kyle swooped in like a superhero. Would Eric do that? He would. Not in the way Kyle did but in his own endearing, bumbling sort of way. He would show up and do whatever she asked. Or she would say, *I need you,* and he would come.

That's not nothing. Until he lost his way, Eric was steady as they come. Perhaps a little in the shadows and, toward the end, lost—as if the more her prospects brightened, the more his dimmed. But maybe he's changed; maybe he realizes it doesn't matter if she's already found her path and he hasn't, and the resentment will be less. Maybe they could start again and be better this time.

She lifts her face to stare through the curtainless window at a flickering neon Oly beer sign, trying to imagine them back together. He would like . . . *love* Ruby. He always wanted them to get a dog. She was the one who said no. She was in veterinary school and dealt with animals all day. She didn't want to deal with another when she got home. Maybe she should have said yes. Perhaps that would have changed things.

Where would they live? She has no money; she's certain neither does he. *The van?* They'd kill each other inside a week. How would they get by? Would she support him until he got a job? She can't even support herself. She imagines them living on brussels sprouts and ramen, and the thought is so depressing she groans.

But it's Eric. She thinks of his long body, his melodic voice, the deep connection that bound them from the first moment they met—eight years ago, yet so close, like it was only yesterday. Memory is strange that way. He was the one who released her from the past, making the darkness recede as the prospect of something brighter moved her forward. It was because of Eric that Finn was able to let go and move on, knowing Chloe was okay.

Noise outside the room causes her to push the thoughts aside. After using the restroom and brushing her teeth, she walks into the restaurant to find Hawk in the kitchen.

"Morning," he says brightly. "Coffee's on." He nods toward a coffee maker near the back door.

She chooses a mug with the carving of a moose on the front from the selection of mismatched cups, fills it, then pulls herself onto the counter to watch Hawk as he expertly chops onions, the rapid rhythm mesmerizing.

A buzzer goes off, and Hawk sets down the knife to pull a tray of biscuits from the oven. The air fills with warmth and dough and cinnamon. He drops a biscuit beside her, and her stomach rumbles as her mouth waters.

She pops a steaming bite in her mouth. "Yum."

He nods and goes back to chopping.

Last night, as she lay in bed, struggling with sleep, his story came back to her. The name Hawk threw her, but when she thought of him as Drew, she recalled a tragic story in which his mom had killed his dad after the dad had kidnapped Drew and his sister and then tried to kidnap his baby brother. The killing was self-defense, but she can't imagine how difficult it must have been to live through something like that.

"How'd you get the name Hawk?" she asks as she continues to break off pieces of delicious biscuit.

"Paul gave it to me. The first time we met."

The skinny server appears, glances at Chloe, and gives a curt nod as if not surprised in the least to see her, then rapidly blathers a hundred foreign words to Hawk that might be a story or might be a rant or might be a combination of both. Hawk nods, laughs, frowns, and adds several "wows" and "huhs" and one "that sucks."

She works as she prattles, creating rolls of silverware.

"Can I help?" Chloe asks when the last bite of biscuit is gone.

The woman nods at a tray of salt and pepper shakers, and Chloe sets to work filling them. The normalcy calms her, and for a long while, she loses herself in the task as she continues to listen to the conversation she doesn't understand.

The woman, finished with the silverware, carries them to the dining room.

"Is she related to Paul?" Chloe asks.

"She's Coast Salish, and Paul is, too, so they're part of a tribe, but they're not related by blood that I know." He dusts his hands on his apron and looks up at her. "If you need a place to crash, you can stay," he says, surprising her. "This is a good place to figure out your troubles and even a better place to hide from them." And she wonders if her worries are that plain on her face.

Her phone buzzes, and she pulls it from her pocket.

Take all the time u need. I'll wait as long as it takes and spend forever trying to make up for this. Yours til the kitchen sinks.

35
MO

Mo almost misses seeing the note.

"Hey, Ace, watch yourself." Kyle nudges her to keep her from stepping on the folded sheet of paper with her name scrawled in Chloe's distinctive left-slanted handwriting.

Her nerves are already frayed, Allen's texts replaying on a constant reel in her brain. Last night, when she climbed back into bed beside Kyle, she was incensed, unable to believe Allen could think she would even consider what he was suggesting. But as the hours passed and the initial shock wore off, she realized his offer might not be as out of the question as she thought. Unless Mo is willing to throw Hazel under the bus, something she's realizing she's not prepared to do, Allen's proposition might be the only thing standing between her innocence and guilt.

"Why wouldn't Chloe just text," Kyle says as he picks up the paper, sounding annoyed, as he often does when it comes to things involving Chloe. He unfolds it and reads out loud, "'On my way to talk to Haze. Didn't text in case the detectives are monitoring your phone. I emailed you the contact info for the lawyer. Go home and take care of what you need to. See you on the other side. Clover.'" Kyle looks up from the paper. "Haze?" he says, his voice pitching high as his brows lift. "What's Haze have to do with this?"

Before Mo can answer, his head shakes, and she watches as his expression goes from confusion to surprise to anger and back again. "It was Haze?"

Mo drops her eyes.

"Haze was the one who was raped?"

Mo can't answer, her voice lodged in her throat. For eight years, she has never once lied to Kyle, yet somehow, over the past two days, almost everything she's told him has been tainted with untruth.

"How could you have kept this from me?" he seethes.

"She didn't want anyone to know."

"I'm not *anyone*," he fumes, and she's unsure if his anger is for her or for Allen or for both. Half a second later, he pieces it together. "Oh," he says. "Allen's the guy you introduced her to at the bar."

She exhales a shuddering breath, then tells him what happened at Black Sands.

"You didn't try to find her?" he says, accusation sharp in his voice.

She shakes her head, tears welling that she fights to hold back, knowing the mistake is unforgivable. "I thought she left with him because she wanted to," she mumbles, the excuse sounding as pathetic as it is. Hazel had never even kissed a guy, and Mo was gone all of twenty minutes. How could she have thought that?

She knows the reason, and the thought causes such intense shame she pulls her knuckles to her stomach to quell the knot that's formed there. It was because she was distracted, and it was the easier thing to think. Her mind was on the FactNews report and her interview with Jake Tapper. Then Chloe got excited about Hazel having met someone, and Mo simply went along with it. But Chloe wasn't the one at the bar. She didn't know how short a time it was or realize how uncomfortable Hazel had been when Mo left. Mo was the only one who knew those things. Mo was the one who didn't give it the consideration she should have, who didn't figure out a way to track Hazel down and make sure she was okay.

"That's the reason you're here?" Kyle says. "Because of Haze?"

Her voice quakes with her tears as she explains about Kora's visit and her theory about Mount Si and Barking Goat Kitchen, the lies she's told piling up and causing Kyle's cheeks to flush red.

"I can't believe you kept all this from me," he says when she finishes.

And so much more. She keeps her face angled at the floor, careful not to look at him as she thinks of the paint thinner, the poem, the measuring cup, and last night's texts from Allen—so many more lies for him still to discover.

"Poor Haze," he says, his voice choked with emotion. He runs his hand hard through his hair. "I think Chloe's right. We need to trust her to take care of Haze, and we need to take care of you."

She nods, tears still streaming down her cheeks as she mumbles, "I'm sorry."

Then she is in his arms, and he is holding her, whispering that he's there and that it's going to be all right. And though they're close as is humanly possible, his strong arms wrapped protectively around her and his warm breath on her hair, in the eight years they've been together, never has she felt so far apart.

36
CHLOE

Chloe is on the 97, driving toward Mount Si. She's been on Hazel's tail three hours, and her butt is numb and she really needs to pee. Hazel's face icon started moving a little after eight this morning, so Chloe got in the van, dropped off a note for Mo telling her what was happening, then followed.

As Chloe was pulling onto the freeway, she got another text from Hunter. It showed a photo of Ruby doing her business, an embarrassed expression on her pretty, pink-nosed face. The caption read, Handle your worries like a dog. If you can't eat it or play with it, just pee on it and walk away.

She laughed, then frowned.

A single kiss is only that, a fleeting moment turned into a notion not tested beyond one exceptional night and a few funny texts. What she had with Eric was eight years and very, very real. He came into her life when she was at her lowest, and his love healed her. He revered her like no one ever has, devotion that bordered on worship.

Which was perhaps part of the problem. No one can sustain that sort of adulation. Eventually you disappoint, or the reverence becomes contemptible. There were times she wanted to scream. *Ugh. Stop. I'm being nasty to you. Stand up for yourself. Don't just lie there and take it.*

Maybe he sensed that. Maybe that's why he left.

But now, he's saying it was a mistake and that he wants to come back. Doesn't everyone make mistakes? Some of them horrible.

Her stomach growls, weighing in on the situation. She hasn't eaten since the biscuit at Barking Goat, the tank is nearly empty, and she has thirteen dollars in her wallet and nothing in the bank. When Eric left, he withdrew almost all the money from their joint bank account, likely assuming she would easily replenish it. What he didn't count on was how low his abandonment would lay her, devastating her to the point where she was barely able to get out of bed in the morning, let alone work.

She understood it was garden-variety heartbreak, the same devastation she'd suffered at eighteen and the sort of thing poets and singers have been crooning about since the beginning of time. Just as she also knew from those same poems and songs that it was possible to never fully recover from it. She'd barely survived eight years earlier, when things had ended with Vance, her life beset with dim and painful longing that had made carrying on seem impossible. Eric knew that, and the fact he could inflict that sort of pain again was almost as hurtful as the wound of his leaving.

She stops at a streetlight and squints through her tears. *Damn him.* Why did he have to ruin things? And why, now, when she is finally getting back on her feet, is he saying he wants to come back?

The car behind her honks, and she realizes the light has changed. She starts to drive again, her brain fuzzy with her hangover and mixed-up thoughts. He left. He hurt her. And yet, still, she is considering taking him back. Why?

She looks at her pinkie and knows. He loved her when she believed herself unworthy of that sort of affection—contemptible, both for the mistakes she'd made and for the pieces they had taken from her. *Ugly.*

Each time she looked in the mirror, that was what she saw—the pink scar on her forehead, her deformed hand, the face of a person willing to leave her family when they needed her.

Somehow, Eric saw past all that. She would never be whole, but when she was with him, it didn't matter. He loved the part of her that remained.

That's not nothing. Eric knows everything about her—the good and the awful—and he loves her in spite of it. He tells her all the time she is beautiful, so much that when she is with him, she believes it. He hurt her, but he also truly knows and loves her, missing pieces and all.

She thinks of Ruby and is certain if her previous owner appeared, she would race up to him, tail wagging as she yipped and jumped with joy, not upset in the least, forgiving him instantly and without a trace of resentment. If Eric showed up, she'd be yipping and yapping all right, but her tail certainly wouldn't be wagging, and she'd be contemplating killing him there on the spot or castrating him in his sleep.

Tears form in her eyes, and she orders herself to pull it together. She's already wasted too many nights crying about this. It's taken three months to rebuild some semblance of a life—moving in with Mo and Hazel, volunteering with Happy Tails, growing her mobile vet business. And while it might not be much, it's something. Does she really want to risk sharing it with Eric, knowing there's a chance he could destroy it again? *Fool me once, shame on you; fool me twice, shame on me.* And she's already been a fool twice when it came to staking her life on what she believed was love.

She does miss him. Sometimes terribly. Being with him was easy, like putting on an old robe—comfortable, warm, familiar. He is smart and funny, and he loves to cuddle and kiss. His body fits perfectly to hers, and he has wonderful hands with long, slender fingers. He reads voraciously and knows a little bit about everything. He can quote poets and kings, cartoon characters and comics, and she's always found that romantic.

Two days before he left, he said, "Your own soul is nourished when you are kind; it is destroyed when you are cruel."

She was headed out the door to work, and the King Solomon proverb was an artful admonishment for the nastiness she'd thrown at him minutes before for having left the laundry in the washing machine so long it had gone musty.

If she's being honest, a lot of the time she was around him toward the end of their relationship, she was her worst version of herself—short tempered and mean. They bickered a lot and laughed less because of it, and each time she thinks about it, she can't really blame him for leaving.

Her head hurts, and she massages her left temple with her fingers. She shouldn't have drunk so much last night. She's never been good with alcohol, a lightweight who enjoys the taste of beer a little too much once she gets started.

Hazel's icon turns, and Chloe follows, turning onto a narrow two-lane road that slices between forests of soaring pine. With each mile, the trees grow taller and the air more verdant, and she knows they are getting close to the falls. She imagines how it might have felt before streets and cars, when Hazel's great-great-great-grandfather rode in on horseback, and she thinks it must have been awe inspiring and somewhat terrifying.

She follows the signs to the parking lot, passes Hazel's Prius parked near the trailhead, and parks the van in a distant spot away from it.

Resting her hands on the steering wheel, she looks out the windshield. The moment of reckoning is upon her, yet she is no closer to a plan than she was two days ago. The problem she's having is she's been in the spot Hazel is in, and she knows how futile it is to try to talk someone out of it.

Most people believe suicide is impulsive, a rash decision made in a moment of deep despair. For some, it is. But what Hazel is doing is not impulsive in the least. After carefully considering her options, she has decided this is the course she most wants to take. The idea is not abstract, rash, or irrational. The opposite. It is well thought out and contemplated from every angle. Not seeing a path forward, she is choosing instead to end the journey, either because she's decided the pain is too much or because she is searching for peace. For Chloe, it was both.

With a heavy sigh, she climbs from the van and walks toward the visitor center. Her first stop is the restroom. They are at the base of the waterfall, so there is no immediate danger. Since Hazel left, she has taken her time, believing she's alone and therefore in no hurry. She drove all this way to get to here, and Chloe imagines she intends to spend some time appreciating it.

As she is washing her hands, she catches a glimpse of herself in the mirror and startles. It happens sometimes, the echo of her sister appearing when she least expects.

When Finn was alive, no one said they looked alike. Chloe is petite, and Finn was tall and gangly. They shared the same hair color and eye color, but Finn kept her wild copper curls long and almost always tied her hair back in a ponytail. Chloe's hair is straight, and when she was young, she would sculpt it in edgy styles and often dyed it different colors based on her mood. But since her sister passed, Chloe has kept her hair its natural brilliant penny color, and every once in a while, one of her sister's quirky expressions will appear in a mirror or passing window and knock Chloe off balance.

There was a time when she actually felt her sister's presence, a lingering after her death, at moments so strong she was certain her spirit was actually beside her. Now, it's different, more like a vestige within, a heightened awareness of consciousness. And when she's struggling, like she is now, she finds herself calling on it, thinking about what Finn might say or do and relying on the warm pressure on her spine or dull pulsing in her pinkie to tell her what's right. She closes her eyes and breathes deeply, hoping for her guidance, but feels nothing but the same distinct sense of dread she's felt all morning.

Returning outside, she follows the signs and sound of rushing water toward the falls. The day is startlingly blue with popcorn clouds and hawks floating high in the breeze. She passes a few people, but the trail is not crowded, and she thinks Snoqualmie Falls is more like a nice park than a grand attraction like Niagara Falls or the Grand Canyon.

She reaches a small rocky beach and finds Hazel standing at the edge looking at the falls—two torrents of white water running over dark rocks with a few smaller streams beside them. A handful of others are on the beach as well, phones and cameras out as they take photos of the water and themselves.

"Hey," Chloe says, stepping beside her.

Hazel turns, and her eyes widen in surprise. "Chloe?" Her brow crinkles. "How'd you . . . ? Oh." She pulls out her phone and taps it a couple of times to turn off Find My Friends.

Chloe's surprised how normal she looks—pretty and plain with a mane of wild black curls around a small heart-shaped face, her head tilted like her mind is somewhere else, which most likely it is. Exactly the same girl she was. Except, of course, she's not.

"This is beautiful," Chloe says, with a nod toward the falls.

"The mountain is named after my great-great-great-grandfather. His name was Josiah. Hence Mount Si."

"Wow," Chloe says like this is news. "So you're like Princess Hazel of Snoqualmie Falls."

Hazel smiles her lopsided grin before turning back to the water. "I thought it would be bigger." She sighs. "I suppose expectation does that, ruins things a little. In my mind, it was a glorious cascade a thousand feet tall."

"It's still nice."

"And there's a rainbow." She points to the left, and through the spray, Chloe can just make out a thin spectrum of color.

"Make a wish," Chloe says, regretting it the moment she says it, afraid the wish will be for the falls to carry her away.

Hazel closes her eyes and lifts her face toward the sky, and Chloe watches as she takes a deep inhale, then slowly releases it. "Done," she says and blinks her eyes open. "Do you know, when I was little, I always wished for the same thing?"

Chloe did as well. She used to wish for a gray dappled pony with a white mane she would name Whisper. The wish changed when she was eighteen and realized there were so many more important things to hope for.

"I used to wish my life would turn out like Marie Curie's," Hazel says.

"Of course you did," Chloe answers with an eye roll. Only Hazel would dream of being the next great physicist.

Hazel shakes her head. "Not because of her career, though that was rad." She smirks, and it takes a second for Chloe to get the joke. Marie Curie won a Nobel Prize in Chemistry for the discovery of radium, hence her life was "rad."

Chloe rolls her eyes again, thinking one in a thousand people might get the joke, but that's Hazel, her brain bigger than everyone else's and just waiting for the world to catch up. Chloe's always imagined how irritating it must be, thinking at the speed of light while everyone else is thinking at the speed of a tricycle.

"You know, your eyes are going to unscrew from their sockets if you keep doing that," Hazel says.

And again, despite how awful the moment and their reason for being here are, Chloe is charmed as she always is by Hazel and finds herself smiling.

"Ever since I read about her," Hazel goes on, "I knew she was like me. Well, not exactly like me, but you know . . . weird smart but that no one would really listen to her. For her, it was because of the time she lived in—women not taken seriously. For me, it's because I'm . . . well, me." She shrugs the self-deprecating shrug that's as much a part of her as her curls.

Chloe wants to disagree, but she understands what she's saying. Hazel's the kind of person who is easy to overlook—like rain on a window, eyes just sort of glance over her—and it's hard for her to be heard. Even at her job, though she's amazing, credit always seems to go to someone else.

"But then Marie met Pierre."

"Ah, Pierre," Chloe says, rolling the name as a name like Pierre should be rolled.

"Yes, and their story's every bit as romantic as his name, best geek fairy tale ever." Her voice is bright, and the normalcy of her enthusiasm is quite frankly terrifying, like it matters not a wink that this might be the last conversation she ever has. And again, Chloe is reminded of her own chilling nonchalance leading up to Mo's razor-close intervention.

"Pierre *knew* how smart Marie was," Hazel says. "And it was because of him that the rest of the world realized it as well. Polonium and radium."

Chloe crinkles her brow.

"More together than apart."

"Oh."

"What they discovered," she says, looking at Chloe like she's dense.

"Cool."

"Don't you see? Their love was like a mystical collision of destiny."

A mystical collision of destiny. Chloe tucks the words away, loving the way they sound. And they make her think of Hunter, wondering if their random crossing could have turned into something as wonderful.

"My wish was to someday find my Pierre," Hazel says dreamily and looks back at the falls. "I knew the odds were astronomically small, but that's what wishes are for."

Chloe tenses at her use of the past tense. "Haze—" she starts.

"Don't," Hazel interrupts sharply, then smiles sweetly again. "Do you know what Pierre said when he proposed?"

Chloe's afraid to know, certain it's going to be horribly romantic.

"He said, 'It would be a beautiful thing, a thing I dare not hope, if we could spend our life near each other, hypnotized by our dreams: your patriotic dream, our humanitarian dream, and our scientific dream.'"

Thick emotions well in Chloe's throat. *Oh, to find someone like that.* And she thinks she might end up borrowing Hazel's wish.

"It's the reason greatness exists," Hazel goes on. "The pursuit of doing something bigger than oneself."

"Haze—" Chloe starts again.

"Chlo, I appreciate you coming all this way, but I'm fine."

She's not fine. She's not even close to fine. Everything she's said proves she's not fine, and Chloe desperately needs to come up with something brilliant to say to convince her of that but has no idea what that something might be.

"They think Mo was the one who made the GHB," she blurts.

Hazel tilts her head. "Who thinks that?"

"The police."

Hazel looks confused, and Chloe realizes she might not have any idea what's happened.

"Mo's been charged with Allen's assault."

"Allen was assaulted?"

"Wow, you really don't follow social media."

"You know I hate that stuff."

It's true. Hazel might be the least connected Gen Zer in the world.

Chloe explains what happened as Hazel shakes her head in disbelief and interjects with, "No way," and "Really?" and "That's crazy," and finally, "They can't really believe Mo did that." And either she has become the world's greatest actress, or she really had no idea what happened.

"Which is why you need to come home," Chloe says. "Mo needs you."

Her head is shaking before Chloe finishes the sentence.

"Haze—"

"No way," she says. "Mo got herself into this; she can get herself out. She's Mo. Bad stuff bounces off her. She'll be fine."

"This is different. Mo's fingerprints were on the measuring cup you put in the dishwasher, the one you used to make the GHB."

Hazel blinks several times, then shakes her head again. "I'm not going back."

She says it plainly, as if saying she didn't enjoy a meal and won't be returning to that restaurant again. But it's her life she's talking about. *Gee, Chlo, thanks for stopping by, but I really don't like this gig anymore, so I won't be coming back.*

"Haze, they think Mo's the one who drugged Allen."

"Maybe she did."

Chloe feels blood rush to the surface of her skin. "Of course she didn't. It's Mo."

Shrug. "I don't know. Mo's a really good liar."

"But you're the one who made the GHB."

"Well, *I* didn't drug him. I didn't even know he'd been drugged. And if I go back and say I'm the one who made the GHB, they're going to think I did."

Chloe blows out a hard breath. She's right, of course. Hazel looks even more guilty than Mo. Hazel was the victim. She's the one who made the GHB. She has no alibi for the night Allen was assaulted, and she took off that night for Oregon. The only thing she has going for her is that Allen didn't say it was her.

"Why'd you do it?" Chloe says. "Make the GHB?"

Hazel toes the ground. "I don't know. I guess I felt like I needed to try it."

Chloe feels the words like déjà vu. For months after the accident, she struggled to make sense of what had happened. The thing about almost dying is it makes you reassess living. For eighteen years, she'd gone through life believing she had some sort of jurisdiction over what happened to her, some sort of say. Then the accident happened, and suddenly she realized she didn't, that she actually didn't control anything.

And once that happens, something inside you just sort of snaps, like everything you thought mattered no longer makes sense, and it feels like you're free-falling or drowning or maybe a little of both. So you thrash around, searching for something to grab hold of, and irrational as it is, you end up back at the source, thinking if you can just get a handle on it, life will right itself and start to make sense again.

"It's why I still sometimes walk in the cold," Chloe says. "Just to prove I can."

Hazel nods, knowing Chloe understands.

"Did trying it help?" Chloe asks.

"Nope," Hazel says, matter of fact. "Basically, it just confirmed what I already knew. The stuff leaves you conscious but out of it. It sucked, just like it sucked the first time."

She looks again at the falls, her gaze fixed on the pounding water, and warmth like a sun's ray radiates down Chloe's spine, the spirit of her sister glowing, urging her not to give up and to somehow find a way.

37
MO

Kyle seethes as he drives, while Mo despairs. Just as she feared, he is insistent that she come clean to the police and tell them her roommate was the victim and that Hazel has no alibi. And that is without him knowing about the measuring cup and paint thinner.

"I'm not doing that," she says for the dozenth time. "Hazel didn't do this, and I'm not dragging her into it for no reason."

"No reason! Are you kidding? The reason is she had far more motive than you did, which means it will cast doubt on the whole damn thing."

"Allen didn't point the finger at her. He pointed it at me."

"Because he wanted revenge, and it's working. He's going to win."

"No," she says with more confidence than she feels. "He's not. I'm going to figure a way out of this, but not by throwing Haze under the bus."

He's silent a second, then slides his eyes her way. "Do you think maybe she did it?"

"She didn't."

They've been on the road nearly four hours, and she's amazed it took him so long to realize Hazel could actually be the culprit—motive, opportunity, nothing to lose. It makes perfect sense, and Mo's brain is screaming it was her. But Chloe was so certain it wasn't, and Mo has to admit, each time she tries to imagine it, she just can't picture it. Hazel's so awkward, and how would she even have managed it? Allen knows who she is, and he's a foot taller and at least seventy pounds heavier than she is. Even if she managed to drug him, how did she get him to the Tenderloin?

Her head hurts. Her heart as well. At some point, Kyle's going to find out the truth, and then what? He will know she continued to keep things from him, important things. She's not sure their relationship is going to be able to survive this. The foundation of love is trust, and she has violated that again and again and continues to do so.

And what happens if Allen does win and the charges actually stick? Does she trust Kyle to stay silent if they end up going to trial? Or will he out Hazel, believing it's the right thing to do?

All this swims in her head and makes her stomach churn until she thinks she might be sick.

How do they get past this? No matter the choice, she sees no way in which it doesn't take on a neon afterglow that affects everything going forward.

If she accepts Allen's offer, she will be spared. But will Kyle ever be able to see past the bargain she made? A deal with the devil that makes her look crazy and makes him look like a fool? Telling the world she wanted it means negating the post she made and all the heartrending, courageous responses it elicited. It means allowing Allen to be vindicated and willingly allowing herself to become another of his victims. It means shaming Kyle with the implication that she cheated on him.

She doesn't want to cry, her tear ducts worn out, but fresh tears well in her eyes. Tomorrow she is meeting with the lawyer Mrs. Miller recommended. She doesn't see how it will do any good. The evidence is irrefutable, and combined with Allen's accusation, how will any jury not find her guilty?

"There might be press waiting when you get to your apartment," the lawyer warned when they talked this morning. Her name is Cece Gutierrez, and she had a voice like a bullfrog. "Ignore them. Your only comment is 'No comment,' got it?"

The idea of reporters lying in wait compounds her stress. Esther's left three messages and texted a dozen times. FactNews's phone has been ringing off the hook, not about the "Babies" report but instead about the sensational story of Maureen Kaminski, heiress to the great Kaminski fortune turned vigilante avenger.

For two years, she's worked tirelessly to build her reputation and her company, pouring everything she's had into making it a respectable source for news, and in less than three days, all that effort's been undone. She told Esther to respond "no comment" to anything not involving the "Babies" report and asked her to let the staff know that she'll be back next Monday and that, by then, all this would be straightened out. A lie, but the only thing she could think to say.

"We need to stop for gas," Kyle says, his voice edged with simmering anger.

He pulls into the station at the exact moment Mo's phone buzzes, causing Kyle to look over, distrust in his eyes that wounds like a knife.

The text is from Chloe: Kyle needs to come to Mount Si. How fast can he get here?

38
CHLOE

Chloe is eating a sandwich that costs more than she can afford on the deck of Salish Lodge, the hotel that overlooks the falls. The idea of Kyle swooping in to save the day came to Chloe when she had all but given up, her mind blank and all hope deflated.

Offhand, she said, "I sure wouldn't want to be Mo right now, in the car with Kyle. I bet he's fuming."

"Kyle?" Hazel said, her head tilting and a spark in her voice.

Chloe latched on to it. "Yeah, Kyle," she said flatly, afraid any sort of reaction might snuff the ember out. She shrugged like it was no big deal. "He came home when he heard what happened."

"He knows?" Hazel said, her eyes growing round and color rising in her cheeks.

Chloe wasn't sure how to play it—pretend Kyle didn't know Hazel had been raped or tell her how upset he'd been when he'd heard the news? She chose the latter. "He flew into a rage when he heard. Wanted to kill the bastard."

"He did?" Hazel said, and Chloe knew she'd chosen right.

Hazel has always idolized Kyle, admiration that borders on worship, and in return, Hazel holds a special place in Kyle's heart. She's like a quirky kid sister he adores and is protective toward.

Chloe actually has no idea how much Kyle knows or how he responded to what he's found out. She assumes he knows the truth or at least most of it. How else would Mo have explained things? But knowing Kyle, his concern is solely for Mo. It's how he's wired, his love like a laser, narrow and intense.

But to Hazel, she said, "As soon as he gets Mo home and knows she's safe, he's turning around and coming right back here for you." She realized as soon as she said it that she might have gone too far, having no idea how Kyle might feel about the idea.

"He's coming here?" Hazel asked, her eyes going glassy as hope emerged, and Chloe felt it like a shock, the sharp remembrance of her own moment of reckoning blazing.

She'd been barefoot on Mo's lawn, looking at a shoebox that held four newborn kittens. They'd been barely larger than gerbils, and their orchestra of desperate mewing had forced her to look away from the siren's call long enough for her to realize how many reasons there still were to live.

"He is," Chloe lied and prayed Kyle would agree to it. He definitely wouldn't do it for her, but he might for Hazel.

For an eternal minute, Chloe watched as Hazel considered it, her eyes flicking side to side as she decided whether to allow the revelation to change things. She turned toward the falls, then looked at the ground, calibrating, or hopefully recalibrating.

Finally, she turned back to Chloe and asked, "When do you think he'll be here?"

Chloe revealed nothing while inside she cheered.

Quickly she calculated how long it would take for Kyle to turn around and get to the falls. "Maybe around dinnertime."

"Oh," Hazel said, sounding disappointed.

"We could get lunch?" Chloe suggested quickly, terrified Hazel would change her mind.

Hazel looked at the ground again, her chin dropping to her chest. "I'm not hungry. I think I'll just go to my room and lie down."

"Yeah, okay," Chloe said, then watched as she shuffled away. "I'll be at the restaurant if you change your mind."

Hazel half nodded and continued on her way, and for a moment, Chloe stayed on the beach, watching the waterfall and wondering how it never ran out of water. Then she pulled out her phone and texted Mo.

Her response came less than a minute later: Kyle's dropping me at the airport in Bend. I'll fly home from there, and he's on his way. Love you.

Kyle the hero. Some things never change.

~

For the first hour, Chloe sat on the deck nursing an iced tea, but when the server started giving her dirty looks, she ordered a caprese sandwich, which she's been slowly nibbling at since.

"Hey."

She looks up to see Hazel freshly showered and dressed in black jeans and a white T-shirt that has rock-paper-scissors caricatures on the front with the words CAN'T WE ALL JUST GET ALONG? Her hair looks just-rolled-out-of-bed wild, like she doesn't care about her appearance, but the slight blush on her cheeks and shine on her lips make it clear that secretly she does—a good sign. What Kyle thinks still matters.

"Hey," Chloe says. "Did you get some rest?"

Hazel nods. Her eyes look less bruised, and seeing her less battered makes Chloe slightly more hopeful.

She takes the seat across from Chloe. "Where's the dog?"

Chloe tells her the story of stopping at the motel in Bend and about Hunter and how Ruby started eating because of him. Then, knowing

Hazel's a romantic, she tells her about her evening at Mabel's and finishes with the kiss.

"So you've already got a new boyfriend?" Hazel says, bite to the tone that is shocking, and Chloe realizes how bad the timing of the story was.

"It was just a kiss," she says with a shrug like it was no big deal, which is another horribly wrong thing to say. Hazel's never had a kiss, and now, it's possible she never will. Chloe's cheeks warm as she wishes she could rewind the past five minutes and suck the words back inside.

"Sorry," Hazel says. "That was uncalled for. I'm happy for you. Hunter sounds great." The words are right, but tension remains, floating between them until, half a minute later, Hazel looks up and says, "Whoa!"

Chloe follows her eyes, and her breath catches. "'Whoa' is right."

In front of them, the falls have turned to fire, the late-afternoon sun sparking off the surface in brilliant flashes of amber and gold and turning the water to flame.

"That's more like it," Hazel says.

"I'll say. Makes sense now why your great-great-great-grandpappy decided to stay."

"He found his gold."

She sighs out contentedly, and together they continue to watch as Mother Nature works her wonder, putting on a magnificent light show as if it's nothing at all.

"Is this where the cool girls hang out?"

Chloe's head snaps around to see Kyle in his uniform silhouetted by the sun, which makes him look even more like the superhero he is—tall, broad shouldered, and golden all over. Eight years ago, he saved seven strangers. Since then, he's saved countless more in service to his country; his proven gallantry is like a suit of shiny armor he wears easily and with quiet pride.

"Kyle," Hazel says, standing, then falling into his chest.

He wraps his arms around her. "Hey, kid."

Then she is crying.

"You're okay. I've got you." He looks at Chloe over Hazel's head. "I've got this." He gives a head jerk toward the parking lot. "You need to go. I don't want Mo to be alone." While there's gruffness in his tone, his love for Mo still blazes.

Like a soldier following orders, Chloe stands, throws the last of her cash on the table to pay for her lunch, and starts for the parking lot.

"Hey," Kyle says, causing her to turn back. His jaw slides forward as he says, "Thank you."

She tilts her head.

"For taking care of them."

Hazel hiccups against his chest, and Chloe feels a lump form in her throat.

She nods and continues on, amazed how much the small exchange meant. While her family never held her decision to leave them against her, it's all Kyle knew of her, and his unspoken judgment has haunted her since.

With the warm glow of dignity in her chest, she climbs in the van and pulls out her phone. The first text is to her dad: Hey Pops, a little low on funds, do you think you could front me some cash?

The second is to Eric: Always forward never back. I'm afraid our paths are no longer the same. Friends til the banana splits.

Kyle dropped everything and flew from Germany to be at Mo's side when she needed him. Meanwhile, Eric ditched Chloe without a word and then, three months later, asked to come back over text. Chloe wants what Mo has. She wants a superhero. Tears form. It's been a long time since she felt she deserved something more than what she has.

Her phone pings with a notification from Venmo. Her dad sent $3,000. The memo line says: More where that came from if you need it. So proud of you.

She sniffles back her emotions. For three months, she's scrabbled and scraped, too embarrassed to ask for help. She feels Finn rolling her eyes.

You're right, Chloe thinks. *I'm an idiot.*

She imagines her dad smiling, incredibly happy to be able to do something for one of "his girls."

The second text arrives as she's pulling from the parking lot.

U were my north star and with u I knew the way. Now u r the ache in my heart and I am lost without u. But I understand. Friends til the ice ages.

The text brings nothing but a wave of relief, and she knows she made the right choice. Eric couldn't even be bothered to spell out the words. She wants better, deserves better. She thinks of her dad and the lengths he would go to for her mom. Her parents have a remarkable love, one that has withstood the worst kind of tragedy imaginable. Mo and Kyle, her mom and dad—that's the kind of love she wants, one without limits or boundaries, superhero kind of love.

39
MO

The Uber from the airport pulls up outside the apartment a little before ten. Mo steps from the car having entirely forgotten the lawyer's warning about the press and therefore is entirely unprepared for the onslaught of reporters. She pulls her suitcase from the trunk and hurries for the door, her chin tucked in the collar of her coat and her brain on fire as they hurl questions at her:

"Maureen, what is your relationship with Allen Redding?"

"Ms. Kaminski, where have you been?"

"Can you tell us when you will be surrendering yourself to the police?"

She punches in the key code for the door and races inside, then chooses the stairs instead of the elevator so she doesn't have to wait as she is photographed through the glass. As soon as the door closes, she collapses to the steps, tears spilling from her eyes and her whole body quaking. She drops her head to her knees, unable to believe this is happening.

Keening as she cries, she bites on her knuckle to muffle the sound.

"Maureen, what is your relationship with Allen Redding?" He is a *monster who has held a grudge against me for years. "Ms. Kaminski, where*

have you been?" Chasing after the friend Allen Redding destroyed, hoping to save her. "Can you tell us when you will be surrendering yourself to the police?"

She cries harder, unable to wrap her head around it. Allen is the criminal, yet she is the one facing charges that are ruining her life and could send her to jail.

Hands trembling, she pulls out her phone. Kyle's message from a few hours earlier is still open: Chloe's on her way and will be there tomorrow. I'm with Haze and we're playing gin rummy. Still trying to convince her to come home. Not there yet but working on it. Sorry I was so angry. Now that I'm with Haze I realize how awful this was . . . for everyone. You are my world. Call when you get in so I know you're safe and so I can tell you how much I love you.

She breathes in and out through her nose, trying to rein in her emotions.

Closing out of her messages, she opens her phone app and dials. "Fitz," she croaks. "I need you."

40
CHLOE

It's almost eleven when Chloe pulls into the Carnival Motel parking lot. Hunter is in the motel office, his work boots on the counter, his guitar on his lap, and Ruby at his feet, and the sight of them in such contentment stretches out her cheeks.

Ruby's head snaps up as the door opens, and then, realizing it's Chloe, she goes bonkers, jumping and yipping and circling, not letting Hunter get anywhere near her, until finally, he says, "Enough," and pulls her away by her collar to step in her place. "Hi," he says, looking down. Then, "Wow." Then, "Is it possible you've gotten even more beautiful in just two days?"

He's lying. She knows she looks like death, her eyes puffy and her hair unwashed. But he's not looking at her like he's lying. He's looking at her as if the moon just landed at his feet.

"You're delirious," she says, but his appraising smile remains as he continues to drink her in, the intensity terrifying, and she takes a step back, breaking the spell.

She nods toward Ruby, who is looking at them expectantly. "I liked the pedicures," she says with a nod toward Ruby's paws, the claws still startlingly purple, and she imagines beneath Hunter's boots his nails are the same.

"Real men wear purple," he says, then winks at Ruby. "And wickedly good-looking girls."

Ruby stands and circles, clearly pleased with the attention.

Hunter looks back at Chloe. "Hungry?"

"Starved."

"Follow me."

They walk through a door behind the counter into a surprisingly stylish apartment—contemporary, tasteful, and clean. It's not big, a studio with a kitchenette along one side, a square dining table with four chairs, a small couch, a built-in entertainment center, and a king bed. Decidedly masculine, the walls are dark gray, the floors walnut, and the couch leather. A single window looks across the street at the forest, and at the moment, an almost-full moon provides a spotlight into the room.

On either side of the window and over the bed are three large black-and-white photos—trees soaring toward light and sky; water running over rocks with a sapling sprouting against the current; a magnificent acorn cap in snow blown up so large it looks like a fallen redwood in a glacier.

"Wow. Who took these?" she asks, stepping closer to the acorn.

Chloe's always been a sucker for art, and before Eric left, her guilty pleasure was coffee-table books filled with images that moved her. Currently, the books are in a box in her ex-boss's garage. The only thing she asked him to keep for her.

"A local guy you've probably never heard of," Hunter says as he cracks eggs into a bowl. "Amateur photographer, goes by the name of Damian Wayne."

"Cool name," she says before getting the joke. The son of Bruce Wayne, a.k.a. Batman, is Damian Wayne. "Funny. Very funny."

"Man," Hunter says as he chops onions, "a girl who knows who Damian Wayne is. It's like God is majorly messing with me. Sends me the girl of my dreams, but only as a tease because the girl's just passing through. That's cold. Icy, frigid cold."

"Seriously, though, these are yours?"

He shrugs like it's no big deal, but the images are stunning, and she knows each required careful planning, patience, and incredible talent. With a smile, she leaves the photo of the acorn to sit on the couch. Across from her are three stands with three guitars—one electric and two acoustic—and she wonders how a man with so much positive mojo and talent ended up owning a motel on the outskirts of Bend, Oregon.

"Come, Ruby," she says, patting her leg. The dog ignores her, her attention rapt on Hunter and the omelet he's making. "Traitor."

"It's your fault. You're the one who encouraged me to feed her."

Chloe harrumphs, but the harrumph lacks oomph, her happiness at seeing the two of them together vibrating all the way to her toes. Ruby looks incredible, her black coat lustrous and her body already fuller, so much healthier in two days it makes Chloe's heart ache with joy looking at her.

Hunter carries two plates from the kitchen, and she joins him at the table. She's about to take her first bite of the delicious-smelling omelet when Ruby starts to bark.

"Shhh, girl," Hunter says as he stands.

He walks quickly into the motel's lobby, and Ruby doesn't bark again but sits beside the door, ears perked.

Through the wood, Chloe hears Hunter greet a guest. "Evening."

"I'd like a room." The voice is deep and gravelly and causes every hair on Chloe's body to stand on end. She chokes down the bite of food in her mouth as Gretzky says, "Just one night."

She prays she's mistaken but knows she's not, the voice unmistakable and coincidence not something she believes in. Gretzky laughs, confirming it, and she thinks Hunter must have made some sort of joke.

"Room's on the bottom floor, just past the pool," Hunter says.

Gretzky thanks him, and a moment later, the door opens and Hunter walks through. "Hey, sorry about that." His head tilts. "You okay?"

She shakes her head, and the fork drops from her hand.

41
MO

Fitz arrives a little after midnight with a cup of chamomile tea and a slice of chocolate cake from Mo's favorite all-night diner. He gives her a wooden hug, which she returns, and then they sit on the couch.

He opens the box and hands her a fork. "Eat," he says. "Cake always makes life better."

She wants to disagree, but surprisingly, she's ravenous, so she takes a bite and realizes he's right. Calamitous as her life is, the decadent chocolate melting on her tongue somehow puts it momentarily on pause.

"Thank you," she mumbles.

"You might not be thanking me when you hear what I have to say."

She looks up at him, not wanting to hear the next words.

"Finish," he says with a sideways smile.

He looks good despite the late hour—his face clean shaven, his khakis crisply pressed, and his eyes bright—and she realizes how awful she must look. She hasn't showered in a day or slept in two. She's wearing old sweats and no makeup and has a zit on her chin from stress.

When the last bite is gone, she leans back and looks at him.

"You were right," he says. "Things are not what they seem." He sighs, then glances down at his lap before lifting his face and leveling his gaze on hers, his ice-blue eyes serious and worried.

On the plane, Mo finally had some time alone to think, and she realized something wasn't right. *Time.* Allen had specifically offered time. Yet when Mo spoke with Ms. Gutierrez, the lawyer assured Mo the longest she would be sentenced to was six months in jail, and even that was unlikely. The charges against her are unlawful administration of gamma hydroxybutyrate and reckless endangerment. While this was no minor thing, Ms. Gutierrez assured her that as a first-time offender with no prior record, she would most likely get probation.

More at stake for Mo is what a guilty charge would do to her reputation and company. She can't imagine Allen doesn't know this, considering he's been talking with the detectives. Yet specifically, he presented a riddle that offered time, and the offer came more than a day after he woke from his coma.

Perhaps it was nothing, but the delay of the offer along with the riddle needled at her, her nose for news twitching. She couldn't help but feel like Allen was toying with her or that she was missing something. Which is why she called Fitz.

"There's more to the charges than meets the eye," Fitz says with a frown, his mouth a tight line that creates deep creases in his cheeks, making him look like the dignified man she knows he will become. He reaches into his messenger bag, pulls out a single sheet of paper, and sets it on the coffee table.

Mo scooches forward, and her brow furrows as she reads the headline: Foul Play Suspected in Death of Accused but Not Convicted Date Rapist. She looks at the header: the Bend *Bulletin*. The article is dated two days ago, Sunday, the day she and Chloe left Bend to follow Hazel to Spokane.

Her eyes widen, and she shakes her head, denying what's clearly in front of her. The photo accompanying the article shows a thirtysomething man with slicked-back black hair and a slender, handsome face. The caption says, *Dr. Grant Riley*.

She reads the article:

> BEND—Police say foul play is suspected in the death of a Bend surgeon found unresponsive in his Eastside home early this morning.
>
> According to a police official at the scene, there were no signs of trauma, but because of the victim's past, foul play is suspected.
>
> Grant Riley, MD, 39, had previously been accused of drugging and sexually assaulting several women over a ten-year period, but earlier this month, all the charges were dropped due to insufficient evidence. Riley had been painted by the district attorney as a sexual predator who used his good looks to prey on vulnerable women.
>
> Riley was accused of assaulting seven women, of drugging them and bringing them back to his home to assault them. Despite the number of women who independently came forward to accuse Riley, the prosecutor in the case decided there were "serious proof problems" and concluded there was "insufficient evidence to prove the case beyond a reasonable doubt."
>
> At the time of the dismissal of charges, Margie Doyle, senior executive at the Rape, Abuse & Incest National Network (RAINN), a nonprofit that provides resources

and support for sexual assault survivors, said this was a great miscarriage of justice.

"Riley follows the typical profile of a serial rapist. He lacks empathy and is without social conscience. Seven brave women came forward to tell their stories, and he showed no remorse, claiming his accusers 'wanted it' regardless of the wrenching testimony each gave that proved otherwise.

"The district attorney did not do their job, and now Riley is free to continue his predatory behavior. All rapists are wolves, but Riley is particularly rapacious, and until he is stopped, more women are certain to fall victim to his depravity."

And now Riley has been stopped, and the question is, Who was it that stopped him? There have been no arrests in an investigation that is just beginning.

Mo looks at Fitz, her pulse whooshing in her ears.

"I told you it wasn't good," he says.

Haze! Haze did this.

"You were in Bend Saturday, weren't you?" Fitz asks.

"Huh?" she says, stunned by the question along with the accusation in his voice. "What? No. I mean, yes. But no. I didn't do this. You can't think I had anything to do with this?"

As soon as the words are out of her mouth, she realizes that he's letting her know that even if it's not what he thinks, it's what everyone else is going to think. Her mind spins with the timing, realizing it's the reason Hazel left Bend late Saturday night instead of in the morning.

"The case has been taken over by the FBI," Fitz says.

Mo blinks. *The FBI?*

"It's now multijurisdictional, a crime in California tied to another in Oregon."

She feels like she can't get air.

"The GHB found in the doctor's system," Fitz goes on, "matched the chemical composition of the GHB used on Allen Redding. Poisons employed in capital crimes are entered into a universal database, so as soon as the coroner entered her report for Riley's murder, it raised a flag connecting it to the Redding case."

"And they think I did both?" she stammers.

Fitz looks at the table.

"I don't even know this man!" She picks up the sheet of paper and waves it in the air. "What reason would I have to kill him?" It takes all her restraint not to blurt out Hazel's name to clear herself. "And if they're so certain I did this, then why haven't they told me I'm a suspect?"

"It's an interrogation tactic," Fitz says. "You bring a suspect in on a lesser charge, then drop a bomb on them when they show up. It's an effective way of catching a suspect off guard and not giving them time to prepare."

She throws the sheet back on the table and drops her face in her hands. "I had nothing to do with that man's death."

"What about Chloe?" Fitz asks, causing her face to snap up.

"Chloe?"

"She was in Bend with you, wasn't she?"

"What?" Mo yelps. "No! Chloe has nothing to do with any of this. She was only there because of me."

"So Chloe was with you and can vouch for you?"

She realizes he's interrogating her.

She almost says yes but then realizes Saturday night was the night Chloe went off with Hunter.

"Mo?"

She feels the blood drain from her face. "It wasn't Chloe. And it wasn't me."

Fitz leans forward, his elbows on his knees. "It gets worse."

Worse? How can it possibly get worse?

"There's a photo," Fitz says, "caught on a CCTV camera half a block from the doctor's home. It shows a woman about your size wearing a jacket very similar to one you've been photographed in, deep cranberry with a fur-lined hood."

He doesn't look at her as he says it. He knows the jacket well. It's the jacket Mo wears all the time, the jacket she was wearing the night she went to the liquor store to get Hazel and then gave her to wear. The jacket is from an exclusive North Face line produced for a single season two years ago. The color is called Marvelous Mulberry, and the silver fur of the hood is curly like a sheep's.

Mo drops her face back to her hands and shakes her head, unable to believe the incredible chain of events that has led her here.

"You're sure Chloe couldn't have done this?" he asks, and she loves him for looking for someone else to blame and his unfaltering belief in her innocence despite all the evidence to the contrary.

"I'm sure," Mo mumbles into her palms.

"Mo, I've got to be honest—this isn't good. None of the evidence on its own is that damning, but taken together, it's pretty compelling. Both crimes have matching chemical markers, you were in both places when the crimes were committed, and you don't have a solid alibi for either. Combine that with Allen's accusation, the threat, the post, the hard evidence, and the CCTV photo, and they've pretty much got you dead to rights."

"But I didn't do it," she says, dropping her hands and looking at him.

His kind blue eyes hold hers. "Whoever you're protecting, Mo, you need to reconsider."

Tears form, and she swallows them back. Eight years ago, she chose to protect herself over someone she loved, and Oz died because of it. "I'm not protecting anyone," she lies.

He gives a low sigh, clearly not believing her, then pushes to his feet. She stands with him.

"People have been convicted on a lot less, and now we're talking murder."

She nods and tries to offer a reassuring smile but fails miserably, her bottom lip trembling.

"I'm here if you need me," he says and gives her another wooden hug.

She walks him to the door and, when he's gone, returns and collapses on the couch as Allen's offer replays in her head: *Tell the world u wanted it.* And she realizes it might be the only choice that remains.

42
CHLOE

Hunter's hand taps nervously on the table, which is surprising because Hunter doesn't seem like a guy who's easily rattled. Though he's a jokester, there's something tough and certain about him.

Chloe explained as best she could why Gretzky is here, though even as she told the story, it sounded insane.

"He's here because you Ex-Laxed him?" Hunter asks, using the word as a verb as if it's a common, everyday thing anyone might do.

Eyes cast down, she nods. "Well, that, and I might have laughed at him when he showed up at our apartment with the runs. And it's possible that while he was driving me to the precinct, I might have told him he suffered from PPS."

Hunter lifts a brow.

Chloe's whole face burns when she says, "Paltry-penis syndrome."

Hunter almost laughs, but it comes out half groan. "He's a cop."

Chloe nods. In retrospect, it was a very stupid thing to do.

"Two types of men become cops," Hunter says. "Those who do it for the right reasons and those who don't." He glances at the crude tattoo on his arm, the X with the line through it, and again she wonders at its significance.

He notices. "I did time," he says flatly. "A long time ago."

Time? As in prison? She tries not to react but feels heat rise in her cheeks and her pulse quicken.

"Six months," he says, "when I was twenty, for stealing a car."

"You *stole a car*?" She doesn't mean for it to come out the way it does, aghast and judgmental, but the idea is shocking. Who *steals* a car? *Thieves. Carjackers. Bad people.*

She watches as he looks away and feels his intense shame.

"Sorry," she mutters. After all, who is she to judge, especially when it comes to mistakes made a long time ago?

"Left me with a bad taste for law enforcement," he says, rubbing his palms on his jeans. "I've met my share of Gretzkys, screwed-up guys who hide behind the badge—cops, guards, parole officers. They're worse than the criminals. At least with cons, you know what you're dealing with. Guys like Gretzky, they have the power, and they know it."

"I can't believe he drove all this way just to harass me."

Hunter goes back to tapping his hand on the table, and it's all she can do not to set her hand on top of his to stop it, her nerves on fire.

"Why's he here? I don't get it."

"To scare you. Rattle you. Upset you. Make your life miserable if possible."

"Check, check, check, and check," she says.

"We need to get you out of here."

"And where am I supposed to go? He knows where I live. And he found me here, a zillion miles from where I live. He's just going to find me again."

"He either tracked your phone or your van," Hunter says. "You can leave your phone with me and take my truck instead of the van."

"This isn't even your problem," she says, losing the battle with her emotions and starting to cry. "I'll figure it out. I just need a minute."

When he doesn't answer, she steals a peek at him to see him scowling. "Some jerk shows up at my motel to harass one of my guests, a guest I happen to be particularly fond of—that is definitely *my* problem."

"Wow," she sob-laughs, "this really is a full-service motel."

He gives a wan smile before saying, "You can't go home."

She shakes her head. "I have to. Mo needs me."

"Chloe—"

"Not negotiable," she says, cutting him off. "She needs me," she repeats.

"Fine," he huffs. "But you can't go back to the apartment. I have a friend who has a motel in the marina."

She shakes her head and mutters, "I can't afford—"

"Free of charge. His name is Ray. And you'll have Ruby with you. She's a good guard dog." Ruby looks up at the mention of her name.

"I'm sorry," Chloe mutters.

"It's not you who should be apologizing," he says with fierceness that's surprising. "You can stay with Ray as long as it takes to get things settled with Mo. He'll look after you."

She sniffles, unable to believe how kind he's being, a man she's known less than a few days. "Thank you."

"Chloe, look at me."

She manages to lift her teary eyes to his.

"When you've done what you need to help Mo, you need to leave. You can't stay in the city." His eyes flash hard like river stones. "Guys like Gretzky, they don't stop. You hear me?"

She nods.

"I don't know what it is about them. Their anger is like gangrene, and the more time that passes, the more it festers and grows."

Chloe knows all about gangrene. Cut it out, or it will destroy you.

43
MO

"Damn piranhas," Ms. Gutierrez says. Mo's lawyer is referring to the media mob outside the building, which has doubled in size since last night; at least two dozen news vans are now parked up and down the street. This has been the final straw for Jerry—her eviction notice was slid under her door at eight this morning.

Pint size but with a bellowing voice that belies her small frame, Cece Gutierrez definitely stands out in a room. Her black hair, cropped to her chin, is threaded with thick strands of silver, and her suit is eye-popping red. Her mouth is wide and her eyes piercing and dark. *Subtle* is not the word that comes to mind.

She sits in the middle of the couch, her feet crossed queen-style. Mo sits across from her in the armchair. And Chloe is on the pouf.

Ms. Gutierrez sizes Chloe up. "Well, look at you. You sure grew into yourself. Damn ugly as a baby."

Chloe laughs while Mo winces at the brashness.

"Looked like a damn extraterrestrial when you were born, pale as an egg, shock of orange hair, oversize googly eyes."

Mo finds herself smiling despite herself. Mo's seen photos of Chloe as a baby, and she did indeed look a little like an alien from a faraway galaxy, one without much food or light. She and Finn used to laugh about it whenever they looked through the Miller photo albums.

The lawyer turns her attention back to Mo. "Well, isn't this a fine mess you've gotten yourself into?"

Mo looks down at her hands. After Fitz left, she emailed Ms. Gutierrez and filled her in on the doctor's murder and Fitz's theory that the detectives were planning to ambush them on Friday.

"Murder on top of GHB poisoning and reckless endangerment—that's quite an escalation in crime. My retainer just went up."

Mo doesn't smile. None of this seems funny, yet everything out of the woman's mouth seems to be a joke. She really wishes Mrs. Miller were here.

"As your attorney, I'm not supposed to ask if you did it, but I'm going to tell you, looking at the evidence, it sure as hell looks like you did."

Mo opens her mouth to tell Ms. Gutierrez she thinks this was a mistake, but Chloe gets there first. "My mom says you represented Christopher Yellen."

"I did. Won't do that again, take on a psycho maniac. I don't care how much money a client's got."

Two years ago, Christopher Yellen was accused of drowning his pregnant wife. The trial ended in a hung jury. It was tried again a few months later with the same result.

She looks squarely at Mo. "You're not a psycho maniac, are you?"

Mo's not sure if she's joking.

"Of course you're not," she says with a small curl of her lips. "Look at you. Jury's going to love you . . . classy, rich, pretty. I take it back. They're going to hate you."

Mo's heart is scatter-firing all over the place. Her future, her fate, and her freedom are in this woman's hands, and she can't seem to be serious for more than a second. Yet there's definitely something compelling about her that Mo can't put her finger on, like you can't quite catch her, her wiliness elusive.

"I didn't do it," Mo says plainly.

"Doesn't really matter if you did or didn't," Ms. Gutierrez says, skewering her with a glare so piercing it's like black lasers shooting straight into the back of Mo's brain. "Only matters what the jury thinks . . . or at least part of the jury."

Chloe nods, while Mo shakes her head. The idea of this actually going to trial, where she will be judged and most likely condemned for a crime she never in a million years could have committed, makes her head pound and her stomach hurt.

Returning Ms. Gutierrez's laser stare, she says, "While it might not matter to you whether I did it, it matters a great deal to me. This is my life. It's my reputation, everything I've worked for, and my future. And *I didn't do it.*"

Ms. Gutierrez frowns and says, "Let's look at the facts. You filed a police report against Allen Redding for a crime you say wasn't committed against you but against an anonymous friend you were unwilling to name in the report." She rolls her eyes like this is entirely implausible. "The next day, you went to Mr. Redding's office, where you publicly threatened him. Then you posted a photo of him calling him out as a rapist. That same night he is drugged with the same drug you claim he used on 'your friend'"—she makes quote marks in the air—"and is found beaten within a couple blocks of where you claim he dumped your friend. And a day later, he wakes from a coma and unequivocally says you were the one who did it. A subsequent search of your apartment turns up a measuring cup with your fingerprints on it and paint thinner residue, which happens to be an exact chemical match to the drugs used in both the assault on Allen Redding and the murder of another victim, Dr. Grant Riley of Bend, Oregon, where you just happened to be at the time of the good doctor's death. And as if that isn't enough, a surveillance photo shows a woman matching your description and wearing your coat near the scene of the crime. Motive. Opportunity. No alibi." She enumerates the points as she says them until all her fingers are waving around her face.

Mo shakes her head. "You're wrong. I didn't have motive. I would never murder someone. I could never do that."

Mo feels Chloe looking at her and feels her struggling to keep her mouth shut about Hazel. They argued about it before Ms. Gutierrez arrived. Chloe got to the apartment a little after noon, and Mo showed her the article about the murder. For a long time, Chloe sat silent.

"Wow," she said finally. "I can't believe Haze killed someone."

Mo nodded, relieved Chloe wasn't defending Hazel as she had before and that it was as obvious to Chloe that Hazel had done it as it was to her.

Chloe shook her head. "It's like that Alfred Hitchcock film, the one where the two murderers switch targets so neither ends up a suspect."

"*Strangers on a Train*," Mo said.

"Yeah, that one. Haze kills the doctor in retaliation for what Allen did instead of going after Allen, knowing no one would ever suspect her because she had no association to the doctor, but she still rights the wrong, like the poem said, making right the stronger might."

"Except this is different," Mo said. "Because she also poisoned Allen, which leads straight back to her."

"You need to tell the police," Chloe said. "I know you love Haze, but there's no way you can take the fall for this."

Mo shook her head. "The only reason Haze did it was because of what happened. And what happened only happened because of me."

"Mo—"

"No, Clove. Don't. Don't tell me it wasn't my fault." Mo had been thinking things over since Fitz had left, and each time she came to the same conclusion. "Everything that happened, happened because of me."

"Not this," Chloe said, waving her hand at the article.

"Yes. Even the murder. I mucked it up. Haze's plan would have worked. Like you said, no one would have suspected her. Her plan was perfect. I was the one who filed that useless police report and was the one who went to Allen's office and threatened him and then made that stupid post. All of that is what led the investigation to me. Not to her. So now, if I tell them it was her, it's to save myself at her expense. Because without me, she would have gotten away with it. No one would have been looking in this direction at all."

"Mo, this is murder we're talking about. Prison."

Mo nodded, then lifted her face and leveled her gaze on Chloe's. "You can't tell."

"Mo—"

"Promise me," Mo said, her gaze fierce. "I need you to promise."

Reluctantly Chloe nodded, but Mo knows she's now seriously reconsidering. Catching her eye, Mo shakes her head, and Chloe scowls but mercifully stays silent.

"My first thought is to go with an insanity defense," Ms. Gutierrez says. "A he-said-she-said crime of passion that spiraled into a brief period of madness. Juries eat up off-the-rocker narratives, especially when it comes to women."

"That's a terrible idea," Chloe blurts, startling Ms. Gutierrez, and she looks over, clearly not pleased with Chloe's opinion.

"Look at her." Chloe waves her hand at Mo. "Does this look like someone who would go 'off her rocker' and randomly start drugging and killing people? This right here"—she waves her hand at Mo again—"is the most rational person in the world, and the jury's going to know that."

Ms. Gutierrez runs her eyes over Mo and frowns. "You've got a point. We might need to work on the packaging."

Chloe rolls her eyes. "How about instead of trying to make Mo look like something she's not, we paint Allen for exactly who he is? After all, he's the one who's lying."

"He's also the victim," Ms. Gutierrez says.

"And he's a rapist," Chloe counters. "What if we can get one or more of his victims to come forward?"

Ms. Gutierrez's brows pinch together. "Could backfire. Going after the victim is always risky. And Allen's quite likable—good looking, well spoken, successful."

Mo drops her face to her hands and groans, finding the idea of the jury loving Allen and loathing her incredibly irksome.

"They won't like him when they realize the things he's done," Chloe says. "And if we discredit his testimony, prove he's a liar, the rest of the case—both cases—falls apart. The search warrant, which was issued on his accusation, would be found invalid, and any evidence discovered in its execution would be thrown out. Right? And no search means no measuring cup and no paint thinner residue. And no paint thinner residue means no link to the murder in Bend."

"If you can discredit him," Ms. Gutierrez says. "Which is a big if. You would have to prove he falsely accused Maureen, and Allen's not the one on trial. Maureen is. While we might have some latitude in terms of disparaging him, it will be limited. And there's a reason his previous victims didn't come forward. Put them on the stand, and any lawyer worth their salt will crucify them on that fact alone. And if it falls apart, which there's a good chance it will, it will look like we were trying to railroad the victim, which will be very bad for Maureen."

Mo drops her chin to her chest. Every word out of Ms. Gutierrez's mouth is more discouraging than the last.

"What if I say I did it?" Chloe says. "If I come forward and say I roofied Allen and dumped him in the Tenderloin?"

Mo's face snaps up.

"Did you?" Ms. Gutierrez says slowly, her gaze steady on Chloe's. "I will remind you, Chloe, I am not *your* attorney."

"Hypothetically," Chloe says, "what if I said I did? After all, I live here, and I'm a vet, so I have a lot more knowledge about GHB and how to make it than Mo."

"Hmmm," Ms. Gutierrez says, her piercing black eyes flicking side to side.

"No!" Mo says. "Absolutely not. She didn't do this any more than I did, and I'm not going to have her life ruined by saying she did." She turns to Chloe. "Clove, I appreciate it, but no. I'll do the insanity thing before I do that."

"Won't work anyway," Ms. Gutierrez says. "Allen didn't finger you. He said it was Maureen, which means the jury will see right through it." She cocks her head, and her smile curls at the corners. "It's amazing how much of your mom you have in you." Pushing off her knees, she stands. "Let me give it some thought. I'll come up with a plan and get back to you tomorrow. In the meantime, lay low. Don't talk to the press. Better yet, don't leave the apartment."

Mo walks her to the door, thanks her, then returns to the living room, collapses on the couch, and buries her face in a pillow.

"Well, that went well," Chloe says sarcastically, then plops on the couch beside her and flops her arm over Mo's back.

"I can't believe this is happening," Mo mumbles.

"What are you going to tell Kyle?"

Mo shakes her head. If she goes anywhere near the truth, he will turn Hazel in, no question. "Nothing," she says. "I need to make this go away before he finds out about any of it."

44
CHLOE

Chloe climbs into Hunter's truck, her eyes scanning. Hunter texted an hour ago—using her phone to text his phone, which he gave her to use. He said Gretzky was still at the motel, which means there's no chance of him being in the city, yet knowing that does not stop her heart from racing with every sharp noise or her eyes from darting down every side street and into every dark corner. She hates that he's succeeding in exactly what he intended to do, to make her paranoid so she is constantly looking over her shoulder and scared of her own shadow.

She drives back to the motel in the marina, trying not to think about Gretzky, which of course only makes her think about him more. She cannot believe he followed her to Oregon. What is it about revenge that makes it so intoxicating? Her dad nearly destroyed their family over it, not able to see past his festering rage. Allen has hated Mo for years over a rejection from college. Hazel killed a man in retaliation for a crime by someone else. Addictive as heroin or crack, it seems to entirely take over a person, toxic and destructive, until it razes everything around it.

She pulls into the lot of the Twilight Motel, a quintessential midcentury relic with an oversize neon marquee covered in stars. A kidney pool is its centerpiece, the aluminum-umbrellaed deck surrounded by the parking lot and rooms.

Summer found the city while she and Mo were away, and the day is hot, and a family with three kids lounges on the deck and splashes in the water. Ray, Hunter's friend, walks from the lobby with Ruby on a leash, and Ruby tries to pull him forward, but like a jackrabbit attempting to tug a Mack truck, all she manages to do is choke herself.

"Hey, Little Chicken," Ray says. She's not sure why he chose the nickname, but he pinned it on her the moment they met and has used it since.

"Hey, Ray, thanks for watching Ruby."

"No problem. Any sign of the *cop*?" He hisses the word in much the same way Hunter did, and she thinks the two men must have met while Hunter was serving time.

"Hunter says he's still in Bend."

Ray gives a curt nod, his expression dark. While Hunter looks nothing like a criminal, there is definitely something menacing about Ray. He's large as a grizzly, and his white-blond hair is long and stringy, his overgrown beard hangs to his chest, and crude tattoos riddle his arms and spiral up his neck. He has the sort of body that looks soft, a wide belly and skinny legs, but Chloe knows there's enormous strength beneath the strata of fat.

He hands her Ruby's leash. "Here if you need me." He pivots back toward the office, and Chloe leads Ruby to their room and collapses on the bed.

Ruby jumps up beside her, and Chloe knows she should tell her to get down because dogs don't belong on beds, but the truth is she's grateful for the company. She drapes her arm over Ruby's back, and Ruby whimpers and nudges closer.

Chloe closes her eyes, hoping to rest, but knows it's impossible, too many thoughts spiraling in her head: *Gretzky, Hunter, Hazel . . . the doctor from Bend.*

She cannot believe Hazel killed a man. Yet she also understands how it makes sense. Hazel has always loved superhero comics and graphic novels, especially the ones that feature science-geek avengers like Spider-Man, Doctor Strange, or Professor X. So believing it was her final act, she decided to use her big brain to carry out karmic justice, just like the poem she left said.

Chloe tries to imagine how she did it but can't figure it out. Did she just walk into his house and put GHB in each bottle of booze in his liquor cabinet? How did she know he wasn't home? How did she get in? The questions spin, Chloe's curious mind fixed on how Hazel pulled it off and finding herself impressed regardless of how she did it. She's a little surprised how unaffected she is by the doctor's death, not feeling bad for him at all, and she supposes it's because of what she read in the article, a calculation of the cost of his death compared to what was most likely saved. He already had seven victims: too many to believe he had any chance for redemption.

Chloe's put plenty of animals down, mercy killings mostly, the pain more than what's left of their waning lives. It's always sad but also a relief, an end of suffering. But also, sometimes, she's needed to put animals down for other reasons. A week ago, a cat suffering from dementia who couldn't remember her owner and attacked whenever she came near. A year ago, a dog who had bitten one too many people when he got worked up. Plenty of animals with rabies—sick animals deemed too much of a menace to society to be allowed to continue to exist. Chloe has no problem with the same reasoning being applied to humans.

Her eyes flick behind her lids as she wonders if she could do what Hazel did, kill someone. She wants to say no, that she couldn't intentionally snuff out the light of a person who still had life in front of them. But she also knows, until they are pushed to the edge, nobody truly knows what they are capable of.

A truck passes outside, and she listens as it rumbles by, her thoughts continuing to weave. She's so tired. She feels like she hasn't slept in a month, her body sputtering on fear, adrenaline, and caffeine.

Hazel, the doctor, Allen, Mo: Good. Evil. Evil. Good.

"Ray will watch out for you," Hunter said this morning.

They were just inside the door of his apartment. A moment earlier, he had pulled his truck in front of the lobby.

"He's a good guy. You can trust him."

Ex-felon, good. Cop, bad. Life is not always what it seems.

Hunter set his fingers on her chin and tilted her face to look at him. "He doesn't get to win," he said.

She wanted to agree but knew from experience that bad guys win all the time. Life isn't fair, and those who cheat hold an unfair advantage. She was still thinking that when he kissed her, his lips brushing over hers before returning to kiss her fully, his mouth melting against hers and his large hands wrapping around her back to pull her tight.

When he released her, he said, "This . . ." He pointed between them. "This isn't over. You don't just get to waltz into my life, tangle up my heart, make me fall in love with your dog, then leave. Gretzky or no Gretzky, this isn't over."

She didn't know what to say to that, so she bit her lip and lowered her eyes, her heart scatter firing with fear far more terrifying than her worry over Gretzky.

"I like you, Chloe Miller, and I haven't said that to a girl in a really long time."

She liked him too. Really liked him. Her pulse pounded. Already, twice, she had destroyed her life over impulsive love. And now, as if she hadn't learned anything at all, she was considering jumping off the same damn cliff.

Hunter didn't give her time to decide. Wrapping his hands back around her, he pulled her into another deep kiss, heat filling her until she could no longer think at all. Ruby tried to get between them, nuzzling her snout into their thighs, but Hunter nudged her away. She tried again, rising on her hind legs and resting her paws on Hunter's arm.

"Uh-uh," Chloe mumbled against Hunter's mouth as she reached down and pushed her away. "This is *my* guy."

Hunter reared back, smiled, and did a fist pump as he spun in a circle. "I love when the geek gets the girl."

Only when she got on the road and was away from his mesmerizing spell did she realize what a terrible idea the whole thing was. She and Hunter had known each other less than two days, actually more like a handful of hours. That was not enough to base a lifelong decision on.

Dream like you have all the time in the world. Live like there's no tomorrow, Finn piped in, encouraging her with one of the many cheesy sayings she loved to dole out when she was alive, a great guru of Hallmark philosophy.

If her sister had actually been there, Chloe would have rolled her eyes and argued, told her that living like there was no tomorrow was what had gotten her into this situation in the first place. But of course, that was the problem. Finn wasn't there, hadn't been for eight years, making it impossible to argue against her cockamamie, romantic view that Chloe should throw caution—and proven history—to the wind.

So what are you going to do, never love again? That's stupid.

Yes. That was the plan.

What Finn doesn't realize—her starry-eyed idealism frozen eternally at sixteen before she ever experienced true heartbreak—is how hard it is to pick yourself up from that sort of pain. It has always puzzled Chloe why falling in love should be regarded as some sort of wondrous event when so often it ends in despair, the scars leaving hard calluses on your heart along with hard-boiled bitterness and deep-seated fear of ever opening yourself up to that sort of hurt again.

Ruby paws at her, and Chloe opens her eyes to see her looking at her, the dog's canine sense of compassion acute.

"I'm okay," Chloe lies and strokes her head.

The scar over Ruby's eye is nearly healed, and she seems entirely content, her happiness restored by nothing more than a little tenderness and love. Does it have to be different for humans? Is it possible to put the past behind and simply move on? To take a chance on Hunter and believe that this time it will work out? *I like you, Chloe Miller, and I haven't said that to a girl in a really long time.*

She thinks of the shame she saw on his face when he confessed to having served time and feels a deep welling in her heart. It was like looking at a reflection of her own soul yet without the contempt, and she wonders if that is why they are drawn to each other—forgiveness of others is so much easier than forgiveness of yourself. And perhaps, in that uncensured view, they find the pieces of themselves they are missing and that finally make them whole.

Like a flickering flame at the edge of her brain, the fairy tale taunts, the two of them together . . . and Ruby. Long walks in the woods, him with his camera, her with a sketchbook.

Her lips twitch with a smile as her pulse continues to pound. The feeling is a little like what she imagines it might feel like to be thrown from a horse, the wind knocked from your lungs so you can't breathe, then air flooding back in when you realize you survived, the relief so strong you just lie there and suck it in as tears leak from the corners of your eyes. The best air she ever breathed after the worst fall she's ever taken, so shocking and wonderful it hurts.

45
MO

Mo's eyes twitch behind her lids as she lies on the couch and runs all the different scenarios through her head. Usually, she's good at making decisions, stomping around boldly, certain of her choices and not second-guessing herself at all. But all of this has become so complicated, each choice fraught with deceit and treachery she never imagined herself capable of. Tell the truth, and Hazel pays the price. Continue to lie, and violate the trust that's been the cornerstone of her relationship with Kyle since they met and jeopardize her future . . . and his.

The problem is, no matter how she looks at it, everything that's happened leads back to her. She might not be guilty of the charges against her, but that doesn't mean she's not to blame. If not for her, Hazel would be in her room right now, reading comic books or coming up with abstract solutions to some existential threat no one else has even considered. Now, who knows what Hazel is doing, hopefully hanging with Kyle and not thinking about the waterfall or about what Allen did or about what she did when she believed there was no tomorrow.

All of it suddenly feels so fragile, tenuous as a butterfly's life, and she feels the slightest false move will destroy her and everyone around her.

Prison—no matter how many times she tells herself it's a real possibility, she simply can't imagine it, being locked in a cell without beauty or the people she loves to bring her joy. She turns her head to look out the windows at the view of the city, the early-evening light casting it gold and umber. She loves this room—the high ceilings, the wide crown molding, the dark parquet floor—and the thought of never enjoying it again makes her heart ache.

Her phone interrupts her mental spinning, ringing with "We Go Together."

With a heavy sigh, she answers: "Hey."

"Hey," Kyle says with incredible tenderness. "How'd it go?"

And she loses it, tears filling her eyes that instantly turn to sobs.

"That good?" he says. "And here I was worried."

She sob-laughs and wipes her nose with the back of her hand, surprised there are any tears left after how much she's cried the past four days.

"Do you like the lawyer?" he asks.

"She's good," Mo manages, realizing as she says it that it's true. Despite Ms. Gutierrez's slightly abrasive personality and unconventional approach, she is exceptionally smart, and Mo knows Mrs. Miller chose well in recommending her. "Good enough to know I'm in trouble."

She feels Kyle tense, and though she can't see him, she knows his expression—lips tight and brow furrowed—ready to jump into action to help.

"I'm still processing everything she said," Mo goes on, hoping to keep the conversation vague to avoid lying as much as possible. "She said she's going to come up with a strategy and call me tomorrow."

"Strategy?" he says. "What kind of strategy? You didn't do it."

She nods. She didn't, but she's starting to realize how little that matters. "How's Haze?" she asks, her energy too sapped to try and convince him of the reality.

"Hard to say. Strangely calm."

"That's not good," Mo says, recalling how "strangely calm" Chloe was in the days leading up to the moment she was planning to leave the living to join Oz and Finn in the ever after. Her decision made, she was bizarrely at peace, unburdened and almost carefree.

"Yeah, I'm concerned," he says. "I think I've convinced her to let me drive her to her parents."

"Really?" Mo says. "That's great."

"I sort of manipulated her into it." There's a glow of pride in his voice. "I called her work. Did you know she quit her job?"

"Haze quit her job?" Mo doesn't know why this is a surprise, considering the circumstances, and yet somehow it is. Hazel loves her job. Her title is geopolitical strategist, which is a fancy way of saying she helps wealthy, powerful people understand how the world works. Using her unique understanding of technology, demography, and economics, she helps her clients prepare for the future, and she's brilliant at it.

"Yeah. Shocked me too. So I called her boss, Ben. Remember him? We met him at that trivia night Haze took us to."

Mo almost smiles. The night was a complete disaster—her, Kyle, and the rest of the contestants sitting around getting drunk as Ben and Hazel answered every question, only missing one about the Kardashians.

"I asked him to send Haze some techy question they needed help with, and Ben was only too happy to oblige. Turned out he didn't even need to pretend. I guess they're working on this really important project, and Haze is the only one who really understands it."

"That's inspired," Mo says, wishing she had thought of it. Hazel can't resist solving problems no one else can solve.

"Yeah. It's not much, but at least she seems willing to leave this place." He sighs out heavily, and she feels his worry. "I'm telling you, Ace, this place is beautiful, too beautiful. It gives me the willies. This afternoon, when the sun was setting, Haze got this dreamy look in her eyes that was terrifying, like if I let her out of my sight, that was it, game over."

Mo's emotions rise again, and she bites hard on her lip to keep them inside. "You'll keep her safe?"

"I'm going to do my best. She's in the shower now. We're supposed to leave when she gets out. My plan is to keep her on task, distract her with the project so she's not thinking about the other stuff."

"Ask her questions," Mo says. "Even if you don't understand what she's talking about."

"Trust me, I rarely understand what Haze is talking about. Doesn't mean I don't enjoy listening. The kid's funny. Even now."

Mo almost manages a smile. Hazel is funny. She's funny and kind and wonderful.

"I wish I could be there to help."

A beat of silence before Kyle says, "Not sure she's your biggest fan at the moment."

And while Mo knows it's true, it still hurts. Hazel is like a sister.

"Plus," Kyle goes on, "you need to focus on your own problems. I know I need to be here with Haze, but it feels wrong not being there with you."

"I'm fine," Mo says a little too quickly, relieved she won't have to face him for at least a couple more days. "Clove's here, and there's nothing really to do. We just need to wait for Ms. Gutierrez to come up with a plan."

"Yeah, but I really want to be home."

Home. Mo looks around the apartment he doesn't know they've been evicted from. *Home is where the heart is.* She just hopes his heart remains when he finds out the truth.

46
CHLOE

The knock on the door sends Ruby charging from the bed and Chloe diving under it.

"Hey, Little Chicken, thought you and Wishbone might be hungry," Ray says through the wood over Ruby's barks. "I whipped up a stir-fry, if you'd like to join me."

Chloe sets her hand on her pounding chest and closes her eyes to still the panic. Ruby peeks beneath the bed frame and looks at her curiously.

"I'd love that. Just give me a minute."

"No rush. Come down when you're ready."

Chloe reaches out her hand, and Ruby licks it. "Yeah, I know, grade A wimp. Sorry, girl."

She pulls herself out and leans against the mattress, her head on her knees and her heart still racing. As she waits for her pulse to settle, she thinks about Mo and the trouble she's in. She made Chloe promise not to bring Hazel into it, but Chloe's not sure she can keep that promise. If Mo ends up in prison, how will Chloe be able to live with that? Her toes ache with phantom pain. It happens when she's stressed. While her pinkie is a source of strength, her missing toes feel more like a haunting reminder of her mistakes.

Ignoring the ache, she pulls on her shoes. "Ready, girl?" she says to Ruby, who needs no encouragement, her tail whipping back and forth as she stands expectantly beside the door. The act of shoe tying is very exciting to dogs.

Together, they head to the lobby, and she knocks lightly on the door behind the counter.

"Come on in," Ray says behind the wood.

She finds him standing at the stove of a small kitchenette wearing a pair of bermuda shorts, a Harley-Davidson T-shirt, and a stained red apron.

"Wow, smells delicious," she says, her stomach rumbling, really hoping it's meatless.

"Tofu teriyaki," he says, turning to her with a wink, and she smiles all the way to the soles of her feet, knowing Hunter must have told Ray she doesn't eat meat. He looks at Ruby. "Chicken for us."

She smiles wider, and Ruby leaves her side to sit close to Ray and the promise of food.

The apartment is worn and comfortable. A brown leather recliner and green tweed couch sit in front of a large flat-screen television, and a sturdy pine table with four slat-back chairs is in front of the small kitchenette. On the wall, beside a door that she assumes leads to a bedroom, is a large photo, definitely one of Hunter's works. Her breath catches at the beauty of it: an older arm and a younger one entwined, both male, with faded indigo tattoos and crisply etched color ones—blurred words, skulls, hearts, thorns, and roses—the juxtaposition stunning. The older arm is definitely Ray's, and she wonders about the younger man.

"Hunter gave that to me the day I was released," Ray says as he hands her a beer, a craft IPA she's never heard of. "He took a photography workshop in prison. He made me and Slack pose three hours, in all different ways, to get it right."

"Looks like he managed it," Chloe says, still mesmerized.

"Totally forgot about it until he showed up at my mom's house the day I got out. Pulls it from the back of his truck wrapped in a big red bow."

He returns to the kitchen as Chloe continues to admire the riddles of life Hunter captured in the frame—love and angst and hurt and hope—so much of it. And while she understands Ray and Hunter and Slack are criminals, the three of them each having done something that landed them behind bars, it's impossible to see anything in the photo but vulnerable humanity and tender devotion.

As if reading her mind, Ray says, "Hunter had no business being in that hellhole. Went for a damn joyride to see a girl and got railroaded for living in a county with a sheriff who was running for reelection and trying to make a point of being tough on crime."

"He stole a car so he could see a girl?" she asks, joining Ray at the table as he sets down two heaping plates of food.

Ray forks a piece of broccoli. "I'd say *borrowed without permission* is more like it." He glances at the photo. "Crazy what some of us will do for love." He drops a bit of chicken on the floor, and Ruby laps it up. "Didn't have wheels, so he borrowed a truck from a neighbor he thought was out of town. Planned on returning it the next day but got caught before that could happen."

Chloe could totally imagine Hunter doing something like that, and if the outcome hadn't turned out so awful, she might even smile at the idea. Instead, she turns her focus to her dinner, thinking how infinitesimal the distances are between fates: a single breath this way or that, and your life turns out entirely different from where you believed it was going.

"This is delicious," she says around a mouthful of teriyaki-glazed carrot.

"Spend enough time behind bars, and you come out appreciating the small pleasures in life—food, beer, and sex." He winks. "In that order."

She laughs. Ray has a great round belly, proof of his priorities.

"Are you and Slack still together?" she asks.

"Until death do us part," Ray says, holding up his left hand to show a tattooed band around his third finger. "Unfortunately, Slack won't be seeing this side of freedom anytime soon. So I suppose it's more apart than together at the moment."

Chloe feels bad for them. She hasn't met Slack, but already, she likes Ray as much as you can like someone you barely know.

Ray's phone rings, and he pulls it from the leather holder on his belt and squints at the screen. "Speak of the devil." He carries the phone into the bedroom, saying, "Hey, Hunt."

It's several minutes before he returns, enough time for Chloe to have finished her dinner and to have washed most of the dishes.

"Leave it," he says, taking the sponge from her hands.

Reaching into a high cabinet above the fridge, he pulls out a bottle. Chloe recognizes it—Blanton's bourbon, the pewter racehorse on top of it the trademark. The whiskey is her dad's favorite and no joke in terms of cost.

"A toast," Ray says, pouring them each a shot. "To justice."

She clinks his glass and swallows it past the lump in her throat, wondering what it is exactly they're toasting.

47
MO

Exhausted as Mo was, it took a while for her to fall asleep, and when she did, Hazel wove in and out of her dreams—fragile and pale as a Lladró figurine and teetering on the edge of a waterfall with raging rapids below. In every vision, she was looking directly at Mo, the expression the exact one she wore in the hospital, a hard wish for Mo to go away, not so much hate as hurt, like she didn't want to be near her.

When Oz died, the only one who knew it was her fault was her. Six survivors remained in the wrecked RV when Kyle and Mrs. Miller went for help. Mr. Miller was gravely injured and unconscious, leaving only her to look out for Oz, a boy of thirteen but with the intellectual capability of someone less than half that. The other three, a family of neighbors—Bob, Karen, and Natalie Gold—were concerned for themselves. There was a moment when things got tense. Mo was boiling snow for the survivors to drink, and Oz insisted she give the water to the Millers' dog, Bingo. When Bob asked Oz to go outside with him so Bingo could relieve himself, Mo thought it was to distract Oz so the rest of them could have water. But when Bob returned, it was without Oz and Bingo. She knew something was wrong. She knew Bob had done something. And she knew she should go after Oz and try to bring him back. But she didn't.

Bingo was found during the search-and-rescue mission; Oz was not. And Mo has never forgiven herself.

This is the same but different. Hazel is still here, and she knows Mo is to blame.

Pushing from the bed, she grabs her phone from the nightstand and, before she can think about it anymore, types: I accept your offer. Rescind the charges and I will make the post.

Allen's reply is almost instant despite it being four in the morning.

Right the wrong to continue on

He's being artful, just like he was the first time, using cryptic language so as not to say anything she can use to incriminate him. She imagines this isn't even his phone but rather a burner that cannot be traced back to him.

She shakes her head. Stressed as she is, she is still her father's daughter, and hard-core negotiation is in her blood. She doesn't trust Allen, and at the moment, he holds all the cards. The only leverage she has is his desire to have the claim she made that he is a rapist disavowed and his reputation restored.

She trembles with desire to double down and put out a public call for his victims to come forward, similar to what Chloe suggested. But she knows it's a fool's move and will only cause more harm.

Dropping back to the bed, she closes her eyes and thinks about what comes next once she does this. FactNews will be over, her credibility as a journalist destroyed. Her employees will be out of jobs; her father's investment will be lost; her dream of creating a revolutionary new way of reporting the news will be gone.

Of course, even if she doesn't do this, the result will be the same. Already, the media is having a field day, far more interested in the drama unfolding around her than the "Babies" story. She can see tomorrow's headline: *Ryan Kaminski's Daughter Involved in Lovers' Quarrel Turned Sex Scandal.*

She rubs her knuckles against the hard knot in her chest, wondering how she will ever recover from this. What is she going to do with her life? This is going to follow her forever.

And when Kyle finds out, she's not sure he will forgive her. How could he? She's confessing to being in a relationship with another man, a man she falsely, insanely, accused of being a rapist on social media and then went on to publicly apologize to. And she will have done it without consulting him, without including him in a decision that permanently altered their lives, and he won't have the benefit of knowing she did it for Hazel, having no idea about the murder charge or the evidence against her.

The thought is so horrible a sob escapes, then another, until she is crying uncontrollably—a complete griefquake made up of two desperate gasps of oxygen with every snivel. Curling in a ball, she squeezes her stomach tight, unable to believe this is the choice she's been left with. Oz floats to the surface of her distraught mind, the way he often does in moments of stress, his face ageless, frozen in time at thirteen. *Don't cry, Mo.*

"Oh, Oz," she whispers and cries harder.

At least twice a year it happens—always on his birthday and usually one other time—intense grief over his loss. She hates that he was never found. It makes it so much worse, like somehow he's still out there, part of the woods and looking for his mom or trying to find his way back to his dad.

The summer after his death, on what would have been his fourteenth birthday, there was a memorial service, and the weeks after were the hardest of her life, the finality and hopelessness destroying her. She understands a body is only a vessel for your soul, but she has never been able to reconcile that idea with her emotions when it comes to Oz.

The thing she didn't realize at the time she made the cowardly choice that cost Oz his life was how much worse shame is than terror, how it stains your soul and never completely washes out, no matter how much you live your life trying to atone for it. Kyle can't understand that because he's never felt that sort of regret. He walked away from the accident with his conscience clear. When he looks in the mirror, he sees himself. When Mo looks in the mirror, she sees a girl who stood by and did nothing while a friend suffered and died.

Her phone pings.

???

She realizes it's been several minutes, and she hasn't responded to Allen's text.

She sets the phone aside. Let him stew.

A moment later, it pings again. She picks it up and holds it over her face.

Let's meet. We'll hit send together.

The willies crawl over her skin; the way he worded it almost made it sound romantic, and she knows it was intentional. Every atom in her body screams at her to say no, knowing that agreeing to meet him is a very bad idea. But she also knows it's the only way. He doesn't trust her, and she doesn't trust him.

She stares and stares at the message until the pixels blur.

Finally, she writes, Ritual Roasters. Eleven o'clock, then quickly hits send before she loses her nerve.

48
CHLOE

Ruby sits in the passenger seat, her head out the window. She loves being in the truck, and Chloe knows whoever cared for her previously must have taken her along when he went places. It makes Chloe happy and sad, wondering what would cause someone who obviously loved the pup to abandon her as he did.

The day is warm and blindingly bright, and despite the calamity of her life, she finds herself soaking it in and, at moments, forgetting her worries and enjoying the refreshing bustle that comes with the first days of summer in the city.

They have a dozen stops today, makeup appointments she needed to reschedule from the time she was away. They left the motel at dawn and have been going nonstop for hours. It feels good to be working, and the distraction of doing what she loves has kept her mind too occupied to spin out of control with worry.

Most of the moments between stops she finds herself thinking about Hunter. Perhaps because she's in his truck, or perhaps because of everything Ray told her last night. She was amazed how similar his story is to hers, both of them done in by a single tragic mistake made for love. He stole a car to visit a girl. She left her family to follow her boyfriend into the snow. Impetuous, foolish choices that irrevocably altered their courses and permanently changed their views of themselves.

The text she got from him last night confounded her— ABCDEFGHIJKLMNOPQRSTVWXYZ—until finally a smile spread across her face.

"He's very clever," she said to Ruby, who was curled beside her on the bed.

Miss "U" too, she texted back.

She stares at the red light in front of her and thinks how easily he makes her laugh. Not only the jokes and stories he tells but the way he tells them, his animated expressions and the way he uses his hands. Finn was like that, perpetually in motion when she talked, which made everything she said far more entertaining and grander than it was.

Finn would love Hunter. Oz too. He's one of those guys who would fit right in with her family. She imagines her dad meeting him and sizing him up, then looking at her and nodding. It's not that her dad disapproved of Eric. He always said he liked him just fine. But she always got the feeling he didn't think he was good enough. He wouldn't think that about Hunter. Hunter's definitely good enough, strong in a way Eric and Vance simply weren't. Her mom would just be glad Chloe was happy. It's strange how much her mom has changed. Before the accident, she was intense and very demanding of her kids and even more so of herself. Now, she never talks about what's next or what each of them needs to be doing to get there, her focus entirely on the present and whether Chloe and her sister Aubrey and Aubrey's husband and their two girls are happy and okay.

She pulls Hunter's truck in front of a blue-and-pink Victorian, then looks at her phone, hoping for another text from Hunter or a response from Mo. She texted her this morning at around nine to see how she was doing, and it's now almost noon, and she still hasn't heard back.

Hunter's phone wallpaper is a photo of him and his mom riding on a bronze woolly mammoth statue. It's very cute, and his mom looks as wonderful as he made her sound—lanky and blonde with a smile bright as the sun. Her hair is short and chic, buzzed on the sides and long and wild on top.

No messages.

"I'll be back," she says to Ruby in her best Terminator voice and climbs from the truck.

Halfway up the steps, Hunter's phone buzzes, and she steps back to the sidewalk. Seeing the number, she answers. "Hey, Mom." She gave her mom Hunter's number and explained it was a temporary phone because hers was getting fixed. The only other people who know she's using Hunter's phone are Mo, Kyle, and Ray.

"What's she doing?" her mom asks in the measured, low voice Chloe calls her mom's courtroom voice, menacing and authoritative at once, a voice that says, *Don't mess with me, because if you do, I will methodically and deliberately rip you apart, dismembering you limb by limb, while enjoying every moment of it.*

"Who?" Chloe asks.

"Mo. Why is she taking photos with that man and posting them?"

"What man?"

"Allen. Allen Redding."

49
MO

"Smile," Allen says.

Mo doesn't feel like smiling, but her lips curl. When his phone clicks, she winces, but it's barely a twitch, like her reactions are on delay and muted.

"Oh, that's a good one," Allen says and holds the screen out for her to see, but her eyes won't focus. She sees only a blurry image of two faces, her synapses not firing well enough to realize it's her and him. Yet sickness roils in her gut—vague, vile comprehension that something bad is happening.

"Need . . . to . . . go," she stammers.

"Oh no, baby, we're just getting started."

She tries to straighten her thoughts, to get her brain to work properly, but it's like trying to stop water from whirling toward a drain.

The last thing she remembers clearly was climbing in the Uber to go to Ritual Roasters. As they drove toward downtown, she started to not feel well, woozy and disoriented. She thought it was stress or perhaps the heat that had suddenly descended on the city. She hadn't eaten breakfast, her nerves too frayed, so that, too, could have been contributing. She guzzled the water the driver had given her, hoping it would help, but as they inched forward in the thick midmorning traffic, she only felt worse.

Then Allen was there. At first she didn't realize who had climbed in beside her, thinking the driver had made a mistake and marked her ride as an UberPool instead of a single and was picking up a second rider.

"Excuse me," she said, her tongue sluggish so it came out slow. "I think there's been a mistake."

The driver's eyes flashed in the rearview mirror, and something about her was familiar, pink lips. But Mo couldn't place it, her brain refusing to work.

"No mistake." It was Allen who answered instead of the driver, and that's when Mo realized the trouble she was in.

She reached for the door, but the child locks were on, and she watched in horror as the driver climbed out, leaving Mo alone with Allen.

Now, it's a little while later. How much later, Mo can't say. Time is swimming—fast, then slow, with lapses she can't recall.

"What should I say?" Allen asks, looking at the photo on his . . . no, *her* phone. Why is he holding her phone? "How about *This time I will love him right and keep him tight?*" He pecks it out, and his mouth skews sideways.

She stares at the device as if it's a magnet, and her gaze is suddenly steel, her eyes fixed and refusing to leave.

"Yeah. That's good." He smiles and pokes the screen with his forefinger.

His left eye is bloodshot, and there's a bruise beneath it. Her focus switches to the wound as she tries to recall why it's important.

"No," she mumbles, dull warning breaking through the fugue.

"Oh yes," Allen says with a twisted smile as he lifts his face to hers. "Don't fight it, babe. Just let yourself go."

She shakes her head, but his words have a profound effect, as if she is unable to reject them. She tries to lift her arm to take the phone back, but her limbs no longer work, and the effort causes her to topple sideways so she is slumped against the door, her eyes still open.

"Time to get you home," he says with glee, and she watches as he climbs from the car and into the driver's seat.

The car begins to move, and paralyzed, she has no choice but to remain crumpled where she is, aware but like she's watching what is happening on a three-dimensional screen rather than being part of it. As her cognition continues to fade, the fight drains out of her. Her last thought before her mind goes blank: *A mistake. What a horrible, horrible mistake.*

50
CHLOE

Chloe knows when she looks at the Instagram post something is wrong. The photo is strange—a picture of Mo in a car with black leather seats, Allen kissing her cheek. The caption reads: *Make ups r the best part of break ups*

Chloe's breakfast crawls back up her throat, and her pulse triples. She's about to call Mo when another post pops up: *This time I will love him right and keep him tight*

Mo is smiling, her face beside Allen's, their cheeks touching. His toothy face is larger than hers because he is the one taking the photo. Signs of the beating are still clear—broken capillaries near his nose, a ring of black beneath his left eye.

All of it is wrong. Mo's grin is strange, and if you look close, her pupils are constricted—pinpricks in pools of blue. Plus, Mo never uses *r* instead of *are* in texts. It's a peeve of hers. And she always punctuates her sentences. And she would never write such cheesy lines. Chloe's blood turns cold as she realizes what has happened . . . *is happening.*

She hurries to the truck as her client calls from the steps, "Dr. Miller?"

"I'm sorry," Chloe yells over her shoulder. "Family emergency."

Leaping into the driver's seat, she taps the phone to life to look Mo up on Find My Friends, then realizes the phone isn't hers but Hunter's, and he and Mo aren't connected.

No matter. She knows where they are. Throwing the phone on the dash, she peels from the curb and floors the accelerator. A block from where she started, she slams on the brakes, missing the bumper of the car in front of her by an inch and sending Ruby sliding off the seat into the dash.

"Sorry, girl," she says, helping her up.

She orders herself to calm down, grabs the phone again, and calls Ray.

"Hey, Little Chicken, what's kickin'?"

Her voice wobbly, she explains what she thinks has happened and rattles off an address.

"On my way," he says. Then he adds, "Wait for me. Don't go in until I get there."

They slow to a crawl, some sort of protest on Divisadero Street—slow, slow, slow—bumper to bumper with no end in sight. Up ahead, she can see the signs but can't make out what they read. She turns at the next corner and snakes her way along side streets and alleys, willing the cars in front of her to go faster.

When she's two blocks from where she's going, she hits construction. Her brain on fire, she slams the truck into a loading zone, grabs Ruby by the leash, and runs down the street. A deliveryman tells her to "watch it." She ignores him, counting each address as she goes: 4323 . . . 4547 . . . 4591.

She nearly takes out a mother with a child walking from a store. "Sorry!" she says as tears fill her eyes for how long it's taking to travel the short distance.

Finally, they reach 4663, a beige brick building four stories tall. Breath heaving, she looks up at the balconies. A young woman in a jogging suit walks from the entrance, and Chloe grabs the door before it closes. Scanning the mailboxes beside the elevators, she finds the one that says *Redding*, then races with Ruby up the stairs.

Allen's door is the second one on the left on the third floor. She doesn't knock, and she doesn't slow. She has no plan and only realizes after she's already crossed the threshold how stupid that is.

Ten feet away, Allen is on a black couch, Mo straddled beneath him. Music blares, Bruce Springsteen screaming about the USA. A flat-screen to the left shows a tennis match but is silent. Over the couch is a large abstract painting. The apartment smells of lemon wax and sweat. Allen's T-shirt is halfway up his stomach, a roll of softness around his waist. Mo's shirt is off, her bra cotton candy pink.

Allen looks up, and his eyes open wide in surprise. Mo turns as well, her face pale and her expression blank. Chloe freezes as Ruby continues to charge, barking and growling and pulling hard on the leash. Chloe's brain continues to spin at hyperspeed, taking in all the details at once: Allen's shirt falling as he stands, the front emblazoned with the logo of a ski resort; his belt undone but his jeans buttoned. He is larger than she remembered. Mo looks small.

Chloe falls back as he steps toward her, and she opens her hand. Ruby charges, launching herself toward Allen. With barely a flick of his wrist, he swats her away, sending Ruby sprawling to the floor with a yelp. Before Chloe can react, Allen has closed the gap between them. "You," he says as the hand that hit Ruby returns to slash her across the face, the blow so unexpected she only realizes she's been struck after she is falling.

The wind gone out of her, she lies wheezing on the floor, the left side of her face pulsing in pain as she watches Ruby get back to her feet and bravely charge again. This time she goes for Allen's arm, gets hold, and clamps down with all her force, her teeth sinking deep into his flesh. Allen cries out and tries to shake her off, but gallantly she holds on.

"Mo, get up!" Chloe says as she staggers to her feet.

Mo continues to stare with unblinking eyes, her head turned sideways like she is watching but not fully awake.

There is a crash behind her and Ruby cries out, and Chloe turns to see her crumpled against a stool in front of the kitchen island.

"Ruby!"

"Clove?"

Chloe turns back to see Mo pushing herself up, her head lolled to the right like she can't quite hold it up. Chloe reaches for her at the exact moment Allen's fist rises.

Chloe rears back with her hands up as she braces for the blow. But miraculously the strike doesn't come. Ruby has gotten back on her feet, and with her left back leg lifted, she is faced off against Allen, hunched and growling. Allen lifts his foot to kick her, and Chloe hurls herself at his supporting leg, barreling into it with her shoulder and sending both of them crashing to the floor.

Ruby attacks, savagely going for Allen's face and neck as Allen tries to fight her off, his hands flailing to defend himself.

Chloe grabs Mo by the arm and pulls her toward the door at the exact moment someone barrels through, causing Chloe to stumble back and Mo to crumble.

Everything after that happens quickly yet in slow motion.

"Hunter?" Chloe says, the name coming out an exclamation and a question, not sure she's seeing right.

Hunter dives at Allen, who is still on the floor, and his elbow smashes across Allen's jaw, snapping his head sideways. Ruby, seeing the exposed vein of Allen's neck, pounces, and Hunter gets hold of her collar half a second before her powerful jaws clamp shut, her teeth missing his throat by an inch.

Allen lies dazed, blood dripping from his right arm and nose.

"Chloe, unplug that light," Hunter says with a nod toward a lamp on the side table beside the couch. Chloe hurries over and grabs it, thinking he's going to smash it over Allen's head. Instead, he uses the cord to tie Allen's hands in front of him. Then he sits on him, his knees pressed into Allen's shoulders. Ruby stands beside them, snarling, her back leg still lifted to keep weight off it.

"Call 911," Hunter says and nods toward Mo, who lies with her eyes open on the carpet, her breath rapid and shallow.

Hands trembling, Chloe manages to punch the keys.

"Hey, Little Chicken."

Chloe looks up to see Ray. He walks past and replaces Hunter, sitting on Allen with an "oomph."

"911, what's your emergency?"

"I need to report . . ." Chloe's voice quakes so badly the words are nearly unintelligible. "There's been a . . . please send police and an ambulance to 4663 Jackson Street, apartment 305."

"Miss, can you please tell me your emergency?"

She looks at Mo on the floor, her jeans undone, her bra pulled up over one breast. The phone still to her ear, she kneels beside her and straightens it. Mo's face turns, tears squeezing from the corners of her eyes.

"You're okay," Chloe says, her composure cracking.

"Hello, are you still with me?" the operator says, and then the phone is being lifted from her hand. She looks up to see Hunter. He carries it toward the kitchen and continues talking to the operator. "Rape" floats across the room, and Mo's eyes, pools of azure with pupils the size of pinheads, connect with Chloe's as she repeats it as a question: "Rape?"

Chloe shakes her head. "No, sweetie. No."

Repositioning herself so she is behind Mo, she pulls her up so she is sitting with her back against Chloe's chest. Ray pulls off the flannel shirt he had over his T-shirt and tosses it their way. Chloe drapes it over Mo, then rocks her back and forth. "I've got you. You're okay."

"Where am I?" Mo mumbles.

"You're safe," Chloe says, kissing the side of her head.

"Is that Hunter?" Her words are slurred and slow, like she's talking through cotton balls.

"Hey, Mo," Hunter says, walking back into the living room.

"Are we in Oregon?" Mo asks.

"I don't think so," Chloe says, looking in disbelief at Hunter and Ray.

Allen tries to say something, but his jaw must be broken, because it comes out garbled. In response, Ray lifts up a few inches, then slams his big body down again on Allen's chest. Allen's face loses color, and he sucks air through his nose.

"How?" Chloe asks, looking at Hunter.

"Damian Wayne," he says. "No one messes with Damian Wayne's girl."

51
MO

It feels like an anvil's been dropped on Mo's head and a ball of gauze has been shoved in her mouth. Her stomach is cramping, and her eyes are filled with tears. She's in a hospital, machines around her. She has no idea how she got here, though there's a faint recollection of sirens.

"Hey, Ace."

She turns her head, slowly so as not to rupture her brain, to find Kyle sitting in the chair beside her, a shadow of beard on his cheeks and chin.

"You're here," she says, her voice like sandpaper.

She watches as his jaw slides forward and locks as he nods. His eyes are red rimmed and swollen, and she thinks he might have been crying. He stands, then sits on the edge of the mattress and takes her hand.

"I'm sorry," she mumbles, the words collapsing into a hiccup of tears. She's not even certain what she's apologizing for, only knows it's bad, that whatever she's done is worthy of begging for forgiveness. Her head spins, and she thinks she might be sick. She closes her eyes and swallows down the acid.

"You're okay," Kyle says, a tremble in his words.

She slits her eyes open, drawing breath through her nose to keep the bile at bay, her brain throbbing, and she wants to say she's sorry again, but the walls are swaying dangerously—pale blue like forget-me-not flowers. The thought is distracting: her mother holding her hand in a garden and pointing as she said the romantic name.

"Pretty," she mumbles.

"What's pretty?"

She blinks to see Kyle, and it takes a second for her to remember that she already knew he was here. He wraps his arm around her, and she leans into him, wishing she could stop the pounding in her skull.

"I have such a bad headache," she says.

"I know." He sets his palm on her forehead. "Does that help or hurt?"

"Helps," she says.

"Rest."

She grips his shirt. "Don't be mad."

"I'm not mad."

She feels his lips on the side of her head, and for some reason, it makes her want to cry more.

"I messed up," she says, knowing it's true but unable to piece the puzzle together, her brain cycling backward but confused about time. "I let Chloe keep the dog," she says, knowing somehow that's where it began.

"I heard," Kyle says without an ounce of anger.

"We're getting evicted."

"That's okay."

"But you love our apartment?"

He shrugs, and she supposes that's the thing about moments like these: they put things in perspective. Things that seemed so important, suddenly you have to work to remember why they mattered.

"That dog saved you," he says, and again she hears the emotion in his voice.

Ruby? Ruby saved her?

Her brain struggles to catch hold of it, but she has no idea what he's talking about; then she forgets what she was thinking altogether and starts to drift away. But just as her eyes begin to close, she jerks awake, bolting upright and setting off a jackhammer in her head. She folds forward, clutching her skull and rocking against the pain as an awful flash of memory blinds her—Allen on top of her, his lips on her skin.

Kyle leaps to his feet. "What can I do? Tell me what I can do."

Nothing, she thinks as her head continues to pound and tears stream from her eyes. *Ruby. Ruby was there. She was barking, and then Allen's weight lifted.*

"Ace?" Kyle says desperately. "Should I get the doctor?"

"No," she manages, drawing breath through her gritted teeth. "Already getting better." She rocks back and forth. "Is she okay? The dog?" she asks, remembering Allen knocking her away and Ruby yelping.

"She's at the animal hospital," Kyle says. "Chloe thinks she might have a broken leg."

Mo rocks harder, the memory like a shadow she can't catch hold of. "How'd I get here?"

"An ambulance. Chloe called 911."

Chloe. Chloe was there as well. More tears drip down her chin. *How?* The thought tumbles.

"Chloe," she rasps.

"In the waiting room," Kyle says, thinking it's a question.

She nods and closes her eyes again, too tired to think about it.

Kyle sits again beside her, and she leans against him.

"Rest," he soothes, wrapping his strong arms around her and holding her tight.

In seconds, his breath grows heavy, and to its steady rhythm, she starts to drift as well, thoughts of Chloe and Ruby weaving through her mind.

Ruby yelping as she crashed to the floor. "You!" Allen saying as he stepped toward Chloe, looking at her as if he knew her.

52
CHLOE

They are in the waiting room, Hunter's hand entwined in hers. Ruby is on the floor beside them, a pink cast on her back left leg, her tibia fractured. Ray took her to the emergency animal hospital in Oakland, then brought her to the hospital an hour ago.

"I said wait for me," he scolded as he handed Chloe the leash, his eyes fixed on the bruised side of Chloe's face.

"I had my mighty guard dog with me," Chloe said, then bent to pet Ruby's head.

The dog looked exhausted, as done in as Chloe. She looked up at Chloe, then plopped down at Hunter's feet.

"Traitor," Chloe said.

Ray clapped Hunter on the shoulder. "Stay out of trouble." He lifted an eyebrow at Chloe.

Since Ray left, Hunter can't stop cooing at Ruby and fawning over her. "Heck of a dog," he's said at least three times. And "I'm buying you a Mabel chicken sandwich . . . make that *two* Mabel chicken sandwiches." And once, his voice choked up, "Never know how to thank you, Rubes," and Chloe could feel how scared he'd been.

"Rubes," that's what he calls Ruby now, or sometimes "Ruby Tuesday," singsonging the name to the Rolling Stones tune, and Ruby seems to like it, mooning up at him with her big brown eyes, clearly in love.

"Want to tell me why you're here?" Chloe asks, still unable to believe he showed up the way he did and glancing at him every other second to confirm he's real and not part of some very real-feeling dream.

He looks sidelong at her. "If I said it was for Ray's charming company, would you believe me?"

"I'll give you Ray's charming, but he's not *that* charming."

He lets go of her hand and leans forward, his elbows on his knees. "I'm warning you, you're going to think I'm nuts, but I'm not . . . well, I might be . . . but in this case, I just had a bad feeling."

"Okay," Chloe says. "Got it. You're nuts."

He half smiles, sits up, then rubs his palms on his jeans like they're sweaty. "Fine. Here it goes. When Gretzky left the motel, I got worried— like, crazy worried."

Chloe swallows and nods, letting him know she was worried as well.

"I know guys like him," he says, "met my share on both sides of the bars when I did my time. Piss on their shoes, and they never let it go. It's like they feed on it. It revs them up and becomes their sole reason for getting out of bed in the morning." He shakes his head and rubs harder on the denim. "I knew he was going to come after you. So what was I supposed to do?" He lifts his eyes to hers sheepishly, as if apologizing. "So I borrowed my mom's car, asked her to watch the motel, and followed."

"You what?" Chloe says, astonished. "You followed Gretzky? From Bend to San Francisco?"

"I told you you'd think I was nuts."

"What were you planning on doing once you got here? Continue to follow him for the rest of his life?"

Hunter shakes his head. "I don't know. Forethought's never really been my strong suit."

Maybe not, Chloe thinks, but chivalry certainly is. She reaches for his hand and twines her fingers back through his. "Thank you," she says, the words thick.

He looks at her, his eyes a remarkable warm brown, not too different from Ruby's, and she thinks how alike they are, two tender souls, unassuming and not violent in the least unless you threaten their loved ones; then they'll fight ruthlessly with courage and valor that are astounding. She leans in and kisses him tenderly, a gentle lingering of lips, her hand on his rough cheek.

The opening of the sliding doors that lead to the rooms interrupts, and they pull apart to see Kyle.

"How is she?" Chloe asks, standing.

Ruby staggers to her feet awkwardly, still not comfortable operating with only three legs. Kyle squats down and scratches her behind the ears. "Hey, girl," he says, and Ruby offers a dog kiss before flopping back to the floor.

Kyle stands. "She seems to be doing better, though she's still pretty confused. The doctor said that's to be expected. She's sleeping again."

He looks terrible, which means he still looks great because he's Kyle, but worn out, his face unshaven and ashen and his eyes red rimmed.

As soon as the EMTs had taken Mo from Allen's apartment, Chloe called Kyle. Unsure how much to say, she kept it simple. "Kyle, Mo's been hurt."

"Hurt? How?" he said, panic in his voice.

Chloe wanted to reassure him it would be okay but wasn't entirely certain, so all she said was, "You should come. She's on her way to UCSF Medical Center."

He arrived two hours later, a man on fire, his eyes wild and tension pulsing off him in waves. The doctor assured him Mo was being well taken care of and offered to allow him to wait in the room, and for the past six hours, that's where he's been.

"Doc says she's out of the woods. Her blood pressure's stable, and her vitals have returned to normal. Now, it's just a matter of waiting for the drug to wear off." He says it as if trying to convince himself, his head shaking and his shoulders folded forward.

Chloe closes her eyes and offers a silent prayer of gratitude for small mercies, knowing things easily could have turned out so much worse.

"Bastard," he seethes. "What makes a man like that?" He bends forward, his hands on his knees, and Chloe sets her hand on his back.

"Bad egg," Hunter says.

Chloe looks at him and thinks again how much he and her dad would get along. One of her dad's favorite expressions is *We need ourselves an eggdicator*, referring to the scale in *Willy Wonka & the Chocolate Factory*'s golden-goose room that determined which eggs needed to be flushed down the garbage chute. He says it whenever he encounters someone he doesn't feel is passing muster.

While Chloe's always liked the notion, she's never been fully on board with it, unable to help thinking about the eggs at birth, before they turned rotten, thinking of a mother holding a swaddled baby and the hope she must have held in that moment. She understands Allen is evil and, at this point, probably too far gone to be redeemed, but it doesn't lessen the sadness she feels for what might have been had things turned out different. And it makes her wonder about the curve in the road or sliding-door moment that altered him and set him on a course that erased all that promise and led him instead to where he is.

"If it makes you feel better," Hunter says, "I'm pretty sure I cracked his jaw."

Kyle straightens, locks eyes with Hunter, and says, "It does." And Chloe's thankful it was Hunter who burst through the door and not Kyle, certain Kyle would not have stopped at just one blow.

Kyle's about to say something more when a voice interrupts: "Chloe."

All of them turn, and Chloe blinks rapidly as, for the second time in a day, a person she loves appears like a mirage.

"Ann?" Kyle says, confirming it, and Chloe loses it and runs straight into her mother's arms.

53
MO

When Mo wakes again, her headache is vaguely less horrific. It's still there, pulsing beneath her skull, and she still feels strange, but her thoughts are clear. She has no idea how long she's been in the hospital. It could be hours. It could be days.

An IV is plugged in her arm, and her throat is parched. She knows it's night by the black sky through the window, a sliver of moon shining. She turns her head carefully and finds Mrs. Miller and Chloe in two chairs beside the door. Chloe reads a book thick as the Bible, undoubtedly a classic. Mrs. Miller works on her laptop.

She must make some noise, because both look up, their expressions so similar it's startling.

"Mo," Chloe says, setting down the book and hurrying to her side.

Tears fill Mo's eyes as she takes in the bruise on Chloe's face and the small gash below her eye, not knowing how she got them but certain it has to do with her and what happened.

"Are you okay?" she asks, her voice sounding like there's gravel in her throat.

"I think I'm the one who's supposed to be asking you that," Chloe says as she picks up the water on the table beside the bed and holds it toward her.

Mo drinks it down, her throat incredibly dry.

"Kyle and Hunter went to the cafeteria for some food," Mrs. Miller says. "We've been taking shifts. And your mom is on her way. She got a flight out of Heathrow and should be here by morning."

Mo tries for a smile but instead ends up crying, and then Mrs. Miller is on the bed holding her, the familiar smell of lavender lotion and Pantene shampoo enveloping her. She sniffles against her, wishing she could contain the emotions, but her efforts only cause her to cry harder. Like a faucet turned on and the handle broken off, she simply can't stop.

She sucks air through her nose, and the tang of Mrs. Miller's scent causes the memory of another, sharper scent to emerge, unclean but coated with pungent aftershave. She jerks away, sending Mrs. Miller jolting to her feet. "Mo?" she asks.

Mo pinches her nose as tears continue to stream down her face, and she looks from Mrs. Miller to Chloe. "Did he . . . was I . . . ?" She can't get her mouth to form the word. She shudders, and bile rises in her throat.

Chloe, realizing what she's trying to ask, quickly says, "No. No, Mo. Ruby and I got there in time."

Mo locks her gaze, holding Chloe's eyes to be sure she's telling the truth as panic continues to course through her veins, her body quaking and her mind on fire. Finally, she looks away.

"Your shirt was off," Chloe says, the words careful, "but your bra and jeans were on."

Mo wraps her arms around herself and sips shallow breaths, knowing she should be grateful but instead feeling horribly violated, her skin crawling and the sickness still thick in her throat.

"You're okay," Mrs. Miller says. "We're here, and you're okay."

Mo looks at her through her teary eyes, wondering what she must think. Mrs. Miller's opinion has always been very important to her, and she's made so many awful mistakes this week; her shame is overwhelming.

"Can you tell us what happened?" Mrs. Miller asks, her voice soft but lawyerly.

Though Mrs. Miller is not a big woman—average height and thin, a marathoner with a body that matches—her intensity fills a room. And when she's in lawyer mode, she gives the phrase *rapt attention* a whole new level of meaning. At the moment, her green eyes, the exact color of Chloe's and Finn's, are locked on Mo's and her head is tilted slightly as her body leans in.

"How did he get you to take the GHB?" she asks.

GHB. Mo knows that's what she was given. She's been told several times. The same drug Hazel was given. It's just so hard to keep remembering, the idea refusing to stick.

"I think the Uber driver gave it to me," she says, recalling the girl turning and offering a bottle of water over the seat. Foolishly she took it, assuming it was safe because it was being offered by a woman. "I think I knew her, or she knew me, but I'm not sure." *Pink lips.*

Mrs. Miller nods thoughtfully, her brain turning. In the bright fluorescent lights, Mo notices the small wrinkles on her face, which she finds surprising and comforting, the same feelings she has when she sees her own mother after not seeing her for some time—evidence of time passing with all of them still here, seconds ticking on.

"Do you recall going to his apartment?" Mrs. Miller asks.

Mo shakes her head. It's so strange to have chunks of time missing, gone, like they never happened at all. "I remember there was a painting on the wall with lots of bright colors."

"A Richard Schemm print," Chloe says.

It's no surprise Chloe knows this. She's like a walking encyclopedia when it comes to modern art. Mo looks at her hands. The polish on her right index finger is chipped, and she stares at it, wondering how it happened, hoping maybe she fought. Though even as she thinks it, she knows it isn't true. She runs her thumb over the blemish, rubbing at it as if trying to erase it.

"Anything else?" Mrs. Miller asks.

In a rasp barely louder than a whisper, she says, "I remember his hand on my throat."

Mo can feel the bruises on her neck, more pronounced on the left than the right—four fingers versus only his thumb—and she bites her lower lip, willing herself not to break down again. Most people think that in the face of terror, the choice is fight or flight, but Mo knows a third, far more likely choice exists: freeze. And that's exactly what Mo did. Again. Just like she did when Oz didn't come back. She starts to cry again, and Mrs. Miller reaches out and gently touches her hair. "Oh, baby."

"I'm sorry," she stammers, embarrassed.

"It's the GHB," Chloe says. "First it dulls you; then it makes you overly emotional."

"Well, I guess we know which stage I'm in." Mo snivel-laughs as she presses her fingers to her eyes, determined not to let the drug continue to have control.

"Evening," someone says, and Mo drops her hands to see her doctor walking into the room, a young woman with sleek dark hair tied back from her face. "How are we doing?"

Mo has always hated when people use first-person-plural tense in a conversation, but she pushes her irritation away and says, "I think better. At least I know where I am."

"Good. That's good. It might take a bit longer before we're completely back to ourselves."

Chloe, who is standing behind the doctor, rolls her eyes, and the small gesture makes Mo feel slightly better. Chloe's still Chloe, and that alone makes things feel a little less like they're spinning off kilter.

Mrs. Miller says, "Mo, Chloe and I are going to let the doctor examine you. We'll go to the cafeteria to tell Kyle you're awake."

Chloe lifts her hand in a small wave, her fingers barely lifting from her side, and again Mo clings to it. Ever since Chloe was a little girl, that's how she's said goodbye.

"How long do I have to be here?" Mo asks when they're gone. Now that her brain fog has cleared, she's anxious to go home. After the accident eight years ago, she spent close to three weeks in rooms very similar to this, and she's had her fill.

"How about we see how we're doing before we talk about what's next?"

The doctor goes about examining her, shining a light in Mo's eyes, checking her heart with a stethoscope, asking her to take deep breaths. She has Mo follow her finger with her eyes, recite her name, the date, who's president. She asks her to remember three objects—red chair, big horse, loud bell—and a few minutes later, she asks her to repeat the objects back. When Mo gets it right, she says, "Good," and Mo starts to cry again, and she knows by the way the doctor is looking at her, her eyes narrowed with concern, that she just blew it, her chance for being discharged erased.

"How about we get some rest?" she says. "I'll check on you again in the morning."

Before Mo can answer, she has turned and is walking out the door.

Alone for the first time, Mo closes her eyes and focuses on her breathing. She counts backward from a hundred in fives, and when she reaches zero, she counts forward in fours. It's a technique she uses when she's struggling with turning off her brain so she can sleep.

Despite the exercise, her thoughts swim, snippets and vague ideas she's not certain are imagined or real. Finally, giving up, she cranks the bed so she's upright and grabs her phone from the nightstand.

Notifications splatter the screen. She scrolls to the bottom of her new messages to see a text left this morning from a number she doesn't recognize: How are you holding up?

She tilts her head, wondering if it's a wrong number, but when she clicks on it, the previous thread pops up, and she remembers Chloe was using Hunter's phone.

Closing out of her texts, she opens her camera, snaps a selfie, and, unconcerned with how she looks, posts it to Instagram. The caption reads: *Earlier today, I was drugged and, if not for the grace of God, would have been raped. I am safe and recovering at UCSF Medical Center, and tomorrow, with my team at FactNews, we will endeavor to uncover the truth about the awful pandemic of drug-induced rapes that is plaguing our society and which has destroyed and continues to destroy countless lives. It's time for the predators to become the prey and for the victims to be heard.*

She hits "Share" just as a call comes in.

"Hello, Ms. Gutierrez," she says, knowing she should care more that her lawyer is calling but truthfully indifferent; the charges against her feel very far away.

"Bad plan," Ms. Gutierrez says with no greeting. "Making deals with the devil is how good people get burned."

Mo nods. There's no arguing. Meeting Allen was a very dumb move.

"Good news and bad news," Ms. Gutierrez says. "Which do you want first?"

Mo doesn't care.

When she doesn't answer, Ms. Gutierrez says, "Allen's been arrested. He's being charged with attempted rape, poisoning with intent to harm, and kidnapping."

Mo assumes that's the good news.

"The receptionist rolled on him before the detectives made it through her door."

"Receptionist?" Mo asks.

"The girl who picked you up and pretended to be the Uber driver. She works with Allen."

"Oh," Mo says, suddenly realizing why the girl was familiar. The hair was different, and she wore glasses, but the pink lips and voice were the same.

"She claims she had no idea what Allen intended to do, agreed to it because he paid her and she needed the money."

"Okay," Mo says, trying to be interested. More bad people. There seems to be no shortage. "And the bad news?"

"Attempted rape's a joke and really tough to prove. He'll be out in a day."

"Oh," Mo says, worn outrage flaring in a halfhearted way. While she could very possibly end up in prison for years for a murder she didn't commit, Allen, who has been drugging and raping women for years, will once again walk away with barely a slap on the wrist.

"So now do you want the other good news?"

"Sure," Mo says, only half listening.

"He kidnapped you," Ms. Gutierrez says, glee in her gruff voice.

Mo sighs out heavily, trying to see how this is a good thing. Allen, along with his morally corrupt receptionist, drugged her, then took her to his apartment, where he would have proceeded to rape her had Chloe and Ruby not shown up when they did.

"Kidnapping carries fifteen to life," Ms. Gutierrez says with undisguised relish.

"Really?" Mo says, a spark of hope igniting.

"Really. And there's footage, clear video from the camera in front of his building, that shows him drag-carrying you inside. We've got the bastard."

"That's great," Mo says, almost feeling it.

"And of course, in light of this new turn of events, the DA is dropping the charges against you, Allen's testimony clearly not credible."

"Just like that?" Mo says. "What about the measuring cup and the murder charge?"

"Fruit from the poison tree," Ms. Gutierrez says, sounding practically giddy. "Allen's identification led to the rest. No judge is going to allow evidence that resulted from it. It also turns out you have an alibi for the murder."

"I do?"

"The motel you were staying at in Bend has surveillance. The owner's an ex-con and uptight about security because of it. The footage makes it clear you didn't leave your room that night. Looks like the jacket was just a coincidence."

Hunter an ex-con? Ms. Gutierrez must be mistaken, or maybe Hunter has a partner. The image of a large man with stringy white hair and lots of tattoos crosses her mind, and she doesn't know why.

"So that's it?" she asks, a sense of disbelief washing over her that this thing that only moments before was so momentous could go away so quickly.

"Yep. Looks like you're coming out of this smelling rosy. Finally, a case where the good guys win. Love that."

"Thank you," Mo says.

"Don't thank me just yet," Ms. Gutierrez says. "I'm not quite done with you. What do you say we take this to civil court and go after Mr. Redding for defamation for those posts he made? Take him for everything he's got?"

"I don't need the money," Mo says, her eyes closing, suddenly very tired and ready for the call to be over.

"You don't, but think about all the other victims who might. I'll work it pro bono, and we can donate whatever we get to a legal defense fund for sexual assault victims." There's something in her tone Mo hadn't noticed before, a low thrum of rage, and Mo realizes this case might be personal.

"Let me think about it," Mo says, wanting to feel the way Ms. Gutierrez does but plumb out of pluck. All Mo really wants is to hang up, curl in a ball, and sleep until it's over.

"Yeah, okay," Ms. Gutierrez says, sounding disappointed. "Get some rest. We'll talk again in the morning."

Mo hangs up and looks at the screen, notification after notification popping up about her post. She sets the phone facedown on the table and, half a second later, reconsiders. Picking it up, she pecks out a text to Hazel: Hey. Thinking of you. She hesitates, then finishes: I'm sorry. I never should have left you alone in the bar.

She hits send and collapses to the pillow, wondering if life will ever feel right again. She knows from experience that, eventually, even the worst pain fades, but it's hard to imagine ever returning to the place she was.

Pieces of time are missing, and that alone breeds a sort of nervous paranoia she can't quite shake, fear and distrust inside her much in the same way she still has deep misgivings when it comes to cold. Her eyes flick behind her lids as she tries to remember the moments she lost, knowing if she could remember, it would help. But hard as she tries, the only memory she has is the same single recollection of Ruby being knocked to the floor and Allen saying, "You!" as he looked at Chloe.

"Oh!" Mo says, her eyes snapping open.

She looks at the chairs where Chloe and Mrs. Miller were when she woke up. Chloe's vet bag sits beneath the one nearest the door, a vintage leather satchel given to her by her dad when she graduated vet school.

You! Allen knew who Chloe was.

Brain throbbing, she pushes unsteadily to her feet and shuffles to the bag. She finds the vial in the main compartment in a black nylon pouch, along with a dozen other medications. Three inches tall and half an inch wide, it is half-full of clear liquid and neatly labeled in Chloe's distinct, left-slanted, precise writing, *Gamma Hydroxybutyrate*. The date is the day after Hazel was raped, the same day Allen was assaulted. She opens it and lifts it to her nose—paint thinner, the smell exactly like what you would expect.

The riddle continues to spin. *Why?* As much as Chloe loves Hazel, she can't imagine her going to the extent of seeking Allen out and drugging him in order to avenge her. Chloe's attitude toward the whole thing was more in line with Hazel's, believing their energy should be spent moving forward and figuring out a way to help Hazel heal.

Chloe left the apartment the night of the assault supposedly for an appointment, but maybe there was no appointment. Did she track Allen down? Go to his apartment? She must have. How else would she have known where Mo was?

Footsteps in the corridor startle her, and she screws the top back on the vial, puts it back where she found it, and hurries back to the bed.

Kyle walks in. "Hey," he says, wearing a fake, bright smile.

"Hey," she says as she paints on a false smile of her own, her thrumming brain continuing to try to work it out. Chloe drugged Allen. But why? And when she knew the trouble Mo was in, why didn't she confess?

Kyle sits on the edge of the mattress, takes her hand, and brushes a kiss across her knuckles. "How you doing?"

"Better," she says.

Because no one would have believed her. Allen hadn't accused her. He'd accused Mo. And Hazel had committed the murder, so to confess to the assault would have made Chloe a suspect in a far worse crime she had nothing to do with. What a mess!

"You sure?" Kyle says, looking at her curiously.

She pushes her spiraling thoughts away. "Yeah. I'm just trying to get my head around everything. Ms. Gutierrez called."

She tells him about their conversation. His expression is dark and stormy as he listens, and each time she says Allen's name, his jaw twitches. The gold cross he wears is outside his shirt, and she imagines he's been praying, struggling with his Christian faith against his fierce craving for vengeance.

"He's going to pay," she says, hoping to assuage it, feeling like they've already lost enough to Allen and not wanting to give him any more. "He's going to prison, and Ms. Gutierrez wants to sue him as well, take him for everything he's got."

Kyle remains silent, his jaw still twitching, the soldier in him not quite satisfied.

"I'm okay," she says, hoping to reassure him, and then she softly touches his cheek and amends the statement to a more truthful one: "I'm going to be okay."

54
CHLOE

Chloe and her mom are in the cafeteria, a cup of coffee in front of each of them and a slice of cheesecake between them. Hunter left a few minutes ago to take Ruby back to the motel so she could rest. As he said goodbye, her mom hugged him hard. "Thank you," she said, the emotion cracking her voice causing Hunter to blush.

Chloe turns her cup between her hands, the warmth comforting.

"Do you plan on telling me what's going on?" her mom says.

"You already know," Chloe answers mostly to her coffee, then sneaks a peek to see her mom frowning. "What?"

"So you're *not* going to tell me?"

Chloe swallows. Lying to her mom is never a good idea, as her mom's instincts for deceit are well honed from representing liars most of her adult life.

"You don't want to know," Chloe says. After all, what will telling her accomplish? Implicate Hazel. Implicate herself. It would only make things worse.

"Really?" her mom presses. "I fly up here because I *know* something's going on, and now you're stonewalling me?"

Chloe shakes her head, though that's exactly what she's doing.

"You know I'm your lawyer," her mom says. "Whatever you tell me falls under attorney-client privilege."

"What about daughter-mother shame?" Chloe says, her eyes still on her cup.

"Mother-daughter unconditional love," her mother counters, then reaches out and sets her hand on Chloe's, and Chloe looks up to see the look she hates, a tender combination of veneration and devotion that feels like a million pounds of bricks on her shoulders, the worship too much to live up to and constantly making Chloe feel as if she's failing miserably and not doing nearly enough to deserve it.

Her mom takes her hand back and tries a different tack: "So . . . Hunter?"

Chloe's cheeks flush.

"I like him," her mom says. "Reminds me a little of your dad."

Chloe's face snaps up. "I thought the same thing."

Her mom smiles, and the expression is so full of hope that Chloe says, "Fine," and then she tells her about the trip, leaving out all references to Hazel and Mount Si and sticking to the lie about driving north to get away from the brouhaha surrounding the assault and because Ruby couldn't stay at the apartment.

Her mom lights up when she hears about Hunter serenading Ruby outside their motel room. "A musician," she says with an eyebrow lift, knowing it's one of Chloe's weaknesses.

And when Chloe tells her about Kyle showing up in Elmer City, her mom's eyes well with love and respect. "He's amazing," she says. Her regard for Kyle is beyond what she holds for almost anyone else in the world.

"That was the same day you told us about the evidence they found at the apartment and the arrest warrant. So Mo drove home with Kyle, and I went back to Bend to get Ruby."

"And to see *Hunter*," her mom trills, clearly excited at the prospect of a new romance in Chloe's life.

"Yes." Chloe rolls her eyes. "And to see Hunter."

Her mom smiles wide, and Chloe goes on to tell her about his apartment and his photographs.

"He sounds amazing," her mom says.

Chloe nods. He is amazing. One-of-a-kind sort of amazing.

"So how did he end up here?" her mom asks.

Eyes on the table, Chloe explains about Gretzky showing up at the motel and how Hunter followed him when he left.

"Wait. Stop," her mom says. "You're telling me there's some cop harassing you?"

"I kind of pissed him off," Chloe says. "He pulled me over for a flat tire, and I didn't take it well, so he arrested me. Then I might have made some not-so-polite comments as he was driving me to the station."

Her mother is frowning hard, clearly not pleased with Chloe but, it turns out, more upset with Gretzky. "And because of that, he tracked you to Oregon?"

And because I Ex-Laxed him and laughed at him when he showed up with the runs.

"Yup. Really didn't like being told he had a small weenie."

Her mom frowns again, clearly not sharing Chloe's sense of humor. "What precinct?" she says.

"Huh?"

"Gretzky, what precinct is he out of?"

"The one near UCSF Medical Center."

"Fine." Her mom stands, her phone gripped like a saber in her hand. "I'll be right back." She marches from the cafeteria.

Chloe watches her disappear, feeling like a little girl whose pigtails were tugged on by the playground bully and whose mom is now taking the bully to task.

Five minutes later, she's back.

"What happened?" Chloe asks.

"He wasn't there. I left a message."

"What did you say?"

"I politely asked him to call me back." But the way she says it belies the nonchalance of the words, and Chloe feels silly for not having told her mom about Gretzky sooner. While her dad is tough, her mom is fierce . . . and lethal when it comes to the law.

"What are you going to do?" Chloe asks.

Her mom issues a shrewd smile and ignores the question. "So back to Hunter," she says, causing Chloe's insides to warm with that amazing my-mom's-got-my-back feeling that never goes away no matter how old she gets. "He followed Gretzky back here because he was worried about you?"

Chloe nods.

"Now I *really* like him," her mom says.

Chloe nods again and confesses, "I think I *really* like him too."

"Wow, a new man and a dog all in a week. Aubrey and the girls are going to be so excited."

Chloe imagines her two young nieces with Ruby and how good she knows Ruby would be with them.

"Does this mean you're finally going to take your cat back as well?" her mom asks.

"Not sure Ruby would like that," Chloe says. "She definitely seems like the jealous type."

"Fine. I suppose we can keep the rodent a bit longer." Her mom says it like she would love to get rid of Finn the Mighty, but Chloe knows secretly she adores the rebel feline.

"Thank you," Chloe says, the words for much more than her mom agreeing to watch her cat.

Her mom takes a sip of her now-cold coffee, acting like it's no big deal. But it is a big deal, and Chloe knows how lucky she is to be surrounded by people willing to risk everything for those they love without ever having to be asked—her mom, her dad, Mo, Hunter.

Her mom's about to say something when her phone rings. She looks at the screen, and a Cheshire grin fills her face. "Ah, Gretzky," she says.

"Ann Miller," she answers in her sweetest voice as she walks from the table.

Chloe smiles as she watches her go, knowing Zeus himself wouldn't stand a chance against her mom and that Gretzky is no Zeus.

55
MO

Mo wakes in Kyle's arms. The dawn is rising outside the window, and the room is dusted in shadows of gold and gray. Kyle snores lightly, his warm breath on her neck. His right leg is draped heavily over hers, and his arm is pinning her chest. Reluctant to leave the moment and step into the next, she closes her eyes, hoping to return to sleep, but it turns out to be impossible, too many thoughts swimming in her head.

Careful not to wake Kyle, she reaches for her phone, hoping Hazel has texted back. She swipes past all the notifications for the post she made and goes to her messages, then scrolls past dozens of texts from work and her mom to find the one left by Hazel:

It is one of the blessings of old friends that you can afford to be stupid with them. Finally starting to see beyond the pain to know the only person to blame has nothing to do with you. I will be home when I've solved the riddle.

Mo has no idea what riddle Hazel is pondering but imagines it has to do with trying to decipher the cosmos that caused this. Relief floods through her veins; Hazel's use of the Ralph Waldo Emerson quote is a sweet nod to Mo and her love of the great writer's work.

You never realize how fragile your friendships are until they are truly tested. A single moment, four lives undone, but only for an instant . . . Hazel safe, Chloe safe, Kyle beside her as she lies safe in his arms.

"Hey," Kyle says sleepily and pushes up on his elbow. "How are you feeling?"

"Okay. I still have a bit of a headache, but it's better. Haze texted."

"Yeah?"

"Yeah." She feels her emotions rising, and Kyle reaches out and touches her cheek with the back of his hand. "I think she's going to be okay."

She watches as he lifts his eyes to the heavens, his way of saying thanks. When he returns his gaze to hers, his expression holds nothing but love, and she is amazed by that.

"I really made a mess of things," she says.

He shakes his head as his Adam's apple bobs in his throat, the fear of having almost lost her still clear on his face. "You, Ace, are amazing."

She's not. She messed up. But rather than argue, silently she vows to do better and never let anything like this happen again. Though even as she makes the promise, she knows it is impossible—things happen, and people screw up. When she left Black Sands to answer Kyle's call, she had no idea the calamity she was about to set in motion.

"I just want to smuggle you out of here and fly someplace where no one knows you," Kyle says, touching his forehead to hers.

"Mars?" she says. "I understand it's the next big thing in real estate, and I would imagine most Martians still haven't heard of the Kaminskis."

He gives a half smile, kisses her lightly, then climbs from the bed.

"I have something to ask you," he says. His voice is serious, and she's certain this is where the rubber hits the road, when he is going to confront her about one of her many lies. Instead, she watches as he digs into the pocket of his jeans to pull out a black velvet box.

She's nodding before he's gotten it free, her head bobbing around her eyes, which have filled again, happy tears this time.

"Let me at least ask," Kyle says, getting down on one knee.

She nods harder, then realizes what she's doing and forces her head to stop, but it only makes her body jiggle.

He shakes his head and smiles, then lifts the lid to reveal her mother's ring, the ring her mother wore every day of her remarkable marriage to Mo's dad—a stunning emerald cut diamond flanked by triangular side stones and set in white gold.

"I know this isn't the most romantic time or place," Kyle says, "but if this week has proved anything, it's that you can't wait for tomorrow to take hold of the things you want today." His voice breaks, and he clears his throat. Then, lifting his eyes to hers, he says, "I love you, Mo Kaminski, and if you'll allow me, I will spend the rest of my life proving it."

She nods again, and he rolls his eyes. "You're ruining the suspense."

"Sorry." She forces every part of her to stop moving.

He blows out a breath. "Since the first moment we met, I knew you were the woman I wanted to be with . . ." His eyes drop. "And I know you won't believe me, but I also knew I wasn't worthy. So I vowed to change, to become better. You did that for me, made me a better man."

He's right; she doesn't believe him. He would have been amazing whether he met her or not. But she also knows his remarkability comes from deep-seated devotion to those he loves, and she was lucky enough to have become the object of his devotion when he was just beginning to discover it.

"For eight years, you have owned my heart, but with this ring, I offer my soul." His eyes move from the ring to her face, so earnest she is reminded again why she fell in love with him—*good*, all of him honest and true and good.

This time when she nods, he smiles, and then she is in his arms, the past week growing smaller as it makes room for the new remarkable future ahead.

56
CHLOE

They are in Hunter's apartment, naked beneath the sheets, Ruby lying on the comforter between them.

"We need to set some boundaries," Chloe says. "Dogs don't belong on the bed."

"You want to tell her?" Hunter asks with the heavy sigh of a contented man.

"You're her favorite."

"And I'd like to stay that way."

"Wimp."

"Mmmm," he says and reaches over to set his hand on her waist.

It's been a little over a week since the incident at Allen's apartment, and she and Hunter have been inseparable. They both drove back to Bend the morning Mo was released from the hospital.

Mo's mom was there, and so was Hazel. It was stunning, really, all of them crowded in the room as Mo was told she could go home—Hunter, Chloe, Chloe's mom, Mrs. Kaminski, Kyle, and Hazel—a great cocoon of unrelenting love.

After Mo was wheeled away, Hazel looked squarely at Chloe. "Thank you," she said.

Chloe started slightly before recovering and giving a shrug. "I always wanted to see the falls."

"Not for that," Hazel said, her dark eyes steady. "Not sure how you managed it, but it was very Amadeus Cho."

Chloe swallowed and looked away, not sure how Hazel had figured it out. Though it made sense. After all, Hazel was one of the smartest people on the planet.

"You knew it wasn't me," Hazel said plainly by way of explanation. "At the falls, you said I needed to come clean about the paint thinner and measuring cup, but you didn't say anything about the assault on Allen. And the only way you could have been so certain I didn't do it was if you knew who did."

Could have been Mo, Chloe thought.

Hazel's eyes glinted like they do when she knows she's being clever. "If it was Mo," she said, answering Chloe's unspoken thought, "she wouldn't have made the deal with Allen. She did that to protect me because she believed I was the one who drugged him, which she wouldn't have thought if she had been the one who had done it."

Her eyes moved to the door where Mo had been wheeled out a moment before. "She's no Amadeus Cho, a mere mortal when it comes to smarts. Agreeing to meet Allen was one of the dumbest decisions ever made in the history of humankind." She looked back at Chloe. "But she's a heck of a friend."

At that moment, Hunter returned to the room, having realized Chloe was still inside.

"Everything okay?" he asked.

"Just chipper," Hazel said in an English accent. She looked again at Chloe. "Einstein said, 'Weak people revenge. Strong people forgive. Intelligent people ignore.'" She shrugged. "I think Albert and I disagree on this one. Made me feel better." With a crisp military salute, she pivoted and walked away.

"She's awesome," Hunter said.

Chloe nodded. Hazel was certainly one of a kind.

"What was that about?" he asked.

Chloe didn't answer, her eyes still on the spot Hazel had been and her thoughts on her parting words. Chloe wasn't sure how she felt about what she had done to Allen. She couldn't say she was sorry about what happened to him. Mostly she was just terrified that it had led to what it had. If he had died, she might have felt bad, but even that was hard to say. But had something happened to Mo or Hazel because of her part in it, that would have destroyed her.

She hadn't set out that night to exact revenge on Allen. He wasn't even on her mind. She really did have an appointment to take care of Mrs. Linden's vomiting cat. Her van was in impound, so she needed to take an Uber. When she was done, the driver dropped her on Haight Street because it was easier than circling around to the apartment.

It was a beautiful night, and Chloe thought she might go for a walk. She loves walking the city when most everyone else is tucked away snug in their homes. There's danger but also freedom, the sleepless wandering about, along with artists and musicians. Liquor stores, bars, diners, and Laundromats are open; everything else is shuttered. It's a whole different vibe than during the day.

She was about to set off when she looked through the window of Black Sands and saw him. He was sitting at the bar, his face exactly like his profile picture, plain except for his overly wide jaw. He had a drink in front of him and was looking at the television.

It irked her, the casualness of it—him sitting there calmly drinking his beer and watching sports while Hazel was a block away, struggling. So she walked in. She must have considered what she was going to do because the vial was in her hand when she sat down. She'd made the GHB earlier that day after her conversation with Hazel, thinking she might give it to Ruby if she didn't start eating.

"Hey," Allen said, looking her over with an appraising glance.

She smiled sweetly. "How are the Warriors doing?" She nodded toward the game.

"Good as always," he said, the words round, letting her know he was drunk.

When he turned back to the TV, she poured what she hoped was a few drops of GHB into his drink, her thought at the time nothing more than tit for tat, to literally give him a dose of his own medicine.

She was shocked how quickly the drug took effect. Within minutes, Allen grew talkative, then giddy, then agitated. He looked at his drink several times as if curious, his brow pinched.

"You okay?" Chloe asked.

"Huh?" He looked up, his pupils small.

"Maybe we should get out of here," she said, her nerves jumping, not entirely sure how the controlling part of GHB worked.

It turned out it was disturbingly straightforward. He nodded, zombielike, and she knew if she had said, *Maybe we should jump off the Golden Gate Bridge,* she would have gotten the same response.

She led him outside. "Maybe I should drive?" she suggested, and without hesitation, he dug in his pocket and handed her his keys.

She clicked the unlock button on the fob, and a late-model black BMW parked down the street beeped.

"Where to?" she asked when they were inside, and he gave his address: 4663 Jackson Street.

Instead of punching the address into her phone, she punched in the name of the liquor store where Mo had found Hazel. A few blocks before they reached it, they hit a stop sign, and her nerve running out, she said, "I think we should get out here."

"Okay," Allen said and stepped from the car.

As soon as he was out, she hit the automatic door locks and drove off, leaving him on the side of the road. Then she returned to Black Sands and parked the car where she had found it, the fob in the center console. She wiped everything down with an antiseptic wipe from her vet bag, then walked home and climbed into bed, unable to believe she'd just done what she had.

At the time, she had no idea it would lead to everything that came after. She thought Allen would stumble his way home and wake up with a nasty hangover. She definitely didn't anticipate him being mugged and ending up in a coma or that he would wake up a day later and accuse Mo of being the one who had drugged him. At the time, she didn't know Mo had gone to Allen's office and threatened him or that she had made the post about him being a rapist.

Every other minute of the following days, she considered confessing, admitting she was the one who'd drugged him, but she was terrified. Her mom assured her the detectives didn't have a case against Mo, and she believed her. After all, Mo hadn't done it.

Only when Allen woke up and accused Mo did Chloe realize the trouble they were in. And at that point, it was too late. If she'd confessed to the crime, no one would have believed her. They would have thought she was only saying it to throw doubt on the case against Mo. The measuring cup with the paint thinner had Mo's fingerprints on it, and Allen had plainly said it was her. Then the doctor was killed, which made things a hundred times worse; now Hazel would be in trouble as well if Chloe said anything. Hazel had followed the same basic recipe Chloe had used to make the GHB for Ruby, and they'd both used the same common paint thinner from their local art store. Which unfortunately made the chemical markers for their separate crimes a match. When Chloe had made the GHB, she'd used a disposable syringe to measure the ingredients, which was why it had never occurred to her to worry about a tainted measuring cup. The whole thing was a nightmare, one bad coincidence after another leaving Mo in the crosshairs as a suspect and Hazel a single confession away from being discovered as the true culprit of the murder in Bend.

"Chloe?" Hunter said, breaking her from her thoughts.

She looked up at him, at his handsome, tired face with his brown, mischievous eyes and concerned smile; then she took his hand in hers and said, "I think I might be homeless. I can't go back to the apartment with Ruby. I don't have my van. And I think I've overstayed my welcome with Ray."

A grin twitched his lips as he scratched his unshaven chin as if considering her dilemma. "I suppose you and Rubes could come back to Bend for a bit. At least to get the van."

"I suppose that might be an option," she said, then pushed up on her toes to kiss him.

They picked Ruby up from Ray at the motel, and Chloe drove Hunter's truck and he drove his mom's car back to Oregon. She told herself she was only staying until she could find an apartment in San Francisco or Oakland that took dogs, a plan that fell apart immediately.

The night they got to the motel, Hunter made her dinner, and she ended up spending the night. Then the next night and the night after that. And now, it's been a week, and she can't imagine going to sleep without him.

Her phone rings, and she reaches over him to grab it from the side table. "Hey, Mom."

"Mo is crazy," her mom says without a hello. "Seriously. Certifiable."

Chloe sits up and pulls the sheets over her nakedness. Hunter yanks them down with a grin. She grabs them back, and Ruby, thinking it's all in great fun, starts jumping around and tugging as well, which is totally unacceptable dog behavior and which Hunter is shamelessly encouraging, both of them pulling at the sheets in a full-blown tug-of-war.

She storms from the bed to the couch.

"Mmmm, mmmm," Hunter says to her naked backside. "Nice view."

She looks over her shoulder and sticks her tongue out at him, then plops on the couch and pulls the afghan over herself.

"What's going on?" her mom says. "Where are you?"

"Nowhere," Chloe says, embarrassed at being caught naked with a boy by her mom, despite being twenty-six and having been in relationships since she was sixteen.

"Well, get somewhere where you can look at Instagram. I'm telling you, she's lost it."

"Hold on." Chloe pulls the phone from her ear, opens Instagram, and goes to Mo's page.

Mo has close to seven hundred thousand followers, and her last post has nearly two hundred thousand views and has been shared close to a thousand times. There are three photos: one of her in the hospital and the two Allen took in his car when Mo was drugged. Despite the rings beneath her eyes, the lack of makeup, and the flatness of her hair in the first photo, she is beautiful—a wounded princess who will capture the heart of anyone who looks at her. The post reads: *This is what a victim looks like. If you are a victim, join me in bringing this dark blight on our world that has been kept too long in the shadows into the light. #thisiswhatavictimlookslike.*

"Do you see it?" her mother squawks.

Chloe returns the phone to her ear. "Yeah. It looks like she's rocking the world."

"What she's doing is rocking the case against Allen. You need to tell her to stop."

Chloe has no intention of telling Mo to stop. She thinks what she's doing is awesome. She thinks of Kora. She thinks of Hazel. She thinks of all the women who responded the first time Mo posted about Allen. It's like Kora said: it's important that victims know they're not alone, and it's important for the world to wake up and realize how rampant sexual assault is and how often the perpetrators go unpunished.

"The hashtag is blowing up," her mom says. "There's no way Allen's going to get a fair trial, which means this is going to be dragged out for years. He might even get acquitted. Is that what she wants?"

"Mo knows what she's doing," Chloe says.

"No, she doesn't. She's mucking it up, and it seems like she's doing it intentionally. Cece's pissed. She says Mo suddenly can't remember anything, not even getting in the Uber."

"Mo said that?" Chloe says, a prickle in her spine. "She said she doesn't remember the Uber?"

"How can she say she doesn't remember?" her mom says. "She remembered that part perfectly. She even knew the brand of water, Aquafina."

She knows, Chloe thinks.

"He might never see the inside of a prison cell!" her mom practically screeches. "The DA is going to have no choice but to plead this out."

And she realizes her mom is right. Mo is mucking it up, but not for the reasons her mom thinks. Mo knows, so she doesn't want the case to go to trial, where the truth might come out. Mo is protecting her.

"It makes no sense," her mom goes on. "They have him dead to rights."

Chloe hesitates a beat too long, and her mom pounces. "What the hell is going on?"

"More than one way to peel an orange," Chloe says. She decided in high school that skinning cats, even in an idiom, was wrong.

"What the hell does that mean?"

"It means, look how many women have come forward because of what Mo's doing. Victims whose voices were silent before."

"Yeah?" her mom argues. "And what about the men they're calling out? No trial, no chance to defend themselves. Guilty by Instagram post! Accusations that could be baseless and could cause irreparable harm. There's a reason we have courts and rules and juries."

Chloe doesn't know what to say to that. She hasn't looked closely at the responses but imagines the thread is endless and that hundreds of men have been named without any proof except the accuser's word.

"All Mo posted was 'This is what a victim looks like.' I think that's brave."

"No. That's stupid. And Mo isn't stupid. Something else is at play."

Chloe doesn't answer, knowing to tussle with her mom in half truths will only lead to more trouble.

"Fine," her mom says with a harrumph. "Don't tell me."

Chloe smiles at her mom's childish tantrum. "I love you, Mom."

"Love you, too," she huffs. Then she adds, "Say hi to Hunter, and don't get pregnant."

Chloe blushes.

"Unless you want to get pregnant," her mom adds. "Then have at it."

"I'm hanging up now."

"Bye, Bug."

Chloe sets the phone down with a happy sigh, and Ruby jumps up beside her, incredibly adept now at getting around with her cast. She lays her head on Chloe's lap. "Hey, girl." She scratches her behind the ear.

The shower is running, and beyond the spray of water and Hunter's soft humming is deep, resounding quiet, the sort of silence that makes her think about how much noise there is in most other places in the world. No cars or sirens or voices.

Leaning her head back, she closes her eyes. "Nice," she says, and Ruby thumps her tail. A branch rustles against the window, and far off, the sound of distant thunder rumbles, promise of a summer storm.

She begins to drift away, then nearly jumps out of her skin when a shock of cold and a wet body land on her. Hunter shakes his wet hair over her like a dog, spraying her with icy droplets, and she yelps and lifts her hands in front of her face.

Ruby leaps and jumps, yipping and howling.

Hunter sits back, his knees straddling her waist. "Missed you," he says with a great big smile.

She rolls from beneath him and stands, pulling the afghan with her and wrapping it around her body. Holding out her other hand, palm out, she says, "Stay."

Both Hunter and Ruby tilt their heads in the exact same way as if considering whether to obey.

Hunter decides first, dropping off the couch to his knees and crawling toward her, completely incorrigible. Ruby follows. And in the next moment, Chloe is running around the room as Hunter chases after her, Ruby circling, jumping, and yipping. And while Chloe doesn't want to get caught, because she is very competitive, she also very much wants to be caught, because being caught by Hunter would be very fun indeed.

As it turns out, the decision isn't up to her. With incredible athleticism, Hunter vaults the bed and catches her in his arms. The afghan falls as he kisses her, and Ruby's tail whips against her leg as, inside, Finn whoops and hollers and cheers.

AUTHOR'S NOTE

Dear reader:

Several months before I started this novel, a good friend of mine told me a story. Her twenty-two-year-old daughter had called. For the sake of this letter, we will call her Katie. She was upset. The night before, she had gone to dinner with a friend she hadn't seen in a while. We will call her Barbara. During their conversation, a disturbing coincidence was discovered that left Katie reeling and unsure what to do.

Katie had asked Barbara how things were going since graduation, and Barbara said not so well. She went on to describe an awful experience from a few months earlier, a night of drinks out with friends that had ended with her in the hospital after she'd realized she had been roofied, her drink spiked with something that made her disoriented and woozy. Fortunately—or unfortunately—she recognized the early signs because she had been roofied before. She took an Uber to the emergency room, where it was confirmed she had GHB in her system.

The event traumatized her. Twice a victim, she told Katie she was now terrified to date or go to bars or even to parties and that her trust in people, both strangers and friends, had been shattered. She was constantly paranoid about her food and drinks and obsessively worried about memory lapses. She had gotten in the habit of texting herself before she left wherever she was so she would have a record of where she had been. She had also started counting her steps, a mental way of reassuring herself that she was there and present.

Bad as all this was, it wasn't the worst part. This is where the story turned particularly disturbing. Barbara knew the guy who had drugged her. He was the one who'd bought Barbara her drink, and she was certain he was the one who had spiked it. Barbara told Katie who he was, and Katie's blood went cold. The guy was the same guy another friend had claimed roofied and then raped her two years earlier. That friend had never fully recovered. She had since struggled with anxiety, depression, and intimacy issues.

And so . . . the phone call. Katie wanted to know what she should do.

When my friend told me the story, my vision turned red and my mama-bear instinct roared. I told her we should find out the guy's name. I wanted Katie to go to the police. I wanted to personally track the monster down and castrate him. My logical mind calculated the odds of these two young women being his only victims and came up with zero. If Katie had crossed paths with two of his victims, that likely meant there were dozens, possibly hundreds, more.

Katie, who had the advantage of having had time to process the information, was more levelheaded than her mom and me and countered our zeal for retaliation on every front. First, Barbara hadn't been raped. She'd had GHB in her system, but there was no way to prove the guy she suspected was the one who'd drugged her or what he would have done had she not recognized the signs and gone to the hospital. And while the other young woman had been raped, she'd never reported the crime because she couldn't remember the specifics and was so traumatized that her only goal was to move past it and figure out a way to put it behind her. Which, of course, turned out to be impossible.

No evidence; no crime. It's why it's so difficult to stop these guys. Frustrated, I went to my local police department and talked to a detective to see if anything could be done. The answer was a sympathetic "not much." Katie could report what she knew to the police in Seattle, and that way, at least the guy's name would be in the system in case, down the road, another case came to light with more evidence, but he doubted it would do much good.

Most date rapists unfortunately know what they're doing. Typically, they target vulnerable victims such as female first-year students who don't have a lot of experience with drinking or people who are already intoxicated, knowing it will impair their credibility should they choose to come forward and try to report what happened. Most are not single offenders. The average number of victims a date rapist has when convicted is six. These are serial, violent predators disguised in sheep's clothing—usually affable young men who know their victims and are able to blend in with everyone else.

Angry beyond words, I suggested we go rogue—call the bastard out on social media and ask other girls to come forward. Katie rationally talked us out of this idea as well. The truth was—like the police—we had no proof. And while none of the three of us believed the two friends were lying or that their stories involving the same guy were a coincidence, we also couldn't justify destroying someone's life on the off chance it was.

So once again, the very thing that made the victims victims—a drug that causes mind-numbing amnesia—was also what protected the perpetrator. And there you have it. The man is free and going about his life while most likely continuing to leave a trail of shattered lives in his wake. Katie said she used to follow him on social media and that he is very successful, a bigwig at an important company who makes lots of money. It is infuriating, which I suppose is why I wrote this story, a desire for some sort of justice even if only fictional, a wish for the good to prevail and for the evil to get their just deserts.

Mo and Chloe gave this story its voice. Some of you might recognize them from my novel *In an Instant*. As teenagers, they went through something harrowing and life changing. I found them remarkable and thought it would be interesting to see how they had developed into young women. And because I was enjoying revisiting them, I sprinkled a few other characters from my past novels in as well. Kyle, Eric, and Chloe's mom, Ann, are also from *In an Instant*. Hunter and Fitz are from *Hadley & Grace*. And Paul and Hawk are from *Hush Little Baby*. I hope you enjoyed catching up with them as much as I did.

Best wishes,

Suzanne

ACKNOWLEDGMENTS

Enormous thanks to the following people, without whom this book would not have been possible.

My family.

My agent, Gordon Warnock.

My editor, Alicia Clancy.

The entire team at Lake Union, including Laura Barrett, Danielle Marshall, Gabriella Dumpit, Alexandra Levenberg, Hannah Hughes, Harriet Stiles, Riam Griswold, Nicole Burns-Ascue, Bill Siever, and Kathleen Lynch.

My sensitivity reader, Nicole Coles, who read the story with a compassionate eye and open heart and whose feedback allowed me to see the world through an altered lens.

The Laguna Beach police detective who took time to explain the frustration of trying to bring date rapists to justice.

DISCUSSION QUESTIONS

1. Chloe categorizes people into breeds of dogs based on their personalities—golden retrievers, chows, mutts, Dobermans. If you were a dog, what breed do you think you'd be and why?

2. Mo leaves Hazel in the bar alone with Allen to take the call from Kyle. Because of that, she thinks she is to blame for what happened. Do you think she is responsible?

3. Ruby plays an important role in the story; her canine story line of emotional healing after being abandoned and finding someone new to love runs parallel to Chloe's. Do you think we can learn from dogs when it comes to forgiveness and moving on, or do human egos and our unique capacity for long-standing resentment make that impossible?

4. Officer Gretzky is an uncaring jerk when he takes the report about the rape. Chloe, irritated by his attitude, puts Ex-Lax in his coffee. Do you think what she does is justified? Do you think it's funny, cruel, criminal? Have you ever done anything like that?

5. "The power of right is a greater might than thou can'st think or speak." This is the final line in the poem left by Hazel, and it explains why she killed the doctor in Bend.

Do you think there are times when it is justified to step outside the laws of society in order to protect it?

6. Mo lies to Kyle. She keeps secrets and makes life-altering decisions without him. Do you think keeping the truth from him in order to protect Hazel is justified? If he finds out the truth, how do you think it will affect their relationship?

7. Allen's brother, James, feels guilty when he sees Mo because he knows about his brother's proclivities. How far would you go to protect someone you love? Would you lie for them? If asked under oath if they'd committed a crime, would you perjure yourself?

8. "Sadness doesn't last forever." There are several references throughout the story to this theme. While the accident eight years ago still has ripple effects on Mo's and Chloe's lives, both believe time heals most wounds. How do you feel about that? Does grief grow lighter with time? How about regret?

9. "What is it about revenge that makes it so intoxicating?" This is another underlying theme throughout the book. "Addictive as heroin or crack, it seems to entirely take over a person, toxic and destructive, until it razes everything around it." Allen, Gretzky, Hazel, Mo, Chloe—all of them experience the festering desire for retaliation, and each acts on it differently, leading to some catastrophic consequences. Have you ever held a grudge or had a grudge held against you? Do you think acting on those feelings ultimately helps or only makes things worse?

10. Do you have a bucket list place—a single place you absolutely have to go in this lifetime?

11. Hunter says Allen is a "bad egg," and while Chloe likes the idea of an eggdicator that flushes bad eggs away, she

doesn't believe eggs start off bad. What do you think: Are bad eggs born bad, or does something happen to make them bad? Can bad eggs be redeemed?

12. Chloe turns out to be the one who roofied Allen and left him in the Tenderloin. Unlike Hazel's, the act was not premeditated and was more of an impulsive choice meant to give Allen "a dose of his own medicine." But Allen ended up in a coma because of it. How do you feel about what she did? Should she have been punished?

13. How do you feel about the epidemic of date rape that is plaguing our society and our legal system's lack of ability to deal with these crimes? What do you think can be done about the problem?

14. There are a lot of references in the book to heroes. Who do you think is most heroic: Mo, Chloe, Hazel, Kyle, Hunter . . . Ruby?

15. An ember of Finn still glows inside Chloe, and she carries Oz's memory close to her heart and lives her life in honor of him. Have you ever lost someone yet still felt their presence, like their passing profoundly altered you or the memory of them is guiding you?

16. Who is your favorite character? Why?

17. Movie time: Who would you like to see play each part?

ABOUT THE AUTHOR

Photo © 2015 April Brian

Suzanne Redfearn is the award-winning author of five novels: *Hush Little Baby*, *No Ordinary Life*, *In an Instant*, *Hadley and Grace*, and *Moment in Time*. In addition to being an author, she's an architect specializing in residential and commercial design. She lives in Laguna Beach, California, where she and her husband own three restaurants: Lumberyard, Yard Bar, and Slice Pizza and Beer. You can find her at her website (www.SuzanneRedfearn.com) and on Facebook (@SuzanneRedfearnAuthor).